THE BODY ON THE
UNDERWATER ROAD

DONOVAN: THIEF FOR HIRE

Chuck Bowie

MuseItUp Publishing
CANADA

MuseItUp Publishing
https://museituppublishing.com

Cover Art © 2018 by Charlotte Volnek
Layout and Book Production by Lea Schizas
eBook ISBN: 978-1-77392-006-1
Print ISBN: 978-1-77392-007-8
First eBook Edition *May 2018

DONOVAN: THIEF FOR HIRE

Three Wrongs

AMACAT

Steal It All

The Body On The Underwater Road

I dedicate this book to my wife and partner, Lois Williams.
Parts of this novel are set in her back yard:
Charlotte County and coastal Maine.
I'd also like to dedicate this book to my brothers and sisters,
who helped me to grow up:
Lynn, Sandy, Debby, Jackie, Bill and Dorothea.

In conducting the research for this novel, I visited the vineyards of Prince Edward County and the Niagara district, in Ontario, Canada. This was, you can imagine, the pleasant part of my research.

A pleasant conversation with John and Jane Murray led me to develop the events in the book that took place on Passamaquoddy Bay, and for that I thank them.

The Rossmount Inn in St. Andrews is home to Chamcook Mountain, as well as one of the best food menus offered in New Brunswick. Thank you, Chris and Graziella Aerni; I wrote several scenes in your wonderful inn.

Chapter 1

RILEY PARKER TOSSED A SHOCK of red hair over one shoulder and searched the side of the bed for her constant companion, a similarly coiffed redhead rag doll. "They're fighting downstairs, Annie-O. Do you want to hide in the closet, or should we watch from the top of the stairs?"

Nodding as if she'd received a positive response, the little girl carried Annie-O to the top of the stairs, just beyond the sight of any raised eyes. Holding the doll as tight as she could, Riley placed her feet together on the top tread and put a chubby index finger to her lips to shush the doll. She cocked an ear, recognizing the voices. Her father, Nick, was speaking to her mother, Tricia, his voice failing to contain cold anger.

"Listen here, you awful…woman. You've been caught red-handed, and you used our bed, no less. It's all I can do to keep my hands off your lying throat. You have five minutes to clear out. And don't go near my girl. I'll try to tell her some lie that makes you look less…*awful* than you actually are. I've advised the bank to not give you the time of day. Give me a forwarding address and I'll wire you five thousand dollars. The pre-nup is clad in stone, so the five grand, together with what you've stolen should be settlement enough."

"Please. I'm sorry. It's over. Don't make me go." Although the voice was muted, Riley could hear her mother was upset.

"Four minutes." His voice was grim.

"Look, it's only money, and you've got more than you can count. I didn't…sleep with him. He just helped me convert some things over to cash. You've made mistakes in the past, and been forgiven for them, haven't you?"

Nick's voice broke. "I never sinned against you, Tricia. You have three minutes left. You can use them to throw lies at me or go get some clothes, I don't care. But if you're here in three minutes, I swear you won't be able to walk out." His voice had fallen to a hoarse whisper, and the little girl had to strain to hear either of them. "I made arrangements to change the locks, and a guard has been instructed to throw you out on your behind if you so much as touch the property fence. Riley and I are going up to St. Andrews for the summer. Don't follow us. Don't phone or write. You're dead to her now, and your two minutes are up. Get out. Get out!" He bellowed the final two words, and a moment later, Riley heard a door close.

Chapter 2

St. Andrews By-The-Sea, New Brunswick, Canada
Eighteen Years Later

WELL, THERE IT IS; THE first girl thrown in the pool by some jock. Riley Parker shook her head. *Do they not know the temperature of an outside pool in early July in St. Andrews? I am so glad to be finished with school and this crowd.* She swished the remainder of her drink and then picked up the broad-brimmed hat resting on the table in front of her. What's a reasonable time to slip away without being called on it, she wondered.

The sun beamed down on the college graduates, and the pergola in the corner was lovely and inviting, but Riley wasn't in the mood. She had a career to focus on, new relationships to develop. A custom-made Riley Parker marketing plan to build. Today was the first day of the rest of her life, and it felt like that. Her chest expanded at the possibilities. She spied Darren working his way around the perimeter of the pool, toward the array of lounging chairs surrounding her. A young woman caught his arm, her ever-so-white teeth gleaming in the sun. He'd spare a minute for her, but it was clear by a self-conscious wave he wanted to talk to Riley. He may want to make plans, ones with her at the center. In her mind, she placed quotations around the word "plans" and grimaced. Riley's future was built for one, for the moment. He was fun, but…perhaps it was time to go for a walk.

Riley flipped a mass of red waves from her face, placed the hat back on her head and stepped away from the Rossmount Inn pool area. She stood for just a moment beside the vegetable gardens, pale green eyes fixed on the incline leading to Chamcook Mountain. Her chin, strong and true was set, along with Riley's decision. On impulse, she followed the route—created to allow for an oxen team's width two hundred years ago—upward and to the right, to where the path levelled off. She was now at the foot of the tiny mountain, a hump, really, and she stood beside an ancient barn. Inside it, she spotted a late model Porsche Carrera. She stopped for a wistful moment, imagining her luscious curls flowing around the driver's headrest and summer breezes eddying across full lips and half-closed gaze. Riley's background as a hotelier-graduate caused her to note the additional inn furniture through the open door of the building. What was now a storage barn had been used to house the serving staff two generations previous.

Riley pulled down on her broad-brimmed hat, tucking errant wisps of hair back where they belonged. Her skin was white porcelain unblemished by freckles. She'd always protected it since her mother had warned as a child freckles were not desirable.

The view from the mountain was pleasing if not spectacular, since she was at the base of the hill and not the crest, so the focus was more on forest. To the left she spied a crude wooden box, compliments of the inn, offering a selection of walking sticks, and strolled over for a closer look. She chose a delicate branch, not a lot sturdier than a switch and, swinging it in the air, headed up the path. The owners of the inn (and therefore the tiny mountain) had posted signs denoting the history of Chamcook. The first posted sign she met advised that the paths up the mountain had been hewn one hundred and fifty years ago. Teams of Massachusetts oxen had hauled the rocks and tools necessary to create a route for horse and carriage, the vehicle of choice of rich New York visitors. Later, work crews dug into the mountain on the inside of the path and offset the route on the outside by placing sturdy granite stones weighing up to a ton. The young lady barely noted the details, her eyes drawn upward along the path.

Riley had thought being a hotel management graduate would somehow feel different from who she'd been a week previous, but it didn't. Riley knew it was merely an "in-the-door" to the next phase of her career. It would take awhile, but she'd eventually run a boutique hotel in the Hamptons. One step at a time.The very next step was to secure a job at the Algonquin Hotel or at the Rossmount Inn, two of the most prestigious establishments in this tiny resort town. She only had one connection, her father, but that, together with her education, looks, and charm would be sufficient.

She paced fifty yards of gentle inclination, rounded a corner that ascended more sharply, and settled into another pleasant fifty-yard section that wound tight around the hill. At this point, she was beginning to feel the elevation by catching glimpses through the birch and ash trees below her. It was dizzying, thinking a single slip on a shiny, wet rock near the edge would send her tumbling a hundred feet down through those slender tree trunks.

At the next corner, the halfway mark, she stopped at a lookout and read the plaque describing Passamaquoddy Bay. Historically, the bay was the reason for the existence of St. Andrews By The Sea, her always summer home, and for now her year-round home. The treeline obscured the town itself, but the wedge of blue bay water, framed by trees on the right and left, was straight out of a tourist photo. Just in front of her toes, though, the mountain dropped thirty feet before the angle of the mountain sloped away from her toward the base. Turning left, she rounded the next bend and headed upward.

Now anxious to get to the top, she pushed her thighs and calves to increase their pace, stopping at times to listen to the breeze soughing through the trees, and tried to catch a glimpse of the occasional chipmunk scratching through the leafy blanket of forest floor. The afternoon sky had greater opportunity to peek through the thinning trees, brightening her path. She rounded the last corner, climbed five wooden steps and, smiling at her accomplishment, placed her feet on solid granite stone. Her eyes followed a three hundred-and-sixty-degree panoramic view that included Chamcook Harbour, the town of St. Andrews, Passamaquoddy Bay, which was the body of water separating New Brunswick from Maine, and on the landward side, a portion of Chamcook Lake. She could see for miles.

Bringing her view in a little tighter, however, she noticed she wasn't alone. Someone—a woman, perhaps—was warming herself on the chunk of granite that sloped down and in the general direction of Calais, Maine. She took a few steps toward the prone form, calling "Excuse me?"

The woman sat up, a smile suffusing her entire face. Her arms and face were the most delicate porcelain tone, and her hair was a knotty rosebush of strawberry blonde curls. The resemblance was unmistakable.

"Hello, Mother. What's it been, seventeen years and two months?"

The woman's smile faltered.

* * * *

Riley paused. She'd actually rehearsed what she'd say, if this moment ever came around. As she practiced, in her mind, the words always came out as "I lost my trust in you then, and I do not trust you now." Instead, different words tumbled out.

"I'd just like you to know your daughter grew up smart. But I was always smart. Can I give you an example? Remember that night you left Daddy and me?" She wagged a finger from side to side, silencing the woman. "I had a feeling it was an important night, and even at five years old, I told myself the story of that night over and over, line by line, repeating what was said between my loving mother and father. So I wouldn't forget. This is what you said, the last words I heard from you until today. You said 'You've made mistakes in the past, and been forgiven for them, haven't you?' And Daddy said '…your two minutes are up. Get out.' Now, as a child, I wasn't sure what it all meant, except for the door slamming." She smiled, her voice sad. "I knew what that meant."

"You have to understand, darling, your father and I…we just weren't compatible."

"What you mean is, you liked to take things from him, and he liked things not to be taken from him."

This provoked a genuine smile from Tricia. "In a sense, you're correct. I may have had an exaggerated sense of what was, ah, ours. And I may have had a…substance abuse issue at the time."

"Yes, I heard that from my cousin Kate. Men you weren't necessarily married to were one of your substance issues, as I understand it. Drugs, too?"

"I never pretended to be anything I wasn't, darling." Tricia's voice lost some of its softness. "I was just a woman passing through life with a marriage partner who didn't have time for me. Listen, when you're alone and don't need to work, you have lots of time to feel sorry for yourself. You begin to think, maybe, there are only a few options available to you. You, ah, pursue them and, next thing you know, you're on the wrong side of a beautiful, expensive door with no money, no connections, and no options. I made a mistake. Hell, I made a wheelbarrow of mistakes, and that day wasn't the last of them.

"But, after an eternity, things stopped working against me. I cleaned up, and I started taking pride in myself. I opened a small business, a nail salon." She flashed a beautifully manicured hand. "And I started over."

Riley unfolded her arms from across her chest, but the dubious look was harder to undo. "Let's cut to the chase, mommy dearest. Why are you here? Do you need a deposit on something? A top-up on an amazing opportunity down in Florida? A second chance? Because I have to tell you, second chances are few and far between in the Parker family. Dad and I have developed an immunity to sob stories." The arms crept back up, crossing themselves once again at her chest, re-building her fortress of solitude.

To Riley's surprise, her words made Tricia's face soften to a smile. "I knew this wouldn't be easy, not that I deserve easy. But, from my heart, I only came here for two reasons: to say something and to ask something. So, here goes." She drew a ragged breath, her face tight. "First of all, I came here to say I'm sorry for screwing up our family. I had everything; well, almost everything, and I pissed it away. I'm heartbroken for having done that. And I know it can't be fixed. But I had to tell you that."

Tricia stopped, staring at the granite at her feet as if fascinated by its existence, as if to wish it was the material of her heart.

After what seemed like an hour, she spoke again, this time in a whisper that was almost drowned out by the breeze. "And if you can find it in your heart, I also came here to ask for a hug goodbye. It was my deepest regret, about that night. Not being able to hug you goodbye. It was…the worst." Her voice strengthened, as if the worst was now over. "So, whaddayasay? A hug for your mother?" Her eyes pleaded.

Riley's eyes welled up. "I—I can't. Father…it's just too soon." It was the young woman's turn to study the ground beneath her, drops spilling onto her white blouse.

"Ah, you can't blame an awful mother for trying." She, too, wiped tears away. "Anyway, I'll be leaving town tomorrow. I have a bit of business to see to this afternoon, and I have to get back to work on Monday. Those nails aren't going to buff themselves, right?" She tried a laugh, but it sounded more like a choking gasp. "I'll be at the Links Lodge, if you…if there's…" Her voice trailed off. "And one more thing. You clearly don't trust me. But there are others, close to you, whom you shouldn't trust. Okay. Enough."

Riley's hand extended a few inches, almost of its own volition, and then fell. "I, um, have to go. The group will be wondering where I went." Without saying anything else, Riley turned and headed back down the mountain, eyes blurred, at a quick pace that turned into a brisk jog. She didn't look back.

Chapter 3

Montauk, New York

HARRY RAFUSE PACED THE LENGTH of the great room of his house in Montauk. This particular great room didn't have the scope of the great rooms of nearby estates. This one was a sixteen-foot-square enclosure that took up almost a quarter of his compact residence. At a million dollars, virtually all of it leveraged against loans, its cost didn't come close to the real estate prices of every neighbor for a mile in any direction. A bedroom, kitchen, bathroom, and compact library completed the elements of the building, but the large front room was its only comfortable aspect. He suspected—no, he knew—the nearby beach just over the dunes was the best part of the property. *Better to have the poorest building in the best neighborhood than the best building in the poorest.* He thought that, not for the first time. There was nowhere to go but up. At the moment, though, Harry had other things on his mind beside property values. He had a cell phone in his hand, and he wasn't happy.

That morning, Harry had received a disturbing call from one of his colleagues. Derek Waugh was his go-to man when art works needed to find their way to a private collector and authorities were not to be involved. In fact, Waugh was skilled at making works of art sink beneath the surface, even the ones that were recently stolen and therefore in the news. But Waugh had let Rafuse down. Harry had an exquisite painting, a twelve-by-fifteen Sorolla, and Waugh wouldn't have anything to do with the painting, or with Rafuse. He'd said people were beginning to watch them both. A recent article in an on-line art trading magazine, *Art Valuables and Collectibles* had in fact mentioned Rafuse as a person whose name had come up in relation to art pieces that had disappeared.

Harry ran a hand through thinning, mouse-brown hair and stepped out into the noonday sun. His broad jaw rested in the open position, just a little, and his narrow eyes squinted in the sunlight. The dog chained to the porch pillar sidled up to him and was ignored for its troubles. Harry was deep within his thoughts. He felt New York, and specifically Long Island closing in on him, and it appeared to be just a matter of time before there'd be a hand on his collar. He had to leave town. But all of his money was tied up in art that was proving to be a challenge to unload. With no liquid assets available to him, it seemed a creative solution might be necessary. Who could he hit up for a place to stay, hopefully on the East Coast, and preferably not more than a day's drive from the big city?

The problem was, once the five boroughs and Long Island were taken out of the equation, his friends and acquaintances were as well. Who was left? He began with existing relatives and then chuckled in dismay. He had no brothers or first cousins, and most of the distant cousins consisted of a series of bridges he'd burned years ago. He wasn't even on speaking terms with many of them. *They wrote me off before I even had a chance*. His face turned ugly, a sneering condemnation reflecting every reaction his relatives displayed, as he endeavored to make something of himself. *Bastards! Here I am, sitting pretty in a million dollar home on Long Island. They should be so lucky.* He swore under his breath, knowing they were all better off than he was, and knowing this wasn't getting him anywhere.

A thought struck him. Parker! Fucking Nick Parker. He hadn't said a word to his cousin in, what was it, five years? The good news was, he hadn't pissed him off in five years, either. They weren't close as third cousins, but they were on speaking terms, and a Parker by blood, however far removed, was still a Parker, right? When was the last time they'd had a real chat? High school graduation. The daughter—what was her name—Riley, had finished university and had gone to study something or other in Canada. They had a monstrous big summer home there, went there every year in May. Maybe it was time to give dear old cuz Nick a ring, maybe wrangle an invite to Canada for the summer. He could find an art dealer up there, one who didn't mind making a profit in exchange for keeping his damned mouth shut.

Canada. Mosquitoes, hicks, no culture, and good old, well-intentioned fool Nick. Could he stand it? *I can stand anything for a couple of months, can't I? Besides, Canada was a million miles away from New York, but only a day's drive. Yeah, Canada could work. I'll call dear Nick, and then put the word out to my Montreal contacts.* Re-entering the house, he trotted up the stairs to the bedroom nightstand in search of his phone directory.

* * * *

Montreal

Some people would argue there's nothing that can beat a Boulevard St.-Laurent outdoor patio bar on the sunny side of a June afternoon. Perfectly coiffed *Québecoise* women walked past, owning the sidewalk. Men in Italian business suits sat beside university students, both endeavoring to extend their noon hour just enough to avoid a critical look upon their return. In the corner closest to the bar, a young man sat, drink in front of him, flipping his phone over and over without glancing at it. He wore espadrilles —no socks—skinny chinos, ash gray tee under a thin knit sweater. Razor-trimmed hipsters sat nearby, but this man's hair was glorious. It would be a shame to buzz it up the sides. His eyes were hidden behind sunglasses, and a slender wooden cane hung off the back of the chair beside him. He was alone, but clearly waiting for something.

Something happened, this time in the form of a discreet buzz from his phone. Yves Palu checked the text message before the first buzz finished. He read, and re-read the words, and a look of rapt satisfaction crept across his face as he replied. "We have a deal. Meet me in St. Andrews, New Brunswick, and let's start something big. I'll bring money, and we'll make it grow." He smiled, despite the unpleasant sensation of damaged nerves dancing up and down his left leg. *I'm back in business, baby!* He stood, ignoring the almost-fresh drink, dropped a bill beside the glass and headed home to pack, his cane barely making a clicking sound on the sidewalk.

* * * *

Montauk

An old Ford pickup rolled down a coastline country lane skirting the North Shore of Long Island Sound, a few miles from Port Jefferson. Moonlight glanced off the remaining piece of his rear-view mirror, but the faint glow on the gray primer coat turned the truck into a ghostly image of itself. The muffler, one of the few things that worked well, burbled low and smooth, attracting little attention. The lone occupant sat behind the wheel, radio off, his left elbow outside the opened window, catching a bit of the late-night breeze. The trucked traveled well under the speed limit, further reducing its engine's sound to a murmur.

Harry Rafuse made an abrupt turn into an almost-hidden drive without slowing, slipped the truck into neutral and coasted the remaining fifty feet. The pine branches caressed the passenger side on the way by, making a swishing sound as the Ford came to a stop near a dark building. The engine ticked as it cooled, but other than that, few sounds broke the still night air. He opened the door. His key was ready as he slid from the truck seat and then took care to bring the door to, but not closing it so as to make the latch sound, and in a moment he was inside the small storage shed.

There were no windows and Harry had the lights on as soon as the door was completely shut. He stood at a slight bend since there was no space to stand properly, peering down the tiny path through the middle of the single room. For a building with such an impoverished exterior, its contents were startling in their grandeur. The rear quarter of the compact room was packed to the rafters with scores of paintings. Beside them rested a few European cabinets and hutches, moving van blankets separating the lowers from the uppers. As he moved to the back, he brushed against wooden crates containing art pieces, mementos, statuary, and vases.

Hundreds of pieces of antique jewelry rested in glass cases on shelves above the crates. Beside him, individually boxed, were unique, one-off artefacts, most of which had proven provenances, causing their value to quadruple. "What do you think, Harry? Have we hit the seven million mark yet?" He grinned in the dim light.

It would have been so much easier to unload it all in the shops of Manhattan, or in the galleries in the outlying boroughs. But these pieces were known. Known to have been stolen, known to be the trigger that would set the police dogs on him. He shook his head. *I'm not going to jail because of laziness. I'll just have to ship them off a ways, set them loose in Canada, someplace I'm not known. That would certainly change my status. I don't think the cousins would turn their noses up at me if I coasted into their snobby driveways in a Ferrari.*

Harry thought of an incident the other day, when a plainclothes detective knocked on his door for a chat. Did he know about the MacQuart estate having been robbed in April? Did he have any information to share regarding a ruby-and-emerald bracelet, turn of the century, crafted in India? No? Was he sure? *Of course I was sure. I was sure not going to chat with you about my business. Jerk.*

But that was an anomaly, a crime of opportunism. More than half of the contents of this room came from a single source. An awful grin began to twist his face. *I get the goods, and the insurance money changed hands. Sure, someone lost out, but isn't that the cost of doing business?*

He laid a hand on the nearest crate, the one containing the MacQuart bracelet. It calmed him to be so close to such wealth, knowing it would soon be shoring up the-cupboard-is-bare Rafuse bank account. He smiled. *Some collectors love this shit. Can't get enough of it.* All Harry saw was crap that needed to be converted into greenbacks.

The cop, together with the news he received from his now-ex colleague Waugh reinforced his need to leave town. The sooner he split this burg and landed in St. Andrews, the better. *And that French guy. He's going to be just the ticket to unload a big chunk of this, once I move it into Canada. He seemed hungry for business. I'll give him the business, all right.*

Chapter 4

St. Andrews

So, THIS IS THE RECIPE for turning your day to complete shit. Riley Parker's sight blurred as she left her home on the Bar Road, heading…she didn't even know where she was heading. An evening away from her friends, coupled with a sleepless night had done nothing to calm her down, so she decided to take a drive. What on earth was her mother doing in New Brunswick—in Canada? Without caring of the exact direction, Riley aimed her BMW Z4 Roadster convertible, an early graduation present, down Route 127 toward the highway.

She'd heard so many stories about her errant mother, beginning at age ten with Aunt Erin warning the little girl Tricia was a drug addict. Later, Kate, who seemed to know everything, took her aside at a birthday party and revealed the many infidelities and multiple crimes of her mother, real and imagined. Her father had corrected the story and had their parents chastise the two girls, but by then the damage was done and Riley's pre-teen life became a fragile shambles.

But that was all in the past. At age thirteen, she'd blossomed. Riley's trademark Celtic bronze curls tumbled down past intelligent green eyes, a pert nose, full, naturally red lips and flawless, milky white skin. With her striking good looks came lots of height, full, sensuous hips, and lithe legs built to run. Grade school was a happy pairing of academic and athletic accomplishment. Riley was by nature a generous, kind person, so even those youths who seemed born to tear peers down couldn't find a chink in her armor. Riley's followers—there had always been followers—stoutly defended her on the rare occasion anyone tried to attack. She grew into a confident, accomplished young woman whose cares seemed to slough off, leaving Riley even more confident and resilient.

Until now. Having her mother appear after all these years made the young woman feel like a vase shattered against a brick wall. She pounded the steering wheel in frustration and then geared down, willing herself to be calm. Ahead on the left she enjoyed the view to the road down to the shore. Beyond the shore lay historic St. Croix Island, the first winter home of one of the discoverers of North America. Of course, the Vikings, and the Spanish had been there hundreds of years before Samuel de Champlain, and thousands of years earlier, the nomadic Asians had topped the North Pole and migrated across the Bering Straits to settle southward. But for Canada, Champlain was among the first to establish a colony. On a whim, she decided to pull over beside the monument and sat staring at the water flowing past the riverbank at the bottom of the hill.

D.A. the cook had told her the island Champlain had camped on that first winter was miles longer than the rocky outcropping that remained today. She studied it without leaving the car, noting the analogy between the worn-away island and her worn-away armor. *Am I three-quarters gone as well?* She laughed aloud at herself, startling a brazen chipmunk that had sidled up in search of peanuts. *What a baby I am! I'm pretty, smart, sitting in a frigging Beamer, going home to an estate where someone will cook my food for me, and on top of that, I have two job placements to consider for the summer. What, really, do I have to whine about? The fact of having Father alone makes me a lucky girl.*

But being lucky didn't answer the questions swirling around in her head. What did Mother want? Why was she here? How long would she stay? She'd said she was leaving today, but would she, if she didn't receive what she wanted? Which was…what? Mother always wanted something.

"This is crazy. I'm going round and around, but I'm not asking the right person. What do you think?" she asked the chipmunk, after fishing around in the glove box for some crumbles from a bag of granola. The tiny animal didn't break eye contact with its benefactor, even as it chewed up the last crumbs. "Well, I think you're right. If I want answers, I have to ask the person holding them. What was the name of the motel she was staying at?" The chipmunk stared back, a mute, solemn look on his whiskery face.

Chapter 5

St. Andrews

TONY HORCROFT PUSHED HIS ANCIENT, two-wheeled wooden cart around the Parker estate building and headed for his third trip to the mulch pile, just beyond the guest house. He took the wider path, not certain the smaller building yet contained its newest occupant—an artist, he gathered. He loved his wooden cart, eschewing anything more modern. "The house has been here for over a hundred years, I don't see anyone jumpin' up to replace it with a trailer. If it ain't broke," and he always made it a point to challenge the room with his eyes each time he growled the words, "then don't fix it."

He loved the handles, worn over the years to better suit his smallish, roughened hands. One side and the back were open, the better to slide pots, soils, and other materials on and off without having to lift them straight up from the back. If he were honest, he'd say its best feature was that no one else on the grounds preferred to use it, so it was always exactly where he placed it. Similarly, it was not a coincidence there wasn't a second groundskeeper.

Tony worked alone. Always had, always would, if he had his way, which he usually did. For example, he chose the annuals, the perennials, and most of the vegetables. It wasn't the owners who chose them. It was Tony who explained why the boxes in the raised gardens were the dimensions they were. In turn, the family, Nick and Riley Parker, were permitted to agree with his decisions. And in exchange, he agreed to stay on another year. It was this way when Nick Parker brought his daughter, Riley the infant, for the first time in 1989, and twenty years later, it remained thus.

The fieldstone path wended its way through the back lawn, leading ultimately to the pebbly beach of Chamcook Harbour, part of the Fundy Bay system. As was his habit, Tony set the cart down where the manicured grass butted up against the line delineating the top of the beach. To his right, the Bar Road traced a path to and then onto the beach, past the tide announcement sign that seemed to direct the driver straight into the water. In fact, this was the case. Low tide at the end of the Bar Road revealed a rough, drivable path that led to nearby Minister's Island, a picturesque, elevated plot of land a quarter mile into the bay.

And as was his wont, Tony took a moment, every time he was in the back yard, to catch a glimpse of the first rocks that protected the shoulder of the newly appeared road. This morning, though, the unfolding tableau seemed unfamiliar. This was an aberrant thought, since it was the same bay, the same road, the same neap tide he'd watched a thousand times, perhaps more. But it didn't seem exactly the same as the last fifty times he'd seen it. Shrugging, he loaded his cart with composted soil and headed back to the front garden. A half hour later, he rounded the corner of the house and traced the flagstone path once again. He parked his cart on the grass a foot away from the top of the beach, lining up his wheel to an almost imperceptible track, just as he'd done a thousand times. He took out a red kerchief and wiped his forehead, taking pains to avoid even a glimpse of the watery road. He wanted clear, first-glimpse eyes to view the watery road this time. Kerchief placed in his back pocket, he blinked once and then turned and stared with stony purpose at the almost bared road.

There were the three large saltwater puddles, still-immersed middle section, and the newly formed road winding up to the island. What was different?

There it was, rolling to and fro with each wave, almost halfway to the island. Was it a lobster trap, cut loose? A bag of rags? He'd seen crazier things washed up. "I suppose I'd better go grab it before it gets caught up in some boat propeller." But he hadn't reached the near end of the underwater road when he stopped dead. It wasn't a trap, or a bag of clothes.

Even from this distance, he could see reddish hair, washing to and fro with each wave. *Riley! Surely not Riley!* The road had fully formed now, and his feet hardly got wet as he ran toward the shapeless form, navigating the large, salty puddles. With each step, his heart sank. *The hair's not quite right, but that could be the sun*. He started to call out, to himself, at first. "Get help. Get help!" His voice grew even as his realization hit home, at the odds of survival. He drew the attention of Mrs. Farr in the Maxwell House, whose home was closest to the road. She waved once and ran into the house, the screen door slamming behind her.

Chapter 6

Niagara On The Lake

SEAN DONOVAN TOOK THE EXIT off the highway to Niagara On The Lake, and pointed the red SUV up the by-way toward his new home. Beth McLean, Director of Communications for the Canadian High Commission to Britain, in London, was visiting Donovan, the new owner of the wine estate. She was grateful the weather had improved since her pre-Christmas visit. The early July air through the open window warmed her face, pleasing her with its gentle gift.

Donovan had driven to Pearson airport in Toronto to meet her two days earlier. They'd grabbed dinner and a hotel room in Toronto and done a bit of shopping the next morning, taking the opportunity to get caught up on the transfer of ownership of the winery and vineyards. He'd wanted to purchase his own winery for years, and over Christmas, he'd arrived at a firm purchase price for Plenitude Vineyards. Taking care with the timing, he'd gathered up most of his money from offshore accounts, paying installments over the winter months. By May Day, the winery was his as an eighty-five per cent majority owner, and he hoped everyone involved was happy. He was.

Where does one conjure up six million dollars? In this case, it was a straightforward answer. He'd been a contract thief. On a case-by-case basis, Sean Donovan had been engaged by a series of individuals within the international arts community. Over the years, others, mostly collectors, had paid him to travel somewhere in the world and retrieve a painting, an artefact or, in one instance, the recorded conversation of a U.S. president. His ostensible career as a government consultant created opportunities, and at a hundred thousand a year it, too, paid satisfactorily. But when one can disappear for three days and return with a year's pay, there was just no comparison to the traditional day job.

His lifestyle came at a cost: his health, his conscience, and a dearth of relationships, to name three. At forty, he was beginning to acquire a few silver hairs at the temple, and he'd picked up the habit of looking over his shoulder and always sitting with his back to the wall. It was time to ease away from that lifestyle and what better way to switch careers than to find something to be passionate about and immerse yourself into it? In the back of his mind, though, there was the seductiveness of the quick dollar, the adrenalin rush, the challenge of the theft...

But, no. He was out of the business. Absolutely.

"It's nice to be back in Niagara."

Sean accepted a peck on the cheek, smiling at the comment as he took her bag. In turn, Beth pulled a large suitcase behind her as they followed the cut granite walkway to the front doors of Plenitude Vineyards. They wheeled past the crew offering wine tasting flights, past the restaurant and followed the hall to the private suites at the end.

Beth hauled the luggage to the middle of the room and crossed the final yards to flop on the bed. "Sorry, when I saw the bed jet lag slapped me around and all my ambition left me. I need a nap!" She squeezed her eyes shut for just a second, knowing full well a pair of washed gray eyes were watching her, a smile just behind them. Her head shot up, a look of alarm on her face. "We're not on a case, are we? Tell me I don't have five minutes to catch a flight to Argentina to save someone's life."

Donovan shook his head, continuing to smile. "One hour sounds fair, or you won't sleep tonight. Then I'm coming to get you. We're having dinner with Jack, the Schmidts, and our fake daughter, Claire." Claire Valentin, newly arrived from Arles, France, had benefitted from Donovan and Beth's sleuthing the previous summer, getting to know them for a brief but intense hour. As soon as she'd finished school, the young lady had presented herself on the doorsteps of Plenitude, looking for an apprenticeship. She was as French as the day was long, and equally at home in the vineyards as she was in the wine production facilities.

Beth nodded, her eyes closing. "I'll take it. Now, go away, or I'll want sex more than sleep. And I really, really want sleep." He closed the door behind him on his way out.

* * * *

Donovan thought about the woman sleeping in the room he'd just left. Now it was to be their room. They'd made a decision the week before, and upon Beth's arrival at Pearson Airport he confirmed he'd made the necessary arrangements, and their plan was a go. They stayed the additional day in Toronto, and he had an announcement for the Plenitude family. He thought about her and the journey they'd taken.

Serendipity had swirled around their first encounters. He'd initiated a five-minute exchange of information at the Canadian High Commission in London and that seemed to be that. A year later, however, it was her turn to make the overture. She'd called in a panic. A fraud was being perpetrated, and the blame was falling all around her ears. He agreed to help, and as they went on the lam, he'd come to appreciate her attributes: wit, insight, ability to retain grace under pressure, and a certain necessary toughness wrapped up in a small, attractive package. Further adventures followed, and they'd grown close.

At seven-thirty, Donovan returned to fetch Beth. Once ready, they strolled down the corridor to the restaurant and joined a small group sitting around the Chef's Table in an alcove near the kitchen. There were no strangers to introduce, as everyone had met everyone else at least once before. Jack and Claire sat beside each other, Anna and Dieter sat next to them, and across from the four they'd set a pair of chairs for Donovan and Beth. Jack and Claire had arrived at Plenitude at different times, but they'd gotten to know each other and, despite their odd couple status, had become each other's confidante. Jack, a widower, had been involved in Donovan's last case. As an RCMP detective called in to investigate a murder at the Canadian embassy in London, he'd worked with both Beth and Donovan. He had been shot in Romania, and sent home to Canada to recover.

During his convalescence, Donovan had persuaded Jack to complete his retirement from the RCMP and become head of security at the Plenitude winery. He'd agreed and, with regular bouts of physio, was almost back to being the garrulous, plain-spoken man he'd been before the shooting. Jack had suggested a few changes around the winery that garnered respect from Dieter and Anna Schmidt, the previous owners. They'd sold a majority share of the winery to Donovan, and it had been as if a weight had been lifted from their shoulders. Now, as day-to-day managers of the winery, their new status meant they weren't encumbered by finances, hiring, and many of the mundane responsibilities winery owners never get into the business to manage.

Donovan and Beth were welcomed with a roar, and they sat down to the second round of wine, the whites already having come and gone. Beth leaned in to ask about Dieter and Anna's son, Kurt. He'd spent the previous six months in Florida, enduring a long, painful, and expensive stay at Tampa Bay General Hospital. The expenses almost bankrupted the Schmidts, but Donovan's purchase of the winery, together with getting Kurt home, returned their lives to an even keel.

Anna shared an update with Beth. "Kurt's back home now, convalescing in a physical rehab facility in St. Catherines. He's doing fine, and we will get him home for good by the grape harvest. He might be strong enough to visit us next month. I'm sure he'd love to meet you."

"That sounds perfect. If Kurt's as nice as you two, it'll be a pleasure to sit and chat with him." She took her seat, fending off the thrust of glasses of wine from two different directions.

"All right, what's been going on lately?" Three completely different answers assaulted Donovan, and he couldn't hear any of them. "Let's try this again. Dieter, Beth needs to get caught up. How's business?" The man with curly silver hair and wire-rimmed glasses sat back, one arm draped awkwardly over the back of his chair. "Three bus tours booked today for later in July, all the students are already working the vines, hosting the tastings, and taking shifts at the restaurant. Some of the musicians are in place, and Anna will get the rest of them signed later this week for August and September. So, business is good. Anna?" His wife demurred, smiling.

Jack leaned in, a dribble from his water glass spilling onto the linen tablecloth. "Just so you know, security is horrible. I haven't seen a murder, a kidnapping, or a theft since I got here." That got a chuckle. "I may have to short-sheet the beds, just to raise the excitement level."

Sean spoke up. "From you, Jack, no news is good news. Am I right?" The new head of security nodded, spilling another drop. "Well, we do have a new star, *L'etoile de la France*" He raised a glass to Claire.

Color rose in the young woman's cheeks. "I'm certain I am not the Star of France, Jack." She folded her napkin, meeting Beth's eyes. "*Bien*. It's been almost six months since my arrival. I cannot say whether I've learned more about the English or the wine making! But it has been an adventure, that is for sure. Where to begin? The winery here is fantastic! It has everything I need to learn the business from one end to the other. At home, we have a simple harvest table to serve guests, with bread and cheese to accompany the wine. Here, I am learning about what wines can be grown in this climate. The restaurant is brilliant, and I cannot wait to hear the entertainment all through the summer and the fall.

"But the best—the important part is I am learning so much about the chemistry of wine making, *le terroir*—the dirt?—and the bottling methods you use in Canada. On the *Côtes du Rhône*, we learn from each other, generation after generation. So, if I may be immodest, we do our way very, very well. But New World winemakers are anxious to try new methodologies, which is exciting. I spend four days a week in the lab and around the tanks and barrels, for which I am grateful. Finally, Jack treated me last month to a trip to Montreal. I swear I spoke only French all weekend. It was glorious! *Merci*, Jack."

The group turned back to Beth and Donovan. Beth set her glass of rosé down, and faced the group. "As you know, I've been Director of Communications for the Canadian Embassy in London for over a year now. The thing is, I was promoted and unexpectedly replaced the previous director in his fourth year of service to that embassy. The usual tenure for diplomats is just over five years, and they—we—don't typically know where we will be deployed. So, I'm sitting on the edge of my seat, in year five, wondering where they'll send me. Unfortunately, it's not a level playing field. Family diplomats—and I agree with this unwritten policy— stand a slightly better chance of being sent to what might be called easier posts, for example: New York, Ireland, or perhaps Australia. As a single woman, I'm considered to be more, um, mobile. Portable, you might say." Her laugh was rueful. "Anyway, I'll let Sean take up the story from here."

Donovan leaned back in his chair. "I'm going to cut to the chase. Beth and I chatted about what we want, where we want to be, and how to achieve that. So a month ago we decided to get married, and yesterday, with all the paperwork in place, we went to a Justice of the Peace, and got married." She raised her left hand from beneath the table to reveal a *pave*-style ring, the tiny washed blue stones clustered around a perfect white pear-cut diamond. She held up the hand, waving it as if it had won first prize. The table exploded, with both Dieter and Jack hurrying over to shake Donovan's hand and receive a hug from Beth.

"What happens next?"

"Of course we told her boss Rory very early this morning, who in turn communicated the news upward. They've given Beth the impression they're looking at positions for her in North or South America. If it's Ottawa, great. If it's Peru, that may be a bit more complicated. We're going to play it as it comes." He shrugged. "She may not be asked to transfer for another year. So, we wait." Donovan's cell phone buzzed, and he begged the group's indulgence while he stepped out to answer it.

* * * *

The people around the table were on their second course and there was still no sign of Donovan. Beth excused herself and headed off in search of her shiny new husband. She rounded the first corner outside of the restaurant and almost knocked him over. He took her hand and guided her through an exit and onto a quiet stone patio.

"You'd been a while, and sometimes calls like this are none of my business, and sometimes they are. Which is it this time, Sweetie?"

Donovan hesitated, framing his words. Smiling, he began. "Remember, just before you conked out, earlier? You hoped I wasn't going to drag you off on a murder expedition to Argentina? Well..." He grinned, eyes dancing.

"No! No way, Sean."

"I'm teasing. At least, for the moment. I pulled you aside to ask a question about Jack." Both faces grew serious. "John and Pegs are visiting friends at a seaside resort in New Brunswick. The ex-wife of the host turned up after more than fifteen years. It gets worse. She turned up a bit the worse for wear. She's very dead. They want to help their host, mostly by trying to keep him out of jail. Soo…"

"Yes?" She squeezed his hand.

"I was wondering, since Jack has recovered from his wounds and is acting a bit bored, why wouldn't we send him, instead of us? I'm asking: Can he handle it?"

Beth paused to weigh all of this fresh news. "He looks great, he did mention the winery is going smoothly, and his life would be in no danger, I suppose. Why don't we put it to him and let him decide?"

"Sounds good. But not in front of the table. We'll go sit at the bar after dinner, just the three of us and we can have a chat." They entered the building and re-joined the group.

* * * *

Jack Miller's knobby, calloused hands played with a fresh pour of Guinness, sliding the draught two inches to the right, and then two inches back. His eyes followed the glass: left, right, left, but it was clear his ears were offering undivided attention to the story Donovan was sharing with him. Donovan's friends, John and Peggy Whiteway, from Minnesota, were summering in St. Andrews at the estate of their friend and John's former employer, Nick Parker, also an American. Nick's ex-wife just washed up on shore within sight of the Parker estate. The RCMP suspect foul play. The family hadn't seen the ex for more than fifteen years, and it seemed a little far-fetched to think her corpse would appear five hundred yards from the estate after all these years. No one had been charged, but Nick and his adult daughter, Riley, were both persons of interest in the case.

"It's time for me to cut to the chase, Jack. The Whiteways want some help to figure this all out and hopefully exonerate their friends. They asked for a hand, and Beth and I just can't leave the winery right now. I don't have to tell you crime scenes don't stay fresh, so…we were wondering—."

Jack's voice was dry. "You were wondering what I'm doing tomorrow morning and for the next week or two. I'll let you two off the hook. It sounds interesting, and I'd love a trip to the East Coast, maybe get my nose into other folks' business. Am I going undercover, or am I to make contact with the RCMP as soon as I hit town?"

"I think going undercover with most of the town is the better approach, but feel free to touch base with the RCMP, just to stay out of trouble. It's a very small town, so everybody will be keeping their eyes on you from Day One. You can tell the RCMP you're a private eye, working for the Parkers. No need to tell anyone else, though."

Beth interjected. "Won't you have a better idea of how to play it, once you get into town and see who's playing what cards? If you fly into Fredericton, rent a car and ease into St. Andrews, you can keep things on the down-low to start with. It's a resort town, so strange cars won't be unusual there. Oh! There's an amazing inn there, with a European chef. It's called the Rossmount. You should definitely stay there. It's actually only a few minutes from town."

"How do you know this stuff?" Donovan gave her an admiring look.

"I had a life before I met you, mister. Besides, I am a Maritimer, so this is practically my backyard."

"In the meantime," Jack interrupted with a broad grin, "give me the Whiteway phone number, and I'll be on the next plane. I guess I'd better pack."

Chapter 7

St. Andrews

JACK MILLER DROVE HIS CHARCOAL SUV into the hotel parking lot on the outskirts of the town of St. Andrews. From Toronto, his flight had made a milk-run stop in Montreal before dropping him off in the small city of Fredericton. He'd rented the SUV there and drove the hour and a bit to the small resort town, arriving at The Rossmount Inn at three o'clock.

The old, perfectly maintained inn was built on an elevation at the base of Chamcook Mountain, a rounded promontory of old geological granite that was the highest in the county. Jack unloaded his suitcase, overnight bag, and laptop and wheeled everything over to a wide set of stairs leading up to the grand front doors. Ascending the outside stairs with luggage required a bit of additional effort. It had only been a few months of recovery since his shooting in Romania. Twenty-five steps later he stood, back to the inn, admiring the waters of Passamaquoddy Bay off in the distance. To his right, an elegant swimming pool replete with a large fish statue, pergolas, and two dozen deck chairs offered up a desirable oasis. He admired the long driveway up to the inn, noting the complete absence of traffic noise.

It was too beautiful a scene to leave. Rather than stepping into the inn, he wandered to the side of the property to view the pool area. On the far end of the line of deck chairs he spied a path leading down into an overgrown meadow. The warmth of the sun on his face was pleasant, and he wagered a walk through a New Brunswick meadow would only increase the pleasure of the sunshine. But he had things to do, registering for a room being first among them. He entered the inn, noting the tiny reception room on the left.

He studied the hallway with his back to the unoccupied reception area, appreciating the beautiful bar opposite, inviting him in. Everywhere else was rich, tasteful dark wood paneling. It wasn't overpowering or gloomy; it did, however, tell the visitor this was an inn a notch above the norm. A grand, sweeping stairway straight ahead, just beyond the dining room entrance, welcomed guests to the second story. The size of the hall, the dining room, and the bar suggested there weren't more than a dozen rooms on the two floors above. Content with what he saw, Jack greeted his hostess, entered the reception area, and asked for a room facing the bay on the second floor. A minute later, he leaned on the door bearing the number Twenty-One and dragged his belongings across the sill and into the room.

After unpacking, he spread the few notes he had across the desk. It didn't amount to much. In the good old days, the days before his wife took ill and he lost her, he would have eased down to the bar, ordered a Guinness or two, remarked it was five o'clock somewhere and downed half of the first draught in a great, satisfying gulp. But his drinking had got out of control, and by the end of last summer, he knew it was time to put on the brakes. He hadn't had a sip since then.

Jack asked himself if he was an alcoholic, joking in his head he couldn't be, because he didn't go to the meetings. In truth, he suspected he and his liver were all right. But the issue was he didn't want to get drunk and slide down that dark alley where loneliness beckoned. Not yet. His new job at the winery brought him into contact with lots of new people, most of them not criminals for a change. He laughed at his own humor. And he had new friends in Donovan and Beth, Claire, Dieter and Anna. And he was about to meet with John and Peggy Whiteway, folks he knew he could be friends with. Someday, he'd be able to sit down and order a beverage and have a quaff without over-thinking it. He reached for the phone and dialed a number from a scrap of paper on the desk. Better let the Whiteways know he was in town.

John and Peggy suggested they meet at the Rossmount for dinner, which gave Jack enough time to make the reservation and at the same time order up a bottle of Chianti. He had the obligatory twenty minutes to chill it and to rest his eyes for a spell. In a bit, he received a call from the front desk. His friends had arrived; did he wish them to be sent up?

* * * *

Jack chose to play host in the broad hallway just outside his small room. This hallway was in the style of elegant older inns, a dozen feet wide and eighty feet long, with a table and three wingback chairs nestled beside the window that faced the bay. He paused, bottle in hand to admire the view. The water in the distance looked enticing, and he remembered the Bay of Fundy was very, very cold. He hadn't time to pull the cork before the Whiteways reached the top of the stairs and turned to approach him.

With greetings out of the way, Jack finished pouring chianti into three glasses—his was just a splash to be subsequently ignored—and they each chose a chair and prepared to get caught up. Peggy looked rested and very cheerful, whereas John confessed he'd turned his ankle that day. They'd had a seafood lunch and decided to walk off the calories on the rocky beach near the tiny lobster packing plant at the far end of the downtown shopping area.

The Whiteways asked after Claire and the Schmidts. John and Peggy had flown up to visit the winery for a long weekend a few months earlier. Jack told them about Claire, how she'd found her rhythm and was a solid contributor to the business in Niagara. He dropped the bombshell about the marriage, pleased the time of day was almost six o'clock and therefore the shriek Peggy sent the length of the hall wouldn't wake anyone up. John and Peggy took a sip from their glasses, John nodding in appreciation to his host for the unexpected gift of a beverage. Politenesses out of the way, Jack asked them to tell the story of the body on the underwater road.

"The groundskeeper found the ex-wife, Tricia, as the tide pulled away from the road."

"He'd been caretaker at the Parker estate for twenty years?"

"Long before Riley came along. He'd known the woman, but hadn't seen her for probably seventeen years. The family broke up about then but the father, Nick, and the daughter, Riley, came with the house, so to speak, so that meant Tony, the groundskeeper, became part of that side of the family, with Tricia excluded from everything. Tony's very loyal." Peggy's tone was rueful. "He's a curmudgeon, but a loyal one."

"Everything?" Jack tried not to jump to conclusions. Let the story unfold naturally and the end would reveal itself to him.

Peggy straightened the folds of her skirt with the palm of one hand. "We'd known Nick, and later his daughter for, well, forever, really. John worked for Nick and his father before him. So when we heard Nick and Tricia had broken up, we weren't surprised. She was kind of…bohemian, one could say. And he absolutely wasn't. He was—*is* straight-laced, buttoned-down. Like John, only worse." She beamed at her husband, who sniffed in disapproval.

"Anyway, back then, Nick took it hard. He had a leave of absence, remember, John? and came here for the summer." Peggy looked up, her memory fresh. "He and John were working on some geological project, and John had to take on a junior partner to complete it. Nick wouldn't say anything about the divorce for years, but once the…body washed up, he of course had to give a statement. We offered to sit with Riley while he went off with the RCMP detective. When he came back, he repeated everything he had said, and at that point we knew something had to be done. He needs help, Jack."

She paused, looking her husband straight in the eye. "But, there's a thing."

Jack grinned. Isn't there always a thing? He tilted his head. "Yes?"

"The thing is, if it was just Nick and Riley, that would be one thing. But they belong to an extended family. And, to our experience, they're not all the same. Nick's true-blue, but his family contains all kinds. Not killers or anything, but they aren't all Nicks."

"Duly noted. Was it anything specific he said, to make you feel so strongly that Nick needs help?"

Peggy looked at John, who spoke for the first time. "We feel that the way Nick presented his side of the story, it makes him look as if he still carried a grudge against her for wrecking their marriage. He didn't re-marry and, well, he still holds some animosity toward her."

Peggy nodded, eyes narrowed. "A lobster trap full. But the thing is, we know Nick. He's a sweetheart, true-blue, if a little dull, and he couldn't harm a fly."

"I see. How long was Tricia in town?" He'd almost called her "the ex-wife," but almost twenty years had passed since the separation. As well, the title seemed to take a little of the humanity from her. In his career, consistent reminders to himself that these were real people kept him closer to the running dialogue of their lives. And he needed that dialogue to eventually tease out the truth.

Peggy answered. "It's a curious thing. Nobody was aware of her presence in the community until her body washed up on shore. The police have placed an inquiry with Canada Customs to figure out when she crossed the border, but word hasn't come back yet. At least, the RCMP spokesman isn't saying if they've heard anything. If she wound up here, though, she probably crossed at St. Stephen or Milltown, which is barely twenty minutes down the road."

"Could she have flown in and rented a car?"

"She could have, but she didn't. They found an old GMC quarter ton pickup, what they call a 'beater,' in the coffee shop parking lot, and the plates are from New York State. It's registered to her, and the coffee shop's walking distance to the Bar Road. One advantage to living in a tiny town, I suppose."

John gave his wife an admiring glance. "A beater. Aren't you the local!" She winked back at him.

Jack had been scratching notes in a small moleskin book during the conversation. He put the book on the table and leaned back in the chair. "Well, that was a very satisfactory update. Now I'd like to know a little bit about the town itself. Give me a talking tour."

John's face became animated. "It's a great little New Brunswick resort town, bordered on two sides by salt water. The downtown core is basically one street lined with shops, and the wharf is halfway down the street, and I might as well say it as think it—the uptown is basically the Algonquin, a massive resort hotel, and an ice arena, which was a gift from Lady

Carmichael, one of the richy-rich estate holders. Behind the Algonquin is Katy's Cove, so, more salt water, really. That's it for retail features."

"And who lives here?" Jack's voice was calm, and his craggy face revealed nothing of his thoughts.

Peggy took up the story. "If you don't count the college students, who basically pack up and go home in June and leaving aside the merchants and clerks, you have three kinds of folk. The fishermen—and a surprising number of them are women, by the way—work mostly out of two wharves. You've seen the beautiful touristy one downtown and there's another in a village up the road called Black's Harbour. There's also a wharf almost out to the main highway, but I don't know if it's used for fishing or just as a container port.

"Because this is a resort town, there are lots of artists and artisans. The hippy ones are scattered throughout the countryside, in cabins, shacks, gorgeous country homes, and so on. There are some very successful artists in town. Many of them live in apartments attached to their shops." She paused to take a sip of wine, pushing a stray blonde wisp of hair back into place.

"And again, because this is a resort town, I suppose, there is a surprising number of millionaires living on large estates around town. It's mostly old money. Many of them have estates on the water, of course, and it should come as no surprise that, because they like their privacy the estates are hedged up and gated in the front, so it's tricky to see what sort of building they live in. That said, we were invited to stay at the Parker estate for the summer, so when you come see us, you'll get a bird's eye view of how the other half lives."

Jack grunted. "Millionaires, eh? What kind?"

"Looking backward a hundred years, some came from the lumber barons, out of Montreal. There are a few bankers, or children thereof. There are a surprising number who originated from the New York area, and their children and grandchildren kept coming back in the summers. In the thirties and forties in July, the trains would put on extra cars for the families, their help, and even their horses. I read about them in the books at the library. Irving Berlin proposed to his girl here, for example. Like I said, old money."

Jack decided to press. "Getting back to Nick and his daughter, if someone was to do a little digging, would they find any…mud?" He watched to see if either of his guests bristled at the implication.

Peggy replied. "We expected you to ask that, because we heard from Sean how good you are at your job. It's okay." She placed a hand, briefly, on his knee. "Believe me, these folks are boring, but in a good way. They inherited some money, earned a bunch more, and stewarded it in a conservative manner, so they want for nothing. They have no need to engage in unscrupulous behavior because they don't have to. Nick doesn't need to behave in an ambitious way, because he is the Chief Executive Officer and President of his own successful company. He has no pressures causing him to act in an untoward manner. Ditto for Riley, to be honest."

Jack nodded, but thought about the intangibles, the oblique pressures that created cracks in the foundations of any house. *Infidelity, greed, addictions, attacks on his daughter, or a brain tumor, for God's sake. There are as many ways to break a man as there are leaves of clover in a meadow. And families have secrets.* He raised none of these possibilities, but nodded again. "Did anyone come up with a theory as to why Tricia appeared after all these years? It seems curious…"

John harrumphed. "We've obviously heard a few far-fetched ideas tossed around, within the walls of the Parker estate. And I'm trusting you to be discreet here, Jack. Nobody actually seems to know for sure, but here are some ideas being batted around: she's after money and hit a low point, based on the condition of her vehicle. Or, she calculated Riley's age and guessed she was graduating this year. Nick is considering taking early retirement, an event suggesting two possibilities. Money, generosity, and forgiveness might be flowing a bit more freely at a time like that. On the other hand, she might have been sniffing around for a renegotiated settlement while he's still in business. He basically threw her out on her ear with a pittance. Don't get me wrong, what she did was unforgivable, but what we're doing here is trying to get inside her head, and it was a difficult job when she was in the circle." He shook his head. "And it's an impossible job, twenty years later."

Jack smiled, closing down the discussion of murder. "Let's go downstairs and have a bite to eat. I hear the food here is above average."

"Above average is selling it short. They have this main course with rows of scallops held in line by an outrageous sauce and the whole thing's sitting on sweet potato puree. All of a sudden I'm starved." Peggy handed Jack the remainder of the wine to return to his room and a minute later they were seated in the lap of luxury.

Chapter 8

Niagara On The Lake

CLAIRE VALENTIN CAME UP FROM the fields, opened the door of the staff entrance to the production area and veered left. She entered what looked like a beach concrete shower pad where bathers rinse sand from their flip-flops. In this case, Claire marched mauve paisley rubber boots over onto the pad to rinse off all traces of mud. The owners were obsessive about all forms of contamination and took additional steps to mitigate any air and ground-based troubles that could taint the wines. The fetching rubber boots looked incongruous when lined up with the dozen black and green gum-rubber boots of her colleagues.

Once in her light canvas tennis shoes, she headed up to the tiny production office to chat with Dieter.

"How are the fields? Have the hawks and starlings put us out of business yet?"

Claire smiled, but her heart wasn't in it. The young woman's hair was a light brown, very straight and just off the shoulders. Her aquiline nose and worried eyes that were deep brown, underscored a Gallic heritage. Her cheekbones were high and her chin strong, and the tight, frayed jeans accentuated her youth. Although a striking young woman when made up and dressed for the evening, Claire seldom went out. Wine was a passion of the young Frenchwoman. She understood the grapes, felt at home around the vines, the barrels, and the bottles. The production building had become home, and she lived and breathed every stage of the process of winemaking.

"The fields are fine. You made good fields, Dieter." She knew he loved praise for his winery and vineyards, and her smile widened as he puffed up, just a little. The reason for coming in from the fields came back to her, pushing all other thoughts aside. "There is one thing, though."

"How can there be a thing, Miss V? It's barely nine on a Monday morning. It won't be Friday for five more days. That's too early for complications." His smile didn't leave his face.

"I took the ATV around the perimeter of the vineyards. Near the road, I found a dozen vines dug up. Here, I wrote down the rows and the field number."

Dieter's smile disappeared. "Dug up? Or dug up and taken? Could it have been animals? Was it in an area covered by our cameras?"

Claire shook her head. "Whoever took them seemed to know where the cameras were. The stolen vines were in the gap between the cameras."

Dieter stared at the ground, concentrating. "But if they took a dozen plants, they must have used a truck, especially if they dug deep enough to get most of the root ball. Perhaps the cameras caught the truck as it approached or left."

"It's possible." She sounded doubtful. "In any case, we need to let Sean know. He's a genius at finding things."

"A genius?" He sounded doubtful. "I'm not sure that's what I'd call him, but he does need to know this right away. Let's go find him." He started to move, but she was already pulling out her phone to message him as they left the room.

Chapter 9

St. Andrews

DINNER WAS A SOMBER EVENT at the Parker residence. Without the liveliness the Whiteways had imbued into the home, Nick and Riley ate in silence this night. On Tuesdays Tony had a standing invitation to have dinner with them, in order to report on the estate home, the guest house, the gardens and the grounds. This was a time to plan any enhancements or maintenance necessary to keep up the property. Tony's heart, however, wasn't in it and recent events had taken the wind out of his sails. He'd begged off, promising to be back the following week to "have a scoff with you."

Tonight was seafood night. The appetizer: crab cakes with a lime aioli were served on a bed of rocket greens, with a bottle of unoaked chardonnay sitting within reach. On the side, Caesar salads arrived in white boat plates. The baby romaine leaves were nestled on the bottom of the plate, dressing dolloped on instead of bathing the greens. Above it all, candied maple bacon demanded attention. The main course was old-school cuisine: coquille St.-Jacques. Fat Atlantic scallops were baked in a white wine sauce, with a ring of cheesy creamed potato around the perimeter of the bowl. They'd had music on as was their habit, but it didn't seem right, so Riley turned it off.

She was quiet to the point of sullenness, but Nick kept trying to shake her out of her funk. "How was the party at the pool? Was it more of a goodbye to the students from away, or a 'let's make plans for the students who are staying?'" He waited, unsure if he was going to receive the dignity of a reply.

Riley stared down, moving a fat scallop from left to right in the white sauce, but not actually tasting anything. "When was the last time you saw

Mom?" The tine of the fork scraped the bottom of the dish, and the ensuing grating sound was exaggerated in the large, quiet dining room.

Nick looked taken aback. "Uh, I don't know. Almost twenty years ago, I suppose. The night she left us. Why do you ask?" It was his turn to become fascinated with the bottom of his dish.

"The night *she* left us? I had the impression she was actively invited to live elsewhere."

"Darling, that's not fair." His mouth thinned to a straight line, and his face revealed signs of peevishness. "You were just a child and couldn't have understood at the time, but the circumstances were…complicated." When he looked up, his eyes were stormy, and he dropped his fork with a clatter. "Actually, they weren't complicated at all. Your mother was stealing from us and cheating on me. She'd taken up with a rogue, or thief —I don't even know what to call him besides bastard—and she wouldn't stop. She left us because she had made it impossible to stay. I gave her three chances…"

"Just like in baseball." Riley's gaze didn't leave the plate, but a flush began to creep up her throat.

"Making a trite comment doesn't reduce this to a trite decision. So, no. Nothing like baseball." His voice bounced off the walls, cutting her from all directions. "Baseball's a game. A pastime. This was a marriage, or I thought it was. She thought it was more daily visits to a bank machine. At some point, I thought we deserved more. So I shut everything down. Look. I don't want to talk about it anymore tonight. Let's just enjoy dinner and I promise to tell you anything you want in the morning. But not now. I'm still upset by her passing. I hated her a long time ago, but no one was more surprised than me to hear she was in town. Did you know? Were you aware she was in St. Andrews?"

Riley looked up to meet her father's eyes just as Mary, D-A's part-time helper as cook, entered the room to prepare for the next course. "Why would I know she was in town?"

The father seemed satisfied with his daughter's non-response, but continued to study Riley's face. "A friend of the Whiteways is in town. Apparently, he's just retired from the RCMP, having done detective work all over the world. He's offered to help clear this up. I suggest we share whatever information we have. He might speed things up with the local police. I'm sure we would all like to resolve this matter so you can begin your job placement. Have you decided where you want to work for the summer?"

Riley ignored the question, resentment mounting. "This isn't merely an inconvenience to a lovely summer resort, Father, or to a job placement, for that matter. This is, or was my mother. Who would want to kill a woman who doesn't know anyone in town? Why? I just don't get it, and I want to understand why my mother died within sight of my home. Is that too much to ask?"

"Look, I don't know! I told you, we can talk about it in the morning. I'll get John to invite his friend the RCMP fellow over first thing, and we can begin to get to the bottom of this. Let's just eat a wonderful meal, and deal with this later."

Nick tried to engage his daughter by asking again about her summer placement, but none of the answers she gave were satisfactory, or even complete. Eventually he gave up and focused on his meal, every single bite of which now tasted bitter. He noted Riley's thumbs moving furiously across her cell phone, her meal ignored. Their rule was no electronics at the dinner table, but this was a battle he knew he shouldn't attempt this evening, so he leaned back, one arm draped over the back of his chair, and let it go.

* * * *

Jack Miller made a sharp left across the Bar Road, bringing the grille of his rental up to the gate. He sipped the dregs of his now cold coffee—one milk, one sugar—grimaced and concentrated on inching the vehicle as close to the metal grille in the stone wall as he could. The cedar hedge flanking each side of the gate extended more than a hundred feet in either direction, and by peering, he could see the wrought iron running through the heart of the hedge. He pushed the buzzer, offered his name, and waited. In a moment, the gate swung open and he eased through. Once up the lane, he parked beside a familiar vehicle and knew the Whiteways were either on the property or on the beach. He headed for the primary portal of one of the grander summer homes he'd ever seen.

A maid answered the door, but a casually dressed man strode up behind her, a welcoming smile on his face. He appeared to be a well-maintained forty-something year old, although he could have been fifty, and clearly in charge. His hair was sandy brown, thinning and perfectly trimmed. The lines around his brown eyes made him appear to have a perpetual squint against sunshine, real or imagined. The lined eyes and permanent tan suggested thousands of hours on the water. His lips were pursed as if he was being forced to make a difficult decision, but his smile was engaging and friendly.

"Welcome to Wooler House. My name is Nick Parker; come in, please." He encouraged Jack across the massive foyer, and opened French doors that led into a formal dining room. A full breakfast had been laid out. It appeared to have been prepared for him. It was an embarrassing offer, since he'd just finished eating an egg-and-cheese biscuit sandwich at the Seabreeze in town.

"I thought we might wish to nibble while we chat. But if you'd rather, we could just have coffee on the verandah." Nick waved to a second set of doors that led straight out from the dining room. Jack noticed an attractive young woman seated at the end of the table, a *pain au chocolat* crescent roll in one hand and a cell phone in the other. Her hair was a wild tangle of red curls, her skin had a beautiful pale cast, and her lips were pouty-full and naturally red. She wore rolled up denim shorts and a red-and-white striped boatneck tee, was barefoot and sported a pair of SALT Randall sunglasses atop the knot of curls. Beside her rested a Cuyana City Walk panama hat. She didn't look up until Nick introduced Jack, at which point she slipped the phone in her back pocket and offered him her full attention.

The Whiteways had been apprised of Jack's arrival at the estate, since it was Peggy who'd suggested that Nick invite him. So it was no surprise when the Minnesota couple rounded the corner to greet Jack and introduce him as their friend. As the trio stepped into the refreshing breeze of the verandah, Peggy gave Jack a hug, and made sure to give everyone else a full-on smile.

The conversation took almost half an hour, with Jack asking questions and each of the others, in turn, responding. At the end of it, he thanked everyone for their cooperation, receiving an assurance from Nick that Tony the groundskeeper would answer any questions posed to him. Jack decided to take a walk across the underwater road, the tide having fallen and the road was still draining. Surprisingly, Riley offered to come with him, and he accepted. John and Peggy were off to St. George to explore an antique shop, and Nick headed back to his office to do some work with his New York colleagues.

"Aren't you going to put on some running shoes or something?"

"Oh, I'll be all right." Riley's response was dry. "With those shoes, it's you who needs to be careful not to slip on the rocks. Many of them are covered in algae." She assessed his clothing, which was civilian casual. He had black leather shoes, beige khakis, and a white, short-sleeved shirt. A thin trickle of sweat began at the nape of his neck, and he hoped it wasn't apparent, but as soon as they hit the shore, an eastern breeze rendered the warm day perfect.

She led the way, her long legs pouncing from one two-foot boulder to another until she was halfway to the water's edge. Jack walked alongside the trail of rocks, assessing his companion, and caught up to her as they reached the road.

"So, it's just you and your dad, plus an assortment of housekeeping staff?"

"Yup. Just us. We like it that way. Daddy's had girlfriends over the years, but none of them stuck."

"Who unstuck 'em, you or Nick?"

Riley laughed aloud at that. "Hmm, no polite limits from you, Mister Miller!"

He didn't grin, part of his attention being on the wet rocks. "No, miss. What if that was the question that cracked the case?"

"Somehow, I'm not sure that's gonna be the case-cracker question. But, good luck on your next one." She glanced over to assess the gravity of the offense against him and was pleased to see the beginning of a smile. "Anyway, to answer your question, I was probably most at fault until I was twelve. After that, to be frank, I was a little boy-crazy, and maybe developed some sympathy for Daddy and his...interests." She bent down to pick up a whelk, tossing it into deeper water. "But at the end of the day, our boy Nick's a busy guy. Busy making money. Busy being busy."

It was Jack's turn to study her. Did he sense resentment in her tone? Had the father emotionally abandoned the daughter over the years? Or was it actually the daughter who was needy, feeling bereft by his choice of work over her? He'd keep his radar up and see what he could catch of this friction, who was rubbing, and who was being chafed.

The pair arrived at the spot where Tricia's body had been found. The circumstances of tides and channel waters precluded having any yellow tape up or placing a marker, but Jack spied a five-pound rock that looked unlike any of the others. He picked it up. "One of these things is not like the others." He quoted a popular children's television show.

"Yeah." Her voice was distant. "I put it there."

"This is a very distinct rock." His voice was admiring. "Granite, perfectly round, elliptically flattened at the top and bottom. Lovely, like a curling stone, but squished even more."

"Over on Grand Manan Island, not far from here, there's a whole beach area composed of rocks like this. We brought home a dozen or more from there, over the years. They end up as doorstoppers all over the house. Daddy and I call them guards, because they stand beside every door. I... wanted a guard for her. I know, it sounds dumb."

"No. That's sweet." He took care to place it back exactly where he'd found it. "When the tide rises, which direction does the water flow? Do you know things like that?"

She chuckled. "I've been boating on the Passamaquoddy, from nearby Oak Bay and Big Bay, Back Bay, and Passamaquoddy, all the way out into the Bay of Fundy proper. I once sailed down the coast to Camden, just my girlfriend and me. We visited some boys and sailed back without incident, so yes, I know the waters around here. When the tide comes in, it moves from there—" she pointed toward the tip of St. Andrews "—and moves across the Bar Road toward Chamcook Lake before sweeping around Minister's Island and back out into the Passamaquoddy. Yeah, I know the water a bit."

After a moment, they turned and headed back to the mainland. Keeping his face down and his attention on each slippery step, Jack rumbled a question to his travelling partner. "I'm sure you've heard by now, you, Nick, Tony—basically none of the folks usually to be considered as suspects have an alibi. You were on your way between events. Your father was in his office. Well, probably in his office. The groundskeeper had the afternoon off. None of you was with anyone overnight.

"The circumstances around...your mother, what with the salt water and all, have blurred the exact hour of death. It leaves us in a pickle. Until some hard evidence surfaces,"—he looked up to see any possible reaction —"and it always does, we may be confined to a very small list of suspects." He waited a split second, and the reaction came.

"Look! You're a stranger here, not a real cop, if I heard right, and you don't even know us. She could have been stalked. Her male partner, if there was one, might have followed her with a grudge. She might have committed suicide, we don't know for sure; did you think of that? But it wasn't me. And it wasn't Daddy, so just go to hell." She stomped three strides and then stopped on a large green flat rock to glare over her shoulder.

"It wasn't us. You have to look further, try harder, and know it wasn't us. Daddy was at home since late afternoon. He couldn't have snuck out, the security would have picked him up. Me, too, for that matter. And Tony is loyal." Riley's voice began to catch, becoming ragged. "This is getting annoying, and I'm regretting ever speaking to you. You should leave us alone." She strode ahead, careless of the rocks underfoot, until she was on the beach with him trailing her by fifty feet.

Later, in the car, he reviewed the conversation, looking for contradictions, hedging, anything that stood out. There didn't appear to be anything on the face of it, but Jack was left with the feeling something had been omitted. She had over-reacted to his last observation. What was she hiding? Was it to protect herself, or was Riley the shield for Daddy? He sighed. More questions. More opportunities to piss people off.

There was something else. The underwater road. Something about it bothered him, left him with a feeling of smoldering resentment. Why? Was there a clue remaining on it? Had there been a clue, long since washed away, to resolve the questions swirling around Tricia and her daughter, Riley? Was there something he should have noted, but didn't? The whole business left him frustrated and upset.

Chapter 10

Niagara

DONOVAN AND BETH ENTERED THE office overlooking the vineyards of Plenitude Wine Estate. Ever since the purchase, whenever Donovan and Dieter were both present in the office, each took pains to avoid sitting behind the main desk. The former owner wished to defer to the current owner, and the current owner didn't wish to offend the former owner. This morning found Dieter and Claire seated, with coffee, in the cluster of upholstered chairs near the fireplace.

"What's up?"

Dieter cast a glum look over to his young companion. "You tell them."

"This morning I was doing the rounds in the all-terrain vehicle when I noticed some vines missing from L4, near the road. They were not cut, they were dug up. I counted twelve holes. While the Pinotage vines were young in that field, they were expensive. We—you acquired them from Germany, as I recall. I looked around, but other than some spilled soil on the edge of the road, I didn't see anything else of note." She sat back in the chair, bringing the coffee to her lips. Her eyebrows were furrowed in a frown, and her glance darted from Donovan to Dieter.

Donovan's eyes narrowed. "Has anyone scouted all of the fields?"

Claire nodded. "As soon as I got back to the ATV, I texted the field supervisors. There was nothing out of the ordinary anywhere else. Do you want me to visit each field personally?" Both men shook their heads in unison.

Dieter jumped in, his voice quivering. "I did some thinking. These were valuable vines that were taken, almost as costly as some of the much older vines, which would be very difficult to steal because of the depth of their roots. And even though they were non-producing vines, the ones they took were easily the most costly ones along the road. The thieves seem to know what they're doing."

Donovan caught Claire's eye and spoke, his voice calm. "Tell me again what you saw. Begin as you were driving along. What direction were you coming from as you approached the vines?" She told him every step of the story in greater detail, finishing by advising there were no footprints she could see. He nodded to Dieter, who picked up the phone and called the Niagara area police. He asked his partner one final question. "Can you think of anyone, past or present, who might wish ill upon the winery, or who carried a grudge of any kind?" *It's probably a simple theft, but we can't gloss over anything.*

Dieter shook his head, his face a study in misery.

"Then we'll begin at the beginning and suss this all out. Every action has a genesis, so we'll approach it from three directions, plus that of the police, and we'll arrive at a conclusion. Claire? I want you to study the production, make sure the vats are secured and the contents read what they're supposed to read.

"Beth, can you review all of the hires? Has anyone been refused a promotion, have any of the supervisors reported behaviors that seem out of place? For example, Claire is new on the scene, is she a troublemaker?" He winked at her as she blushed. Dieter started, but caught the wink. It seemed to calm him down. Claire appeared ready to jump at the slightest sound, but her hands were steady and her eyes bright.

Donovan continued. "Dieter will of course be reviewing all the production processes, and making sure whoever touches anything does it exactly the same way every time. Claire will continue to report to him."

He caught an unasked question. "Me? I'll be wandering about, looking into corners." Donovan didn't elaborate. He picked up his phone and sent a supervisor over to L4 to secure the area and, as there was nothing more to say, they parted until the police arrived to take statements.

Chapter 11

New York State

HARRY RAFUSE STARED AT THE last of twenty-seven cases, big and small, to be shipped to the Canadian border, resentment all over his face. He'd boxed and moved them from the storage shed in the countryside to his Montauk home, leaving behind the furniture that couldn't be easily shipped. Each had multiple stickers directing it to the address of a buddy in Eastport, Maine. Each was to have been shipped to one of eight different names, but at the last minute, he took a chance and, with a combination of promises and threats, persuaded the lone man to hold the boxes until he received a PM message on his cell phone. He hadn't worried about some Customs staff sitting in a Maine office, since he had a plan to bypass Customs. State to state...what's the worry? And he'd deal with getting the artwork across the water when the time came.

In fact, he hadn't been the least bit concerned someone would wonder where all these boxes were coming from (or going to). It was frigging Maine. Why the hell would the kinder, gentler state be wasting their time worrying about boxes being moved from one place to another? It wasn't worth the bother of trying anything more complicated. It was the middle of nowhere, for God's sake.

The crates would leave today, so he'd be rid of the last of them by lunchtime. Today, he'd packed his truck, cancelled the newspaper, utilities were to be shut off at five, and Harry would be on the I-95 North by seven tonight. Then there was the matter of the dog. A few gentle hints to acquaintances went unrewarded, so he'd decided to drop him off on a country road, on the way to the highway. *Someone'll collect him up*. He sat on the sofa, watching game show re-runs until the phone rang. It was his new buddy, Yves Palu, the Canadian from Quebec, so that was all handled.

He could relax. He went to the fridge, pulled out the last beer, made a sandwich, and sat down on one of the few sticks of furniture left in the living room.

Harry Rafuse was all set. In a few long hours, he'd make an appearance at his cousin's home in Canada, reinvented as Nick Parker's artist-in-residence. He chuckled, mouth full, as he wiped some mayo on the corduroy sofa with the side of his hand. The map at his side suggested it would be a long fourteen hours to get to St. Andrews. No problem. He'd made sandwiches, and he could pee in a jug. What were the milestones? Connecticut, Massachusetts—Go Bruins—New Hampshire, Maine, and thence across the border.

Harry had been to a not-for-profit art collective that morning, asking questions of the artists and instructors, picking up tid-bits on technique and supplies. And he looked the part of a starving painter. He'd worn a poop-brown sports jacket with elbow patches and his oldest jeans. Under the jacket he sported an off-white chambray LL Bean shirt, his only recent purchase and had taken off his socks to go barefoot in a pair of scuffed topsiders. He ended up spending seventy-five bucks on a couple of blank canvases, three brushes and a mittful of the minimum number of tubes of paint needed to begin a piece. Harry had never held a paintbrush. Hell, he'd never put any kind of brush to anything except to his teeth, and that but once a day if he thought of it. Just before walking out, he had sprung an extra tenner for a pocket-strewn canvas bag that looked as if it had come from an army-navy store. For credibility.

Hell with this; time to boogie. "Come on, dog. We're goin' for a drive. Not a long drive, in your case." He grinned, revealing the tiniest piece of lettuce between a lateral incisor and cuspid.

Chapter 12

I WISH I COULD GET laid, right this second. I wish some bitch would just walk in this bar, and... Yves Palu's thought were interrupted as he shifted in his chair on a patio in Old Montreal. His new best buddy, Harry Rafuse, had called from New Brunswick. Harry had landed in Canada and was settling into his new digs in some mansion on the East Coast. Although his car had been basically empty save for a battered suitcase, some painting supplies, and a passport, it was clear within a few days, Rafuse would be up to his ears in art and collectibles. These pieces desperately needed to be sold to folks who didn't care about who the actual owner was at the moment. If it had provenance, it had value. And if it had value, Palu wanted to broker its sale.

He ran a hand through luxurious, thick, dark, wavy hair. It was his best feature, superior by far to his scruples, ethics, or morals. Palu had been a broker of stolen goods until he landed on the wrong side of his ex-girlfriend's brother, an asshole named Donovan. The bastard had a protector, and when things went sideways, Donovan's benefactor arranged for Palu to go for a ride. Gaia's agents had chatted with him, explained the facts of life regarding Donovan, and invited him to leave Donovan alone. Then, they invited him to leave their limo. The vehicle was going almost fifty miles an hour at the time, and a year later, Palu was the owner of a cane, together with an assortment of pins and wires that invariably drew the attention of airport security.

His mind went back to the more pleasant issue of this new East Coast collection. One piece in particular stood out among Rafuse's bragging. He claimed to have a Manet, a holdover from the job at the Isabella Stewart Gardner Museum, in Boston. The museum had been home to thirteen paintings from the Masters, comprising half a billion dollars in art, the Manet being among them. Of course, it hadn't sold after disappearing. In fact, none of the art had surfaced since the 1989 robbery.

It is notoriously challenging to sell famous art pieces. The logistics of making the piece available to the folks who can afford it are brutal, if one wishes to avoid tipping off the collector who'd previously possessed the piece, as well as the insurance companies wishing to offset their payouts. Yves knew this, but the challenge of marrying up a Manet to a private collector somewhere in the world was thrilling to him.

First things first. It was almost time to head east. Rafuse was probably a reasonable craftsman in the art of acquiring stolen pieces and re-selling them. But he wasn't Palu. Palu had spent a lifetime in the business, first in France as a youth, and later in Montreal. He knew which end was up and had a sixth sense about the timing of the sale. Seldom had he been caught in the middle of a deal—the Donovan affair being wildly notable in its exception—and his delicate touch might be helpful in moving such a significant shipment of goods from New York to New Brunswick to, well, anywhere in the world. He rubbed his thigh and the knee below it.

Donovan. How he hated him.

The thought of him, his stupid sister Madeleine, anything to do with him. He'd even soured on Montreal because of the painful memories of that week, a year previous. First, Donovan's sister had stolen his newest acquisition at the time, and then Donovan had burned his entire life's collection before his very eyes. That had almost done him in, but it seemed not to be enough. He thought again about the injury to his leg, rubbing the knee containing the prosthetic patella, and thinking of the months of rehab that brought him to this moment.

So it was with some measure of anticipation that he thought of leaving Montreal and heading to the seashore in summer. Of course, losing his entire art collection was a blow to the psyche as well as to the wallet. How could he finance a few weeks in a toney resort town? He'd learned from a grifter, at nineteen years, the best way to finance something was to find someone who wanted the same thing you did and convince them to pay for it.

Palu thrummed his fingers on the tabletop beside his drink. Who could he tap? What about Eddie's boss? He and Eddie had fallen out, once his collection had gone to shit. Eddie was a low-status middleman and a complete piece of shit, he thought. But he could bypass Eddie and go straight to Michel. Michel might front him some funds, in exchange for future considerations and a quick turnover of his cash. *No fucking Manet mentioned, though.* The Manet would be his meal ticket for the next several years, and the more cuts, the smaller the piece of pie. *To hell with that nonsense.*

He decided to try it. Now, what would the request be? Could he get by on five Gs? The problem with five thousand is that it's chump change, and only chumps shoot low. He'd get no respect from a piddly amount like that. Better to double it and risk taking a cut in the negotiations. He knew he'd pay dearly at the back end if he was going to borrow from a loan shark, but he needed that small investment, to get the job done. What was a hundred-per cent markup on a ten G investment when he stood to make a few million, maybe more? Smiling, he downed his drink and dialed a number.

"Hey, Rafuse, Palu here. I expect to be in town in a day or so...yes, I'll be alone. Did the goods arrive yet? No? Soon? Ah. Then I'll see you Friday. Find me a bar with a patio good for conducting business. Yes, I think we're going to have a profitable summer, but one should never pass up the opportunity to share a drink on a summer patio, my friend. *A bientot.* See you soon."

Chapter 13

Niagara On The Lake

THERE'S SOMETHING WRONG WITH THIS *picture, and it's not just the stolen vines*. Donovan lay on his back in his apartment at the Plenitude vineyards, studying the ceiling for finishing flaws, of which there were none. Beth slept facing the wall, her breathing quiet. All he could hear were the crickets outside their open window, together with whisperings of disquiet. In his mind, he went over the theft of the vines, from Claire's announcement to the re-enactment by the Ontario Provincial Police. With the facts as they now stood, there was about as much chance of recovering the vines as a New York cop had of getting back a bicycle.

It wasn't just the vines that had him staring at the shadows playing across the ceiling's empty expanse. As the new owner, he saw at least a half-dozen problems swirling up around him as a result of this theft. To begin, would there be more? And was it an inside job; someone within the Plenitude family? And which was more likely: pure theft or revenge? Was it someone he knew (and trusted), or someone he couldn't possibly trace? The biggest problem, which began as a small dust storm in the back of his mind, was coalescing, growing stronger. Would he be instrumental in resolving this theft? After all, as a thief himself it was in his wheelhouse. The reputation of the winery depended on this issue being resolved. He sighed, and Beth reached behind her, patting his hip without changing her position.

"It's okay, Sweetie, go back to sleep." And she did.

But, ten minutes later, Donovan rose and sat in the chair facing the window and stared at the darkness on the other side of the screen. Three thoughts tumbled around in his mind, connected, yet in contradiction to one another. The first, most recent thought was he had got married. After a life mostly spent in solitude, he'd made a decision to link all of his actions to another. Could this reversal in his past approach to life ever be reconciled with the solitude he'd built? Because, being half of a team was still…alien to him, at the moment. He glanced over to the bed where his incandescent life partner lay, unaware.

At odds with this was, when he'd finally found a home, it ended up being a winery filled with people, many of them strangers. They didn't love him and want him to be happy. They just wanted a bed and a paycheque. He shouldn't care about this idea of finding a home and yet, understanding it needed to have strangers inhabiting it. He mostly didn't care, but he was confident everyone didn't adopt strangers, invite them into his home and then tell them what to do, every day. It was, to him, anomalous and strange. *But what about my life, to date, isn't different from the norm?*

Finally, as he thought about having spent his entire adult life in the business of separating individuals from their possessions, it was becoming clear to him that he was no longer a thief for hire. His skills didn't just melt away overnight, but they'd been rendered redundant. Something had changed, erased clean from deep within him. And, rather than feel purged, he felt the hole that had been made. And he didn't entirely like that, because, if in a matter of one single year a chunk of him that large could be wiped away, was he not in danger of becoming invisible? He passed a hand over his gut, home to his decision-maker. It felt the same as it always did, but that didn't reassure him, at least not tonight.

* * * *

Next morning, Donovan and Beth had a brief breakfast meeting with Claire. They'd ordered a platter of latkes and sour cream, an asparagus-and-cremini frittata topped with Vermeer cheese, and a pot of extra-hot coffee. The women chose seats turned to the wall of windows so as to enjoy the vines, while Donovan sat facing the door, as was his wont. Once the eating slowed, thoughts turned to the matter at hand.

"Somehow I feel this is my fault." Claire didn't hide the worried look on her face. "I was supposed to be monitoring those fields. What if I had gone by a half hour earlier? Perhaps I would have seen them and called somebody."

Beth patted her hand. "They did their work in the night, I'm pretty sure of it. They were long gone by dawn." She smiled at her rhyming skills, despite the seriousness of the situation and the look on her friend's face. "Besides, how on earth can one woman monitor every vine in every field in the middle of the night? You're good, Claire, but security isn't actually in your job description." Claire's head nodded in agreement, but her look remained doubtful.

Donovan leaned in. "No, but it's in mine. I'll be working on the theft, but I suspect it's not about twelve vines. I'm afraid this is the beginning. So, rather than putting all my—*our*—energy into finding the vines, I think we need to anticipate something else happening. Dieter and I were chatting about it, and we've ordered two dozen more security cameras. Claire, I'm taking you out of the fields—" he held up a hand to silence her "—and if you're willing, I'm putting you in charge of the entire production facilities: the lab, the vats, the barrels, the bottles. The kitchen extension out there that's part of it. Anything inside of the buildings there, they all belong to you for now. It'll mean longer hours than your job description says, but probably not more time than you've been putting in these days." The tightness around his mouth softened. "We'll get you a bonus: a plane ticket home for after the harvest. You put in a lot of hours, Sweetie."

Beth nibbled on a bite of croissant. "I'll come visit you in the prison Sean just gave you." She patted the young woman's hand. "But I agree with him. Leave the fields to the field staff. The vats are just as important as any part of the operation, and you need your most trusted workers in the production area."

Claire nodded. "It would be a relief to focus on one thing, and as the Chief Winemaker, Dieter just doesn't have the time to stay in the production area. But we need to do twice as much testing, clean and sterilize everything to the best of our abilities." She sat back. "I can do that."

Beth raised a finger, almost as if in class. "There's just one thing, Sean. You may be responsible for everything including security, but you're actually not responsible for security, if you know what I mean."

"Jack." He sat back, waiting to see where this was going.

"That's right. It's all well and good he's out east solving crime and comforting good friends. But at the end of the day, wasn't he hired to be here, working on things like this?"

Donovan pursed his lips. "I suppose. But he's there now, and I'm here. The dog's off the porch, so to speak. Hard to undo that."

Beth shook her head, a stubborn look hanging about her like a dark cloud. "Well, can we think about it for a bit? Dieter is here. Claire is here. We can go to St. Andrews, and see what we can do there. And Jack can come home to do what he knows best. Place people where they can do their best." She raised one quizzical eyebrow.

He shook his head. "I'm not sure about that. Wasn't it just the other day you were begging me not to drag you off somewhere?"

"I never beg for anything." She put her hands on her hips, piqued. "Look, just think it through and see if what I'm saying makes sense."

Claire sat, glancing from one to the other.

"Okay. I'll think about it." *At the same time, I'll be thinking about Dieter worrying that I'm abandoning him, and I'll be thinking about how much money I have sunk in this business. Do I really want to stroll off for a couple of weeks while the place goes to hell?* Aloud, he suggested they finish up breakfast and do a tour of the winery, just to check things out.

Once alone, Donovan and Beth picked up where they'd left off. "Are you serious about us going to New Brunswick and calling Jack back?" His eyes faced forward, his gaze darting from visitors to staff as he surveyed the great room.

"Yes, I am. You didn't hire Jack out of some misguided sense of sympathy. The man is a career cop, remember. And we'd have this ex-RCMP detective watching over us from inside the winery. I just think it makes sense. Besides, we aren't positive this is the beginning of a rash of trouble." Her chin jutted out.

Donovan smiled, defusing the tense aura hanging about them. "You're probably right about us switching with Jack. Probably." He emphasized his last word. "Give me a few hours to process things. If I can't come up with something solid to beat up your argument by dinner this evening, we will give Jack a call and discuss it."

"That's all I want, you know. Just show me you heard what I said, and then you can do what you think is best. Deal?"

"Deal."

The couple headed down the double balustrade to the lower floor. Jimmy the Attendant stood at his usual post, not too far from one of the hogshead wine barrels that flanked the corridors going east and west. Jimmy's tie was slightly askew, his white shirt tugged up just a bit from his pants, and yet his broad smile and guileless eyes absolved him of everything. Jimmy was easily the staff member receiving the most positive comments from visitors, with his natural charm and casual understanding of what people wanted to hear.

"'Sup, boss? Ms. Boss?" This elicited a warm smile from Beth, who wasn't impervious to his looks and charms. Donovan enjoyed watching the harmless flirtation. Jimmy, in his understated fashion, had stuck by Donovan when his ex, Nadia, was killed a year earlier.

Donovan crossed the bottom of the stairs to sit on one of the hogsheads. Beth leaned on the railing at the bottom of the stairs, watching. "We have a little problem, and even at that, Jimmy, I may be exaggerating things. You heard of us losing a dozen vines down by the road? I'm a little concerned we may get hit again, and I'm not sure from which direction."

Jimmy's eyebrows wrinkled into a frown. "Anything I can do? I love this place, and wouldn't want some ass—guy to screw things up."

"As a matter of fact, you can. Here's what we need. I know you have an awesome memory for faces, but if you could maybe keep track, on paper, of who comes down here and which direction they go, whether to the meeting rooms or the production and storage area, well, that would help us a lot."

"Sure. Starting when?"

"Starting day before yesterday, if you can."

"I can. Want a daily report in writing? I could type it up at home at night, have it on your desk first thing every day. Well, second thing." Jimmy was notorious for arriving late.

"Not necessary. If you could scribble the information on a note pad, that would work great for me. Oh, and could we keep this on the down-low? Just show it to Beth when she comes visiting. I'll tell Dieter what you're up to. Oh. One other thing. Listen to what people say. Somebody knows something, and if we can piece together three or four isolated comments, we might just be able to put two and two together."

"Done, boss."

"Thanks, Jimmy," Beth interjected. "We're going to take a stroll past the meeting rooms and then down the other corridor. Just before you leave for the day, could you take a quick pass through the rooms? I'm being a little over-zealous about someone staying behind after hours, I'm sure, but..."

"But why take chances, right? I'm on it."

She smiled in gratitude.

As they passed from meeting room to boardroom to private dining area, Beth quizzed Donovan on the activities taking place in that part of the winery. She learned Anna was most familiar with the east rooms: the meeting areas, and Dieter was more familiar with the production and storage areas along the west wing. Sean told her visitors who were at the winery on business other than tasting or dining in the restaurant were usually brought downstairs. She suggested he ask that Dieter recollect exactly how everything looked in the production and storage area from visit to visit and flag anything out of place from one walkabout to the next. Donovan repeated his suspicion this whole thing was overkill and expected nothing more than perhaps a few more vines might get picked off.

"All the more reason to consider packing our bags, Sweetie. Jack will have this wrapped up the day after he gets back."

"You're not giving me much credit as a superhero crime solver."

"*Au contraire, cher*. I'm giving you all the credit in the world. Your talents are needed a couple of provinces away. Let Jack do Jack's work, while you visit the seedy underbelly of St. Andrews By The Sea, not that a place with a name like that conjures up crimes and misdemeanors." She tucked her hand in the crook of his elbow as they found their way back to Jimmy and the staircase.

* * * *

Over dinner that evening, Claire contrived to sit beside Beth. She contributed to the conversation around the table, but chose moments when the discussions became animated to chat in a low voice with her seat mate.

"Beth, I was wondering if it would be acceptable for me to speak with my father about the problem we're having here. I could leave out all the details, but the thing is, he has been in the business for a very long time. When you consider what he has learned from the generations before him, he knows a lot." She nodded at the significance of her statement. "A lot.

"I thought I'd ask him, if he wanted to do bad things to a winery, maybe put it out of business, what would be the things that could be done? *Que penses-tu?* What do you think?

Beth scanned the table to see who was watching their conversation. Dieter was holding court with his perspective on whether Aussie wines were overrated, versus their New World counterparts. "Here's what I think the problem is. If word was to get out Plenitude was in trouble, what would that do to the value of the wines? Would buyers lose confidence? So anything you do or say would have to be in total confidence and not a word of it can go beyond your father.

"Why don't you catch Donovan after dinner, take him to a quiet corner and propose it to him? He's met your father so any guidance he gives you will be based on his acceptance of risk. But I think it has to be his call."

Claire nodded, her face a study in seriousness.

Beth smiled. "All right, then. Let's see what all the fuss is about this roast chicken Provençal. I suppose you just call it chicken, given the recipe comes from your backyard.

Her companion smiled again. "I may have had this once or twice. I'm sure it is delicious. Everything here is delicious."

Chapter 14

St. Andrews

HARRY RAFUSE CHUGGED INTO THE seaside town of St. Andrews, the rattletrap Ford on its last legs. He'd overshot the exit from the main highway and found himself at Cosmo's, a seafood takeout on the side of the road pointing toward Saint John. Judging from the lineup at the takeout window, it seemed worth the expense to order a seafood platter.

"Clams, scallops, and haddock," she'd explained. "What sort of sauces would you like? We have remoulade, tartar, and aioli." At that question, he suspected he was in good hands and ordered all of them. Belly full, he turned the vehicle around and sputtered back toward the highway exit.

On the edge of town, he spied a coffee shop and passed on the chance to give the tiny town a once-over. Once inside, he asked what their most popular coffee was.

"A double-double."

"Say, what?"

"A double-double. That's a medium coffee with two creams and two sugars." The clerk waited, her eyes on the television flat screen across the room.

"I'll have that." He took the hot paper cup over to a corner, noticing the relative absence of customers. *Gotta like a small town. They roll up the sidewalks at nine o'clock, except on Sundays, when it's six.* An older woman and what appeared to be her adult granddaughter sat chatting two tables over, without regard for who heard them.

"That brother of yours takes the cake; his so-called fiancée is sitting in the front seat on the crazy train."

The younger woman nodded. "I know, eh? When the police arrived at their apartment, Kevin's head was busted open and there was coke powder all over the living room floor. She said he tried to take her coke, and she wasn't having none of it. She smacked his head with a frying pan. And her, seven months pregnant. Imagine. I wouldn't have been surprised if her water'd broke right then and there. Was she ever surprised when the cops hauled the both of them in, instead of just him!"

The older woman took a sip of tea, gathering up her purse in preparation for leaving. "They'll be the death of your mother. What's to become of their apartment, if they both wind up in jail?"

The younger one smiled. "Except for the fact it comes with a cat, I'd love to take it over. That is, if the landlord hasn't evicted them over it all. If they did get thrown out, rent controls won't be in place, the rent'll go up, and then I don't want it." She rose to follow her companion out of the shop. "I'll call tomorrow. We'll see."

Harry sat alone in the shop, watching the headlights of the occasional car as it rounded the corner toward town. Night had fallen and even through the café window and into the parking lot, he could spy some of the stars in the clear sky. *Where's my phone call?* As if in reply, his pocket buzzed and he retrieved his cell phone.

"Yes?"

"It's Yves, from Montreal. Can you talk?"

"Yup. I just got in to Canada. I haven't yet seen my bed, or the house it's sitting in, but they let me across the border, so I'm happy. Where are you?"

"I am still in Montreal. I have some business to tidy up, but I'll be there in a few days. Your first job is to find a place to store our products, and then —"

Rafuse's voice showed he was ruffled. "Lissen, Mr. Palu. I'm fine here. There's no need to get me organized. I'll take care of my end of the business. You just worry about your job, got it?"

Palu's voice came back, smooth, low, and without any sign of defensiveness. "Of course, of course. What I meant to say was, as soon as I arrive, I would be more than happy to help you in any way that I can."

"I'll be fine. You just come along as soon as you can. I took all of four minutes to drive the entire length of town, an' I'll be slitting my wrists if I have to rot in this place more than a month. So, do your part for my well-being and get your ass to New Brunswick." He smiled in spite of his bad mood. "Hey, they should use that as a tourism slogan."

"I'm glad to see that your bad mood has passed." It was Palu's turn to get snippy. "What do I bring with me?"

"At some point, you're gonna need a one-ton truck or a cube van to move product. And you're gonna need money. Lotsa money." He smiled into the phone without letting his voice reveal a tiny pang of mean satisfaction. "One more thing. I don't think it's a great idea for you to stay in this town here. It's too small. Better you should stay nearby but not too close. I crossed the border at another town, about fifteen minutes away from here. A place called St. Stephen. That way you can stay out of the public eye. And the public eye of St. Andrews is as nosy as fuck.

"That's about it. You arrive, we carefully audit my collection, you either buy it outright or I consign it to you for sale. And by consign, what I mean is, you've pre-sold a piece, and our agreement extends only as long as it takes to get the piece into their hands and the money out of their wallet. Are we in agreement?"

There was a pause wherein Rafuse imagined he was being cursed at. Harry waited, not in the least bit anxious.

"Agreed. I'll be there in…a day or so. Two, at the most."

Rafuse decided to soften the discussion, and his words were released as if in a whisper. "You know, we'll both be considerably wealthier in a month. This'll all work out, man. Okay, then. Catch you on the flip side." He rang off and took a gulp of his now-tepid coffee." It was time to go greet his host with broad hugs and pats on the back. *I should practice smiling. Don't want to scare the bastard. Maybe a shave might make me look more presentable. I hope the battery's not dead.* He headed to the rusty pickup, not looking forward to these next few hours. *Keep telling yourself it's only a month. Anyone can survive anything, if they know it's only a month with a payday at the end of it, right?* Not fully convinced, he started his truck at the second attempt and turned left, looking for a street sign that read The Bar Road.

* * * *

Harry Rafuse waited at the closed gate to his cousin's estate, his sputtering old beater barely turning four hundred rpms, and his eyes staring in raw hunger at the property wealth amassed on the other side of the wrought iron. A lithe young woman rounded the corner of the main building in the twilight and, with barely a glance toward him, kept walking to the entrance and then in. *There's the daughter, pretending to not know me. I'll suck up to her, get on her good side and she'll let me in on all the family dirt.* He was in no hurry to enter the estate, not quite having his speech prepared. Nick had already said he could stay a week or two, but had not actually agreed to a month-long sojourn.

Without warning, the gates slowly eased open, and Harry almost stalled the pickup in his haste to scoot through while he had the chance. In the time it took to idle the hundred feet to the front entrance, Nick Parker strode out onto the verandah and leaned on the white painted railing, waiting with a welcoming smile.

"Cousin Harry. Welcome to Wooler House. Riley? Our cousin from New York is here; remember Harry?" Harry's view of the verandah was obscured as he rounded the beat-up fender, and by the time he'd reached the first step, Nick's daughter was standing beside him, eyes on Rafuse like a teacher on her students during an exam.

Nick continued. "You must be exhausted. We'll have you bunking over there," he pointed to the guest house, "but first we must feed you. The cook's gone to bed, but I asked her to leave a meal for you, for whenever you arrived. You are starved, aren't you?"

"I wouldn't say no to a home-cooked meal. Perhaps just a snack."

"Then come in, please. You can put your things away after you've eaten. Sorry about the mess. I've been upgrading the security system, and we thought that, if the walls are open, why not put fiber optics wiring in for sound, videos, stuff like that? Would you like a glass of wine, by the way?" He led his guest to the dining room, while Riley headed to the kitchen to fetch a tray.

"I never was much of a wine drinker, Nickie, but a beer or two'd go down good after a long trip like that. Hard to believe a quiet place like Maine is so big. I dunno what I was thinking, but once I got through

Massachusetts, I figured I'd be here in about a half hour to an hour." He chuckled. "It didn't quite work out that way, and here we are, at ten o'clock at night. Sorry 'bout that." He crossed the threshold, not offering to take off his dusty shoes or wash his hands, and followed them into the dining room.

Between bites, Harry explained how his house in Montauk was being renovated and his painting schedule was completely upset. It was very handy, he said, a "nick-of-time" intervention, no pun intended, to have received this invitation to visit his cousins. He was not reminded that it was he, in fact, who had invited himself, but that was a detail (and a habit) Harry often glossed over in the course of a lifetime of impositions.

"When did you take up painting, Mr. Rafuse?" Riley played with a slice of gruyere.

"Oh, you know, late in life, is I guess a good way to answer that. A few years back." He stuffed a mouthful of bread in, as good an excuse as any to preclude answering more questions.

"And how have sales been?"

The bitch just won't let it go. He swallowed. "Just starting to take off recently, in fact. I'm, ah, experiencing a minor cash flow challenge at the moment, but a coupla nice commissions should be comin' in at the end of July."

Nick watched the corners of Harry's mouth turning down, even as Riley's eyes began to twinkle. "I'm sure you're going to have a lovely, creative period here, Harry. Stay as long as the spirit moves you. If you need anything, just let me know and we'll see you get it. The guest house has a kitchen in it, or you can have cook bring you meals as well, if that's your preference. Her name is Donna-Ann Horcroft—we call her D-A— and she's here Monday to Friday. Her husband Tony's on the grounds weekdays as well. And on the weekends we eat out or fend for ourselves.

"There's one other thing. We have a lovely couple staying with us. John and Peggy Whiteway, from Minnesota are here for the summer. They're staying in the third floor suite, so I expect you'll see them from time to time. They gallivant, to use their word, so even we don't see them at every meal."

"Mostly at dinner," Riley added.

"Yes, mostly at dinner. I'm sure you'll like them."

Harry cast a significant look toward Riley, wondering if she would end up liking him. It wasn't looking good, at the moment. "It's my intention to hole up, maybe try to get caught up on my painting. Time is money, so they say, and I lost a shi—bunch of it, what with the renovations. To make a long story short, other than the odd trip around the coast for inspiration, I'm gonna have my nose in the tripod."

"Easel." Riley whispered it, almost to herself.

"Yeah. Easel. I must be tired." Rafuse couldn't completely hide the look of loathing he shot at his cousin. A second later, the look was gone, as was the last bite on the plate. "I suppose I should hit the hay. It's been a long day."

As Nick held the door open for him, Riley called out. "I'm looking forward to seeing your work, Harry."

Without turning to acknowledge the words, Rafuse responded that he didn't generally show his works in progress. "Ah," was all she said. Riley studied the cheese as Nick studied Riley. He closed the screen door after Harry, without letting it slam.

Chapter 15

Niagara On The Lake

EARLY SUMMER MORNINGS IN ONTARIO can be spectacular, yet often understated. In the fields around Brantford and Delhi, if the tractors and sprinklers are silent, you can hear the asparagus growing. In the east, near Brighton, the fog wisps in overnight from Lake Ontario, and just after dawn the long-haul tractor trailers brush it aside as they carry food and comestibles east on the TransCanada Highway to the Maritimes. In Niagara On The Lake, with the exception of the starlings, hawks, and the occasional field worker, the vines sit still, leaves embracing the sun as it rises low from the east end of the fields to warm them. The solar heat offers precious BTUs to fatten the grapes, building sugar reserves within each purple or green morsel. And it's quiet. Oh, so quiet.

Claire Valentin entered the processing area, ignoring the rubber boots she'd worn into the fields every day since arriving straight from the south of France. Her boss asked her to stay in the lab, so there would be no need for boots this week. She'd moved to Niagara looking for employment and a chance to learn, and apparently, agri-crime was the lesson to learn now.

Her thoughts turned to how she'd come here in the first place. Donovan had confided to her later that Dieter, the employer at the time had been hesitant, unsure if Claire was part of a deal-breaker clause. Dieter had worried that failing to hire her might interfere with his efforts to buy him out. Dieter had engaged many apprentices over the years, but didn't like strings attached to employment offers. In hindsight, he was pleased with Claire, but at the time had been worried about every detail of the sale of his baby, the Plenitude Winery.

Before starting her day, she did a quick walk-about, ascertaining everything she had studied the evening before was exactly the same this morning. Nothing appeared to have shifted overnight, so she began a second, more focused study. Every tap, spigot, bung, and plug was tested, both for its use as well as to see if any foreign substance had been introduced into the receptacle vessels.She opened each tap, just a little, and closed it again, noting the degree of strength required to break the seal. Did it take exactly the same torque as it took the time before? As she moved from the barrels to the vats, Claire thought about her missing-then-found cask of pinot noir, back in Arles, France. A year ago, Donovan and Beth arrived at her father's winery, unannounced, and after a few questions, proceeded to find it hidden in the family's machine shed.

No accusations had been made at the time, but she suspected it was her father's lifelong friend who had hidden it in a fit of jealousy. Nothing like that had ever happened to her family before, and she was surprised at the hurt and fear it had raised within her. It had felt like an attack, a personal assault on her family. And it raised similar feelings within her, here in Canada. She felt guilty, to this day, that she was unable to share the secret with her father, but only bad could come of sharing.

Her mind turned to the matter at hand. Was this activity at the winery the result of a resentful employee? Was it as random, as Dieter assured everyone on the team, or as potentially damaging as Donovan thought? Was it indeed just the theft of vines by outsiders looking to make a buck? Shrugging, she moved on to the next task.

Claire found it in the lab.

She'd walked past it on the first trip through the room, unaware anything was out of place. On the second review of the stainless steel testing table, on the glass shelf above it, she studied every graduated beaker and hydrometer. One of the tall, narrow beakers was set right side up. Her heart sinking, Claire's short frame leaned over the table and she put her nose eight inches away from the tube. A meniscus of colorless liquid occupied the very bottom. Almost sick to her stomach with worry, she slid the glass door open and looked again, without touching anything.

I didn't use that beaker, or put it back that way. Who did? And what did they do with it?

Beakers are used, among other things, to measure the specific gravity of the must in order to determine alcohol content as the juice turns to wine. What had been done with this one? She stared at the room, at the vats, and at the scores of wine barrels in various stages of maturity. One of the staff could have used it, and for any one of a hundred reasons. She'd be sure to ask, of course. But they hadn't, of that she was certain. Claire's hands punched empty air in frustration. The vandals could have done anything to any of the containers!

A quiet thought formed, inducing even more panic. She'd tested almost all of the taps and bungs. Any fingerprints would have been destroyed or replaced by hers, and she couldn't recall if any of the taps were closed differently from before. She'd ruined any chance of collecting evidence. A second thought careened into the front of her brain. Was she alone in the building? She drew in her breath, listening for any stirring. The fact she'd just been through the entire production area calmed her somewhat, but someone had been here, fewer than eight hours ago. Someone malevolent, whose presence clearly meant destruction of the crop, and therefore Plenitude's reputation. The wines and the winery went hand-in-hand; to destroy one was, inevitably, to destroy the other.

Claire realized she'd been holding her breath and exhaled, shoulders dropping in both panic and defeat. It was time to share this burden. Where was Donovan? She hurried to the door separating the production building from the winery. Pulling it open, she crashed into the man she sought.

"Hey! What's the hurry, Clairissima? And why that look?" He drew her away from him, reading her face. "I don't like that look, even on a pretty face."

At the point of tears, she explained what she'd discovered, and ended by pleading with Donovan, "Please tell me I'm over-reacting. Tell me someone merely wanted a glass of water and thought it was cool to drink from a laboratory beaker."

Donovan continued to stare at her, causing Claire to wonder if she'd grown horns, or if her hair had turned green. With a gasp, a third devastating thought came crashing down on her. "You think it was me, because I was the one who found both crimes! Well, it wasn't me.

Plenitude is the best thing that's ever happened to me. I-I would never…" Her face dissolved into tears, and Donovan found himself comforting her, assuring the young lady he thought no such thing. He led her toward the office, where he assigned someone to watch over the lab and to keep anyone from touching the beakers.

Dieter had gone to St. Catherine's, so the next thing to do was to call the police. That out of the way, he again turned his attention to his apprentice. Claire began to squirm, but before he could reassure her, Beth waved through the glass doors, and he signaled for her to enter.

"What's going on, guys? Did you find some more missing vines?" Seeing the look on Claire's face, Beth dropped the attempt at humor and hurried over to put an arm around her. "Now I'm concerned. What *is* going on?"

Claire burst into tears, drops spilling over her already-pinked cheeks. "Somebody has done something terrible in the lab, and he—" she pointed at her accuser, "—he thinks it's me."

Donovan raised a hand to quell Beth's glare. "No. I don't. And this is why I don't like dealing with people. They think they can walk into my brain and tell it what it's thinking. Well, that's not how it works, folks. I think what I think, and you—" he jabbed a finger at the pair of women, "—you don't get to guess what I'm thinking. Ask me, and I'll tell you." He sat back, waiting.

After a moment, Beth spoke. "Okay, Mr. Smartie Pants. Tell me what happened, tell me why Claire is upset, and then you can tell me what you were in fact thinking. And no more finger-jabbing!" She winked.

Donovan and Claire filled Beth in on the most recent event. While they waited for a detective to arrive, Donovan looked over to Claire. "It's about two or three o'clock in France, correct?"

She looked puzzled. "I suppose so. Why are you asking this?"

"I want to call your father. I have some technical questions I want to ask him. What's his number?" Beth nodded in approval, while Claire remained puzzled.

When the phone was answered, Donovan reverted to French. "Monsieur Valentin, it's Sean Donovan calling, from Canada. Quite well, thank you. Yes, Claire is fine as well. She's very bright, and the winery is lucky to have her working here. I'm actually calling about the winery. We've had an instance of vandalism, two, actually. In the first case, a dozen expensive vines were stolen. Yes, I expect your daughter would have mentioned that." Claire nodded in affirmation.

"This morning, however, something has taken place that might have graver consequences. We suspect someone may have poured a contaminant into one or more of our production vessels. No, we don't know what's been done yet. That's why I'm calling you. In your opinion, if you wanted to ruin something in the production area at this time of year, what would you hone in on? The vats? Ah. I suppose so. We'll be checking everything, but I really wanted to know where to start. A chemist? Good idea. Thank you, sir. *Merci*." He handed the receiver to Claire. "He wishes to speak with you."

"*Oui, Papa? Bien, oui. Non. Non, toute est correct. Oui. Je t'aime. Bye-bye*." She placed the receiver in its cradle. "He wanted to know if I am safe, and do I want to go home. I said no, of course. I am not leaving." Beth leaned over to take her hand and give it a squeeze.

Donovan began to pace. "Monsieur Valentin suggested we get a chemist in as soon as possible. When the police get here, I'm also going to ask them to test our vats. The chemist can work with the police to do a tox scan, see what they can come up with." His face was lined with worry. "That said, I'm thinking the entire harvest is compromised. It may come down to losing a year, versus losing our entire name. But let's not say anything until we get the testing done twice."

Donovan sent Claire to the production area to sit with the field manager he'd called in earlier to watch over things. Once the door closed, he met Beth's eyes. "Okay, now I wish Jack was here."

Beth nodded, pausing for a moment before speaking. "Sean, remember me awhile ago, cringing at the thought of going east? I thought we might have to change cases with Jack, and now I'm sure of it. I know how smart you are around crime, and let's not get into how you became this smart." A trace of a smile began to form on her mouth. "But it occurs to me Jack has spent his career—most of his life—solving crimes. We need…"

"Yes?" Donovan knew what was coming, wanting her to say it.

"I'm fine with going to St. Andrews and taking over where Jack left off. Is there a way you could make that work?"

Donovan twirled his chair to face the French doors and the fields beyond. After a long minute, he spoke. "What you're saying is I'd be better at working on a murder than I would at security breaches in a winery. Or, Jack would be better at security breaches than me. Either way, I'd be looking at leaving Plenitude to others while I go help friends of friends." He sighed. "I've never owned anything worth anything in my life, until this. I sank everything into this place. It'd be nice if I can keep it. What I need to work out, is whether I should let the Whiteways down and work here with Jack."

Beth came over to stand behind her new husband. "No one would blame you if you put the winery first, but whatever you decide, a decision has to be made."

"It's okay. I've already decided." He rose. "The police are here. Let's take a walk through the lab."

Chapter 16

New Brunswick

JACK MILLER TURNED A GLASS of Guinness around and around, studying the beads of sweat collecting around the girth of the beverage. He hadn't drunk alcohol of any kind in the past year, following a year of heavy drinking. Losing his wife had thrown him into a spiral of self-pity and grief and, at a certain point, he'd decided enough was enough. But a lifetime of holding a drink left him staring at his hands, wondering what to do with them in social situations. So he'd taken to ordering a beverage, usually a Guinness, and leaving it to rest beside him as he conversed with colleagues and friends. It comforted him and reduced the number of times he'd been obliged to explain his decision to not drink.

As the glass twirled above his single table at the inn, he thought about Tricia Parker, the body on the underwater road. Why had she been killed? Where? Who'd done it, and how much time had passed between the time her life had been snuffed out and her discovery? So many questions and no answers.

She was American. Why was she even here, in small-town Canada? It was understood Tricia had no relationship with her daughter, Riley, or her ex-husband, Nick. Or so he'd been told. This was something he'd have to dig into, just to be sure. People are funny, in what they will reveal and what they choose not to. But people don't travel to another country, except for business or pleasure. Which was it in this case? Somebody knew something and sitting alone in a hotel, charming as it was would garner him nothing. He rose, put the beverage on his tab, and headed to the RCMP detachment office on Hawthorne Street in nearby St. Stephen.

* * * *

Constable Wilfred Norman met him with a nod and a bilingual greeting. There was a stack of forms on the desk in front of him, and he flipped the one he was completing over on top of the pile, effectively obscuring any private information Jack might glance at. The compact office was familiar in its routine features: four desks, paired and facing one another, a television tuned to the CBC news channel and beside it, a telecom screen listing events on a banner format, a door leading to the single cell, and a coffee maker standing guard beside the washroom. Jack noted the duty sheet, counting eight RCMP officers. The constable was thirty-ish, tall and lean, sported a military haircut above his tanned, chiseled face. The overall impression was no-nonsense.

"What can I do for you?"

Jack pulled a chair up to the desk and sat down, eyes meeting the officer's level gaze. "My name's Miller. Jack Miller. I'm investigating the death of Tricia Parker, on behalf of the Parker family."

"Are you family?"

"No. But I have a letter from Whitehead and Speede, notarized and signed by Nick Parker and his daughter, the only family she has—had in the country."

Norman smiled. "That's actually very helpful, Mr. Miller." He crossed over to a filing cabinet and pulled a file folder from the top drawer. The folder was labeled *Parker, T*, and the officer placed it in front of his visitor. "What...sort of credentials do you have? You realize, I'm sure, that this is an ongoing investigation, and you carry absolutely no authority to act here."

Miller smiled, pulling out his RCMP badge. "I still have this for the moment, although I'm no longer active on the force. My retirement comes up next month, and I'm on vacation leave until then, so technically, I'm an off-duty cop. It seems I've not actually used up my vacation time, over the years, so I've been on leave these past months. I do realize I have no authority here, and it's my intention to bring every scrap of information I gather straight over to you. I'm a friend of the family, with no vested interest other than that. I'm not being paid, for example."

Norman leaned over the desk to shake Miller's hand. "Thank you for your years of service, sir. I'm glad you understand about the Force's approach to the case. Rules are rules, as you know."

"Yup, I do. I just need to get started, and a conversation with you, or, better yet, a glance at that file would be a nice start." Norman's response was to retrieve two sheets of paper from the folder, make a point of returning the folder into the cabinet, and then slide the two pages across the desk. Miller peered down and began reading.

Four minutes later, he came up for air. Constable Norman was looking at him, half of his attention on the radio advising of a burning barn in progress, half waiting for comment. Jack leaned back in his chair, making it creak. He tapped the desk beside the papers.

"That's quite a story. More holes in it than a chicken wire fence. The autopsy is enlightening, though. The body wasn't in the water more than nine hours, so it probably fell in or was thrown in around midnight. At that point, it would have been mid-tide and rising, in the hours leading to midnight—which makes me think she was thrown in, from the wharf or somewhere nearby as the tide was coming in. The body would have drifted around the point and back to the Bar Road during the late-night hours. It's a pretty fast tide, isn't it? I've been reading about the Bay of Fundy."

"That's right. We haven't done our homework on the possible distance above and below the wharf to ascertain where the corpse might have put in, but as soon as we can chat with the scientists at the Huntsman Marine Laboratory, we'll have a better sense of all that." The officer leaned forward. "I had a quick chat with one of the fishermen, though. He maintains if the body fetched up on the Underwater Road, to use his words, it was tossed in at Katy's Cove. He seemed pretty confident."

Jack cast a shrewd glance at the RCMP constable. "Have you been assigned here long?"

Norman shook his head. "Two months next week. I'm just down from Nunavut, so it still feels like I'm in a tropical city. I'm originally from Fredericton, though." They shared a chuckle at St. Andrews being considered a city, let alone a tropical one. "It's fair to say I don't have a good enough working knowledge of Charlotte County, for sure."

Jack's finger followed a passage in the document. "It says here the local RCMP arrived on the scene first."

"That's right. Local officers are called in, and once the class of crime is established and the scene is cordoned off, the major crimes unit is called in. Since the tide was going out as the body was found, we had approximately six hours to study the body *in situ*. By three o'clock, we had to remove the body, verify there was no additional evidence around it, and the water was lapping at the feet of the officers as they finally removed the remains from the scene."

"So, nothing beside the body? No ligatures, weights, packages?"

The officer shook his head. "Nothing whatsoever. Her clothing was intact, and the only sign of struggle was a contusion on her scalp, which may or may not have come from contact with the sea bottom, and marks around her throat, consistent with strangulation. Again, we need to speak with a coroner and a forensics specialist to rule out what actions could cause which results." He threw his hands up, palms out. "I mean, after tumbling around in seawater all night, coincidental things are bound to happen to the corpse. Prints and DNA, for instance, wash off nicely with a good saltwater scrubbing. It's going to take someone smarter than me to sort all that stuff out."

Jack nodded in agreement, and Norman finished his thought. "There's this saying I remember from one of my criminal courses: 'You can keep pulling bodies out of the water all day long, or you can go upriver and see why they keep falling in.' I'm leaving the science to the PhDs, and I'm going upriver to see what's going on."

"I hear ya. If I hear anything in my 'travels upriver,' I'll give you a holler."

"That would be great, Jack."

* * * *

Yves Palu left his room at the nondescript motel situated on the road leading out of St. Stephen. The Route Number One Diner, his destination, was less than half a mile toward town, but with his leg, he felt more comfortable driving the short distance. As he limped in, the one occupied table contained a couple of young men seething with attitude. He ordered a club sandwich with a poutine, and the muttering began.

"Looks like we got a Frenchman in our town. I tole ya we shoulda put a wall up on the Quebec border." Both men laughed harder than the comments warranted. They waited a moment to see if the stranger was getting upset, but it was as if he hadn't heard at all.

A moment later, they started again. "On the limp are ya? No more than you deserve, I bet. Do all Quebecers limp? I bet they do." This elicited more laughter, but still no reaction. Bored with their game, the men limited themselves to tossing over a glare from time to time.

It seemed as if the pair was just killing time, because Palu finished up his meal, paid and left the diner without them moving more than their mouths. On the way out, stopping at the only other car in the parking lot, Palu pulled out a thin blade. He stabbed each of the tires on the driver's side and then hurried over to his vehicle. He got in and drove off without a backward glance, thinking one flat tire was an annoyance and could be changed on the spot, but two flat tires would require the services of a towtruck.

Fifteen minutes later, he parked his car on Water St. in St. Andrews, within sight of the wharf. At seven-thirty, the sun had dropped and shops would be closing soon and pedestrian traffic had slowed. He limped down the short paved area leading to the wharf and began what was for him the arduous trek out the length of the wharf. Ignoring the gulls, the gentle lapping of the waves on the pilings, or the pink-to-mauve sky, he hobbled over to the left. Palu peered over the edge of the wharf, to where the last populated boat was tying up for the night.

After watching the pair of fishermen clean the deck, hose the poly crates and tie down all the loose gear, Palu called out that the ropes tying the boat to the wharf seemed awfully loose. With patience in his voice, the fisherman noted the tides raised and lowered the boat a greater distance than anywhere else in the world. "Tight lines would swamp the boat, and then where would we be?"

Palu grinned a winning smile, apologizing for being such a landlubber. A few general comments later, he steered the discussion around to the nearby shore, pointing across the water. "Is that New Brunswick or Maine?"

"That's Maine."

"Any problems with the US Coast Guard?"

The man stopped coiling the rope at the bow and looked up at Palu. "Now, why would I have any trouble with the US Coast Guard?"

Merde! I pushed too hard. "What I meant was, do you have much contact with them? I have a cousin in the Coast Guard and I was wondering where he works. So, if he patrols this area, do they ever come over to the Canadian side?" He paused, wondering if the fisherman bought what he was selling.

The man in the boat appeared to be somewhat mollified. "Truth be told, they don't come over at all, as I recall. Maybe when they're off duty, by car."

His mate piped up from the stern, where he was stacking buckets. "I bet Billy'd know, not that he's the kind of guy to share things without getting paid."

Palu smiled. "Billy? Would you mind telling me his full name and how I can get hold of him?"

The captain's face darkened, but he conceded an answer. "That would be the infamous Billy McLeod. You'll probably find him at the Red Seal, just over there." He pointed to a watering hole on Water Street, closest to the wharf.

"Just look for the guy with a rum and coke in his mitt and a scowl on his face." The man at the stern grinned.

A few minutes later, Palu was seated at the bar of the Seal Cove Pub and Eatery, checking out the patrons. He failed to spy anyone sporting a rum and coke drink. After a chat about the weather, Palu considered asking the bartender about him, but thought better of it. If Billy was the guy Palu wanted, he would by nature also be that guy who didn't like people prying into his personal affairs. Disappointed, he finished his whiskey and limped out. Tomorrow's another day. There will be time to find the right fellow.

* * * *

Harry Rafuse sat in the passenger side of Billy McLeod's pickup truck, just off Route 127, in Chamcook. Occasionally, a vehicle's muffled roar would sound, but a discreet wall of trees ensured the truck and its occupants stayed alone. The path, barely recognizable as such, carried on another twenty feet and then dipped precipitously downward toward the rocky shore. A squirrel scolded them for just a moment, and they were once again alone.

"Want a drink?" Billy reached behind the seat, pulling out a Pabst Blue Ribbon from a cooler. Icy droplets flew as he gave the can a brief shake, tapped the bottom with a broken fingernail and cracked it open. Without waiting for a response, he handed it over to Rafuse, who accepted it. With a little grunt, he returned to the cooler and produced a second beer. "So, what are we talking, here?"

Harry smiled. "We're talking business, my friend. A few days ago, I sent a shitload of parcels to Eastport, in Maine—"

"I know where Eastport is."

"Sorry. I just want to be clear, that's all. Anyway, it would be helpful… really helpful, if I could get those parcels over to St. Andrews in the next few weeks. The thing is—"

"The thing is you're not interested in the St. Stephen or Milltown Border Services." His voice was flat. "You'd rather have a more, ah, customized service for your parcels. Maybe one with fewer prying eyes?" Billy took a long pull on his beer and offered a shrewd glance toward his guest. The setting sun sprayed horizontal white light off the water and up through the trees, causing MacLeod to lower the windshield visor.

Rafuse looked back, taking the man's measure. He saw a solid man in his forties, piercing blue eyes and unruly hair escaping from the sides and back. A touch of gray sprinkled through the brown curls. He noted the lines around the eyes; the harvest from years of heading out eastward on the water as the sun rose above the horizon. The firm set to the jaw, a scatterling of scars across the raised knuckles on the hands, and the size of MacLeod's shoulders all told a story. A tough story. If a man was capable of smuggling numerous cases of art across an international border, this might be that man.

"I take it we're talking about a shipment or two from Eastport, across the water?"

Rafuse nodded. "And you'd get a good day's pay for it."

"Up front?"

Harry Rafuse paused. He'd expected this question, sooner or later. And owing to his current impecunious state—his wallet had less than three hundred US dollars in it—there would be no possibility of fronting the cash to Billy. Unless…unless he was able to separate cousin Nick from a few thou. "I'll say yes. Up front. The end of summer would work a helluva lot better for me, since I expect to be a rich man by then. But I can probably scratch up a few thou in the next week or two." He winked at the fisherman. "In our line of work, trust between strangers only goes so far, right?"

MacLeod's mouth tightened, just a little. "About as far as I can throw you. With that out of the way, I think we should come to terms. What's the value of the shipment, how much space does it take up, and how many trips do I need to make?"

"We're talkin' twenty-five boxes, some of them are just over two cubic feet, a dozen of them are three-by-three by six inches thick. So, one or two trips should do it, I expect. One trip."

"You're talking through your hat, buddy. I'm counting two trips, but if you tell me the exact number and size of the crates, well, maybe I can squeeze it all into one trip. The second trip would cost you ten times as much as the first, on accounta the risk. Now, what was the value of the shipment?"

Rafuse's eyes narrowed. "I'm giving you no disrespect, sir, but that doesn't concern you. I'm willing to pay you a generous amount for each trip. Why can't we leave it at that?"

Billy leaned back, tossing an empty can out of his window and into the bed of his truck. "I suppose so. Okay. Ten thousand. Per trip."

"I was thinkin' three thousand for each of two trips."

"Seven thousand."

Rafuse's voice took on a whiny tone. "I was thinkin' three thousand." He paused."How about two up front before each trip, and two after I receive the goods from each trip?"

Billy MacLeod nodded. "Five thousand up front for the first trip, and ten thousand if there's a second load. Someone's doing all the heavy lifting, risk-wise, and it ain't you." He jabbed a finger, solid as iron, into Harry's chest.

Harry's voice toughened. "Just so we're clear here, these goods are incredibly difficult to sell. If they were to, say, disappear, they wouldn't be worth shit to anyone. They'd be almost impossible to fence."

Billy's laugh was harsh. "I'd be offended, if I didn't know who I was dealing with. Let's just say we understand each other as clear as spring water at high tide. Let's get you back now. I'll call you with possible dates and times, and we can see what works. The weather's gotta cooperate, the alibis have to be set, you have to be nowhere near the job when I get there, and I have to have the right feeling, right here—" He patted his gut. "—and right here." He tapped his temple. "Don't call me, don't recognize me on the street, don't introduce me to anyone, got it?"

Harry laughed, a genuine belly laugh. "You make it sound like this is my first time. Well, it ain't. I won't make any mistakes, and I'll thank you to do the same. With that out of the way, I'm feeling good about finding you. You don't sound like you're interested in getting caught, either. Okay, take me home and I'll wait on a call from you."

"It could be as long as three weeks, so don't shit your pants waiting by the phone."

"I got it. You'll tell me and I'll jump."

Billy MacLeod nodded, not knowing whether the man was joking, and not caring. He put the truck in reverse and backed out of the brush and onto the road.

Chapter 17

St. Andrews

AT FIVE PAST MIDNIGHT, THE cell phone burst into life beside Jack Miller's bed. It played the melody to *Isn't She Lovely*, one of his wife's favorite songs. Jack was always careful to have his phone on vibrate during the day, but preferred the sentimental announcement ringtone in his private time. He sat up, alert, even as he hit the green icon.

"Miller here."

"Hi, Jack. It's Donovan. Sorry about the time. This can't wait. Things have gone down the crapper here at the winery. You know about the dozen vines that were stolen? Something else has cropped up. It appears that someone has broken into the lab and compromised some, or all of our wines."

If Jack wasn't wide awake before, he was now. "What do you mean, 'compromised?' Did somebody poison something? What did they go after: bottles, carboys, casks? Vats, for god's sake?"

"That's the thing, isn't it. We don't know yet. The first tests have come back, and it seems as if one full wine barrel had enough sugar added to it to ruin the contents. That's a hundred and eighty bottles wasted. If that's the extent of it, we'll be okay. The problem is we can't know yet whether any of the other vats have been screwed with. Dieter is running a full set of chemical testing on everything in sight. The place looks like a police crime scene, which it is, effectively."

Jack glared at the news coming from his phone. "Shit." He shifted his weight on the bed, all of a sudden aware his luggage was staring back at him out of the corner of his eye. Sensing where this was going, and trying to wish it away, he took a stab at steering the direction of the conversation.

"Do you want to send me the photos, together with a description of what happened? I could maybe—"

"I want you to come home, Jack. You're my head of security, and you're better at this kind of thing than me. My winery is too important to leave it in my hands. That sounds like a joke, but I'm not laughing."

"I see." Left unspoken were Jack's thoughts around the St. Andrews case. Was he to just pull up sticks and abandon Nick and Riley? What about Donovan's commitment to John and Peggy Whiteway? He sighed. "And time is of the essence, right? The first forty-eight hours and all…"

"That's right. Please tell John and Pegs how sorry we are. On the other hand, maybe it'll take the sting out a bit if you told them Beth and I are going there to take over. If you explain our situation, perhaps they'll forgive us."

Feeling as if a load had just been taken from his shoulders, Jack let out a deep breath, exalted. "So, we won't leave the Parkers in the lurch?"

"No. I'd prefer to be here, don't get me wrong, but Dieter's got the wine experience covered. With you here, we have the security under control. The police are local, and therefore understand how big a deal this is to the wine region, so they're all over it. And they've assured me they'll keep it discreet. Either of us can handle the security issue. So, we switch. I really need you here. I can imagine what it must be like, to be pulled off a case, but this is the best solution I could come up with."

"What does Beth think? I can't imagine this is the honeymoon she imagined." Jack's voice was dry, and his sympathy could be heard over the phone.

"Actually, it was her idea. She noted in this case you are the best man for the job. I agreed, and here we are. So. When can you leave?"

"Depending on getting a seat, I can fly out tomorrow."

"Beth's in the process of writing up everything we know about the Plenitude case. You'll find Claire very helpful, surprisingly so for someone so young. She's taking it personally. Will you be able to do a similar update on the Parker murder? They've determined it was murder, haven't they?"

Jack thought about everything he knew up to that moment. "I'd bet a lot on it being a murder, but the RCMP haven't heard from the coroner yet, or else they're keeping mum. I'm gonna say yes, someone killed her."

He thought about what he'd just said. A lifetime of training taught him never to jump to conclusions without the evidence. In this case, though, everything pointed to a person or persons getting Tricia Parker out of the way, for some unknown reason. How else to explain her showing up in a foreign country, uninvited, almost twenty years after a messy divorce? How else to explain a body washing up, literally, on the doorstep of a family that had disowned her two decades earlier? He shook his head. "Here's something I won't put in the notes, because it comes from a gut feeling. But man! This family carries secrets. And none of them are alike, so they each need a personality profile created. I'm not saying they're all lying, but the truth isn't coming out. Here's my other hunch: I stand to be corrected, Sean, but this is a murder. And I don't know, frankly, if it's a one-off. You could be walking into a viper's nest."

At the other end of the line, Donovan was silent, obviously pondering Jack's words. "All right, then. Get me a report when you can. Beth and I'll be gone by the time you show up. The only thing missing from my report is this, and it's something you'll already have thought of. I hate to say it, let alone think it but we have to consider this an inside job. It's one thing to grab a dozen vines from the side of the road, but they were recent plantings, and strangers wouldn't know the provenance of those particular vines from a pickup truck on the highway, and at night. It gets more personal still when they walk into my lab. I'm running on instinct here, but don't discount it being an inside job."

Donovan intimated as much, and Jack had indeed been considering whether it could be someone employed at the winery. *But don't rule out anything.* "Got it. I'll try to be at Plenitude tomorrow evening. Can you get one of the staff to pick me up at Pearson Airport?" Hearing a single word in the affirmative, Jack rang off and then called downstairs to advise he would be gone in the morning. He requested his room be reserved for his friends Sean and Beth,without any interruption, if that was okay. That taken care of, he packed, wrote up the requested report, sent it to Beth because he remembered her email address, and tried without success to get back to sleep.

* * * *

In another part of St. Andrews, Riley Parker sat on a beach log, staring at the spot where, at low tide, the underwater road would be. A few tiki torches were stuck in the sand at either end of the log, and the fire pit in front of her glowed red, the coals snapping. Minister's Island loomed in the moonlight like a gray castle, just offshore. It seemed like it would be nothing to trace the few paces to the shoreline, step onto the road and just walk across. She shivered, knowing just how cold the water was, how strong the tide would be, and aware as well she'd be passing the spot where her mother had been found.

A man's voice called from behind her, startling her from her reverie. "Hey, Darling. It's after midnight."

"Dad! It's called sneaking up behind someone. If I'd been using a stick for drawing in the sand, you'd have got a whack, you know."

Nick Parker sat down beside her. A half-dozen two-inch pipes had been driven into the sand so that only a foot of metal was left exposed, and a fire stick had been placed in each pipe for ready access. He pulled one from the nearest pipe and dipped the point into the embers. "You were quiet at dinner."

"Not much to say, I guess."

"This is very hard, discovering your mother that way."

"Dead, you mean?"

He smiled. "I remember asking you when you were a kid if you were being sarcastic to me. You answered 'No.' but in a sing-songy tone so I'd know you knew exactly how to employ sarcasm. This one sounds a little more like you're being passive-aggressive."

"Would you rather have a robot, who doesn't feel anything? This is my mother! It just...sucks."

Nick put an arm around her shoulder, and she rested her head in the crook of his neck. "The coroner's report comes tomorrow, so we might learn a bit more about what happened. I think once we learn the details, we'll be less upset—a bit less upset—over what happened to your mother."

"You never say her name, did you notice that?"

He patted her arm, where his hand rested. "I used to hate your mother for what she did to us. But over the years, I just tried to put her out of my mind, and I think I succeeded. I wanted to think of Tricia as someone I used to know. As for her name, well, I think not saying it was just a habit, something I got used to doing."

"Or, got used to not doing."

Nick laughed. "I suppose so. Anyway, I came down here for a reason, and it wasn't to call my twelve-year-old baby girl up to bed. You're an adult now, and a beautiful, really smart one at that, so you can stay up all night every night, if you wish. But I just got some news from Peggy. She was making tea to go with some cookies she'd found, and I was just closing down the house when I bumped into her in the kitchen.

"She'd just got a text message from Jack. Apparently, there's been a change in plans at his place of employment. There are some crimes taking place at the winery where Jack works as head of security. He's been called back."

"Oh, that's great. A lot of good he's been." Bitterness swirled around her tone, melding with the smoke from the bonfire.

"I know. But there's a bit of good news. The winery owner and his wife are coming here to work on the case. Apparently, they are both very good at solving crimes. He's a security consultant, and she's a director of communications at the Canadian embassy in London. Jack's written a report on what he's found to date, and he'll pass it on to the folks who arrive tomorrow. Their names are Sean and Beth."

"So, we're trading in a retired cop for a couple of pretend detectives? Will they be staying with us? The house seems a bit…crowded, with John and Peggy, who I like, and Harry, who I don't like." She squeezed his hand. "You know it's always better when it's just you and me, D-A and Tony. Why can't we just let the police figure it out?"

Nick watched the waves lap at the shoreline for a moment. "I see it this way. The Canadian police are good. Really good. Eventually, they'll figure it all out, I'm sure of it. But every moment they don't is a moment when you and I are…upset. These summer months are precious, darling. Every minute flies by, and the next thing we know, it's our last September before you fly the coop. I'll be back at work and you'll have begun your career in earnest." He withdrew the fire-poking stick from the embers. The tip glowed red-black in the dark. "I'm not asking you to forget her, or what happened to her. I'm saying if we have a couple of friends with unique skills, maybe we'll get to an answer sooner."

"I suppose."

"I'm going to bed. I'll see you in the morning. Maybe we can go for a drive or something."

Riley shook her head in the dim light. "I'm going for my orientation at the Rossmount Inn. Tomorrow's my first day of work as a non-student. It'd have to be a quick drive, sometime around lunch, based on my split shift."

Nick rose and turned to face his daughter. "Then I change my earlier statement. Go to bed. There's very little employment more tiring than serving people. It's exhausting. Get some rest, you'll need it. I bet if we worked on it, we could slip away over noon to grab a bite. Let me know if you're up to it." He kissed her forehead and headed up the beach.

Riley continued to sit on the log, staring at the red core of burning coals beneath the final stick of firewood. Her father's words careened inside, confusing her. "I'm not asking you to forget your mother." *Wasn't he, though? Get the murder solved and sweep everything under the rug? The Parkers were good at sweeping things under the carpet. At secrets.* After a minute, she got up, placed the remaining loose stick back in the pipe receptacle, and studied the area around the fire, ensuring it was contained and couldn't spread.

A wisp of fog insinuated itself around Minister's Island and began the brief journey over the water. *I'll leave when the fog hits the shore.* But the sweeping fog became mesmerizing, conjuring images of her mother. She saw Tricia beneath the ghostly specter of the granite of Chamcook Mountain. And she saw herself spurning her mother's overtures. She'd left, without accepting or, worse, offering a hug. What would it have hurt, to offer a simple embrace, and perhaps a pat on the back? But no. She'd left, refusing this gesture. Tears welled up. Were they sorrow? Guilt? Riley buried her face in her lap. She wept until she could feel the wisps of fog caress her, wisps of betrayal.

A moment later, Riley headed up the beach, away from the shoreline she'd kept company with through the evening. Her eyes rose just in time to see Nick's overhead bedroom light flick off. *Please, please don't be the one who killed her*. Riley's bare feet touched the steps of the verandah and a moment later she had locked the door and turned off the hall light on the way to bed.

Chapter 18

Niagara

JIMMY TALLON LEANED ON ONE of the pair of hogshead barrels adorning the base of the staircase leading to the meeting rooms and production area. Standing one floor beneath Plenitude Winery, he thought about the recent developments in his employment, a preoccupation that seldom took place in the run of his week. Jimmy liked things simple. What had happened, however, was hard to process. He prided himself on his extensive, intimate knowledge of the premises and it concerned him, to have jerks running around the place wrecking things. He'd been thinking of anything he might have witnessed in his travels around the restaurant, production, service areas, even the fields on his way to and from work. He shook his head. Nothing sprang to mind.

The notion of concerning himself with crime was an aberration. While Jimmy was no angel, he'd never had run-ins with the law. A pint of Jägermeister may have slipped out of the LCBO liquor store without being accounted for. Speed limits were really just a suggestion, as far as he was concerned. Once, just once, he'd poured a cup of sugar into the gas tank of some asshole who'd got his cousin pregnant and wouldn't man up. But Jimmy was by nature a gentle man who couldn't wrap his head around folks doing very bad things just to be bad. The other thing was, Jimmy loved his job, and it worried him to think Plenitude could go under because of something he might be able to fix, but didn't try hard enough.

First, some expensive and hard-to-replace vines had been stolen. Now, police were upstairs, taking fingerprints from the lab. They'd told the staff everyone had to submit a sample of their prints. He wasn't sure what this would accomplish, since he loved everyone at Plenitude and couldn't conceive of any of them having a hand in this. Surely, when someone was finally caught, it would be some douche from Toronto, not someone he'd worked beside for a few years.

But how was he able to fix this? Beth and Sean had told him it wasn't his responsibility to find the guy and previously, Jack had told all staff to keep their eyes open for anything different or suspicious. But that was just a general warning. His role on the team was merely to keep his eyes open and let Beth know if he saw anything unusual or anyone behaving strangely. He could do that. It didn't seem like much in the way of action, keeping your eyes open for bad guys. Jimmy ran a hand through black wavy hair. Perhaps he'd corner the guy. *That would get me a raise and a promotion! Well, a raise.* There weren't many jobs Jimmy liked better than standing around chatting all day, so he'd be happy to stick with what he was good at. A raise was never a bad thing, though.

He'd brought a tiny notebook and a ballpoint pen with him, and between visitors to the lower level, he created two lists for each area of the winery. The list on the left was of every individual who passed through his line of vision, with the exception of the restaurant, the bar, and the wine tasting bar. In the column on the right, he indicated if the visitor was unusual, and if so, when had they been there. He updated it for the morning and, shrugging, slid the narrow booklet into a back pocket just as the sound of Anna Schmidt's assured footsteps predicted her arrival.

"Hello, Ms. Schmidt. How are you doing today?"

"Very good, Jimmy. And you?"

"If I felt any better, there'd have to be two of me. What about Kurt? How's the recovery coming?"

Anna's face retained a neutral pose. "It's a long recovery. We're confident he will be his old self in no time. School in September won't be possible, but perhaps after Christmas…" Her voice trailed off and a faraway look entered her gaze.

"I heard Jenna from the wine tasting bar is seeing him. Is that still happening?"

Anna attempted to stifle a smile and mostly succeeded. "I try not to pry into my son's affairs. I will say it's gratifying that he has a few friends who care for him. It's been a bit tough for him these past many months. It's ironic—" She paused, as if weighing whether to reveal a secret. "He's getting better, of that there's no doubt. But it seems with every month we move toward a full recovery, the more he's become bitter about some things. I suppose it's something to do with the recovery process. He has lost a year of his young adult life. I'd be bitter too." She offered an embarrassed smile, sure she'd revealed more about her private life than she meant to.

Jimmy nodded. "That makes sense." He, too, wasn't sure where all this sharing was coming from. Anna was not by nature someone forthcoming with her inner thoughts."Anyway, give him my best. He should come by for a visit, as soon as he's feeling up to it."

Anna nodded. "I agree. I'll tell him you said so."

* * * *

Claire Valentin sat on the sill in the doorway to the production building for Plenitude Winery, her bare feet warming in the morning sunshine. The foreground view offered row after row of vines that were pruned to perfection and on the other side of the sill lay the laboratory which, lately, she'd been calling the scene of the crime. She glanced back over one shoulder at the closed circuit camera that had been installed the day before. *Why weren't you there a week ago? You would have saved us a lot of trouble if you had captured our intruder*. Rebuking inanimate objects was only one of several unusual behaviors she'd recently indulged in. Claire had also taken to visiting the vats in the middle of the night and turning on her heel when walking alone, to catch imaginary stalkers.

Crazy. I'm going crazy.

She'd also flirted with the notion of returning home. Mere Valentin was now sending a text every day, imploring Claire to return home to France. But there were compelling reasons to stay, loyalty and stubbornness being just two at the top of the list. And she'd grown to love this place of employment and new home and friends these past few months. No, abandoning the team was out of the question, but if she wasn't going to leave, by God, she'd do everything she could to solve this mess.

Jack arrived from New Brunswick last evening. She knew Jack had spent an entire career solving crimes with the RCMP. Surely he'd make a difference. Jack felt like a father to her. She remembered when he arrived, still recovering from gunshot wounds, and she recalled how hard he had worked on his rehab exercises. He'd been on a case in Romania when some men driving by in a truck had shot him and his companion. "Filled me full of lead" was the way Jack had explained it to her. He didn't seem to mind talking about it and made it sound like it was just another day on the job. It gave her shivers, though, thinking about what he'd gone through.

He'd awaken soon and had promised to meet with her, over a cup of coffee. She found it interesting; he wanted to meet with Dieter and Anna, Jimmy from downstairs, Karen the manager of the restaurant, and Lars, the head of housekeeping. But he didn't want to meet with everyone at the same time. She'd be very interested to see how he proceeded, but she was equally intrigued to know if things were going to be different. Would she be asked to work all night and sleep all day? Was he going to assign a handsome policeman to follow her around, perhaps guard the door while she was sleeping? She may have to wear pajamas when she slept. Claire blushed at the thought.

What was going to happen next? *Jamais deux sans trois*. (Two things never happen without three.) It was just a superstition, but she'd heard it enough times to worry. She flipped her hair back. Off in the distance, she could see the field workers tending their vines. Would they find another act of theft or vandalism? How many more instances like this could the winery endure before going under? She'd never had to think such grown-up thoughts before. It was sobering to realize her father's winery was equally vulnerable to disaster.

Claire sighed, uncrossed her feet and stood up. Time to take a walk through the production area. Again.

Chapter 19

St. Andrews By The Sea

"I SURE CAN PICK 'EM," Beth returned from the long meadow beside the Rossmount Inn, passed under a copse of trees and back into the shadow of the inn. Once past the garden, rife with edible flowers and micro-greens, she brushed a cluster of devil's paintbrushes aside to enter the pool area. The sofas under the far pergola invited them, but Beth spotted a tiny figure, struggling at the edge of the water. Upon closer inspection they found a fat bumble bee, legs moving slowly, wings sodden and thorax swollen with water.

"Just lift him up with your hand, Sean."

"Nope. One sting later and he's dead and I'm in pain. What else have you got?"

Beth shrugged, looked around and in a few seconds handed him a leaf. "Here you go, wussy." The bee crawled onto the leaf and Sean laid it onto the concrete edge. The bee crawled off the makeshift lifeboat and proceeded to draw a crooked wet line with his body parts. Upon their return, the bee and its line were gone, and the leaf had blown back into the water.

Later, Beth stood at the window of their second-floor room. "That's Passamaquoddy Bay over there, and this inn is just dripping with Victorian ambience. I'm getting my honeymoon after all!" She waved an arm to present the room. "Thanks for this." Beth leaned over to hug her husband, who was sitting on the edge of the high bed.

"There's the little matter of a crime to solve, but I suppose we can look past the murderers to view the scenery while we're here. This is my second trip to the Maritimes, and you were with me last time, when we visited Prince Edward Island."

"We were on the lam as I recall and barely knew each other. And now we're married. You sure can fit a lot into a year, by the way."

"What can I say? I'm a busy guy. And speaking of busy, let's head over to the Parker residence after lunch.The sooner we get started on this, the sooner we can wrap it up and go home."

Beth grinned. "I bet you say that to all of your honeymoon wives."

His response was to swat her behind. But there was no mistaking this as merely a vacation. They'd flown into Fredericton just before ten in the morning and chosen a nondescript gray Impala to rent at the airport. The short trip south to St. Andrews was a rural study in greens, with grasses, brush, bushes, and trees contributing to the palette, and occasionally relieved by glimpses of a granite hill face, or startlingly blue water. Now that they were in town, though, it would be all business. "Time to get dressed." He glanced at his cell phone. "It's almost one. We can grab a bite to eat downtown, and get over to the Parkers before they leave for the afternoon."

* * * *

Nick and Riley Parker had gone to Cosmo's Diner near Oven Head to celebrate her first day of work and because Riley's schedule was a split shift, they'd decided to take their time over lunch. They hadn't returned by the time Donovan and Beth pulled into the security gate. John and Peggy Whiteway were waiting, though, and let them in. The two couples walked down onto the beach, with Peggy doing most of the talking.

She indicated who lived where, both on and adjoining the estate, including offering her impression of the housekeeping staff, Tony and Donna-Ann—a very positive impression—and of the most recent guest who'd arrived around the same time as the murder had taken place. Peggy's opinion of Harry Rafuse wasn't as glowing an endorsement.

It was almost low tide, so the quartet walked out onto the Bar Road extension and across to where the body was found. Beth looked farther along the road, to where it rose from the shoreline and met the crags and grasses of Minister's Island. Donovan's gaze dropped to where a single rock looked unlike any of the others surrounding it. Peggy, who was watching Donovan's every move, murmured Riley had placed it there.

"Has Nick been available to Jack, when he stopped by to ask questions? How about the guest, Rafuse?"

To their knowledge, everyone had been cooperating. Jack hadn't had time to get to know any of the townies; it was their understanding he was about to do that before places and roles were reversed.

Beth interjected. "What was he looking into, with regard to the townies?"

John, who had been kneeling down to feel the frigid water, looked up to meet her look. "It seemed to me to be a long shot, from what I understand. St. Andrews is mostly comprised of tourists, artists, students, fishermen, and rich folk who summer here. It's a funny thing, though. They're all called 'locals,' with the exception of the ones who own estates. The irony is, the ones with estates have certainly been here longer than the students and most of the artists. But every community has its own eccentricities, I suppose."

Beth nodded. Donovan had already read Jack's report, but wanted another perspective. He asked Peggy to give him an overview of Riley and Nick Parker. Any shadows in their past? Was there any strange behavior in recent days?

"As far as Nick is concerned, I haven't noticed anything at all different. He gets up at the same time every day, which is about three hours before John and me. He works four to five hours a day, usually in the morning. This can change if Riley suggests an excursion. So, we're talking about a man with a fairly regimented schedule. He doesn't stay up late, come home drunk or consort with gangsters." Her voice sounded a bit defensive, Donovan noted.

"And the daughter, Riley?"

Peggy smiled. "I've known her since she was a wee tiny button. She's precious, was beautiful then, inside and out and still is, as anyone who spots her can see for themselves. Yes, her behavior is different from before the... from before. But that's to be expected, isn't it? Her world's been turned on its ear, so of course she's been moody, staying up later than usual and eating irregularly, if at all." Her eyes met Donovan's, challenging him.

Beth put a hand on Peggy's shoulder. "When he was trying to save my life in London, I once asked him if he suspected my neighbors. He said he would suspect my grandmother, until she could prove him wrong. It's just how he has to be, until the answers start to come." She patted Peggy's shoulder with a light touch.

Somewhat mollified, Peggy continued. "So, the sun rises and sets on Riley, as far as I'm concerned, you betcha. And Nick is a hard, hard worker, honest as the day is long, and his worst fault, as I understand it, is he lets his relatives take advantage of him."

"They sponge off him?"

"Well, John and I have our suspicions about Rafuse, who just invited himself up for the summer. And there are a couple of cousins back in Montauk who he's bailed out a time or two, the last time being in '08, during the Wall Street shit-throw. He's covered payments, advanced funds and, at one point, even stored his art on their walls so they could look successful for their clients. He's just an all-around good guy, Sean."

John piped up. "But he doesn't go around bragging about this to all and sundry. We know it only because I've worked with him for over twenty years and we've known him even longer."

Donovan began the walk back to the beach. "What about Riley? Any drama in her life?"

"You mean, in addition to graduating with honors in Business a year early, followed by graduating from hotel management, and class valedictorian at that? This girl is special, but she's no drama queen, that's for sure. To be frank, Riley hasn't had time to get in trouble, and that's a fact."

"Yet, the only connection we have to the murder victim is Riley and her father, Nick. It's a long way to go to get murdered on a relative's doorstep. I'll look everywhere, but that house there—" he jerked a thumb toward their immediate destination "—is holding secrets, whether the Parkers know it or not."

Peggy shook her head, but had no satisfactory response to offer.

While they waited for Nick and Riley to return, Peggy introduced Sean and Beth to Donna-Ann, the cook and housekeeper and to Tony, the groundskeeper. They sat around a farm table in the kitchen, a tray of scones and a fat earthenware bowl of homemade raspberry jam placed before them to eat with their tea. D-A was a talker, approaching but not reaching five feet tall. She offered up a businesslike approach to house management. It was also clear she had challenges sitting still and seemed to need to be working all the time. Most of her responses were tossed over her shoulder as she prepared the *mise-en-place* supper tasks.

"It's a shame about poor Tricia. She didn't treat Mister Parker very well, but no one deserves to be murdered and thrown in the bay, do they?"

Donovan stared into his tea, since Tony wasn't saying anything and Donna-Ann had her back to the table while she fussed around the granite countertop. "Why do you say it was murder?"

Her response was low, soothing. "Well, dear, folks with half a lick of common sense don't fall in the water in fair weather, do they." It was offered up as a statement of fact, and he put it down to a regional affectation, asking a question without making it seem like a question.

"So, she fell off the wharf?"

The cook turned to face the table, wiping biscuit flour on her apron. "Well, Tony overheard some of the fishermen chatting, down at the Red Seal Pub. They were saying if poor Ms. Parker washed up on the road as the tide was going out, then she probably was put in five or six hours earlier, somewhere around the point. So, probably not the wharf at all. They may have drowned her nearer the point, a few hours later than that. In that case—" she cast a significant look, "—she probably was tossed in around Katy's Cove area." She paused, her face screwed up in thought. "Of course, someone at the campground might have seen something about that time, since we're talking around dawn. No. It was one or t'other: Katy's Cove or right at the point."

Donovan and Beth turned to Tony, who sat quiet, looking self-conscious. Finally he spoke. "That's what I heard. I don't spend a lot of time gossiping, but what they said struck me as makin' a lotta sense."

"Did anyone else hear them?"

"Nah. Fishermen keep different hours from normal folks. They're on the boats at three-thirty, and they've worked a hard day by mid-morning.

So there was only two tables being used at the pub: the one I was holding for the boys and the one with the fishermen."

D-A piped up. "Their next question is going to be, 'Why were you there, Tony?' Might as well tell them that part."

Tony assumed another embarrassed look. "I work on the estate as you know, an' I'm good at my job, as you might not know. This place is probably the best-kept property in St. Andrews, and I'm not bragging. Others say it as well. One of the reasons the place looks so good is because I get together with some of the other groundskeepers, you know, to compare notes.

"Yesterday was the day some of the groundskeepers chose to take stuff to the dump first thing in the morning: rugs, broken chairs, things the owners have no use for. On days like that, we all go to the dump to watch the burning."

"And?" D-A left the one-word question dangle in the air.

"And, we pick out any choice items before they get destroyed. Then we go to the pub and get caught up over a late breakfast."

Beth spoke up. "Why do they burn it? Couldn't you just take the things you want and walk away?"

"Oh, no. Can't do that. As long as I remember, caretakers have been told to stand over the furniture and stuff and watch it burn right down before they leave. I understand from the old guys the owners wanted to make sure nothing could be taken and re-used. It's only been this past ten years that we are allowed to help ourselves."

"So, the burning was to make sure no one profited from re-selling the goods?"

Tony squirmed. "Not exactly. It's more of a 'we don't want to see our property in someone else's home, making it look as if we had to sell things to make ends meet.'"

Again, a voice piped up from the sink area. "It's also a bit of not wanting others to have what they have. Mister Parker's not like that, though. He's very generous and doesn't care about looking rich. He doesn't put on airs."

Donovan tried another tack. "What about the extended family? Are there any Parker relatives in St. Andrews, or even in New Brunswick?"

The cook answered by giving her head a small shake. "Of course they have relatives back in New York, but they don't seem to want to come here. Mr. Rafuse appears to be the exception." She turned to face them, floury hands on her hips. "In all my years, and I grew up near Bocabec, just down from the Bar Road, I've never seen a Parker other than Nick, Tricia, and Riley. Until this year. And Mr. Parker seldom talks about them. He'll discuss his business back home, his colleagues, restaurants, and plays, almost everything except for his relatives."

"Is he ashamed of them?"

She weighed the question before responding. "No, I don't think so. Perhaps a little disappointed in them. They're not a tight-knit group, nor particularly successful, from the sound of things. They all inherited good jobs and grand homes together with a bit of money, but for some of them, it all seems to have evaporated over the years." D-A came over to the table, and when she spoke her voice had a confidential air to it. "I wouldn't say anything under normal circumstances, but this isn't normal, to my mind. Every now and again, poor Nick—Mister Parker—would get a call and it would be one of the cousins from New York, I call them the cousins, no matter what their blood designation is. It's not so easy to keep up with who's who when they never visit, and after all, I'll never meet them so I don't really care who or what they are to the Parkers."

Tony grumbled at his wife to get back to the story.

"Of course." She didn't appear to be put off by Tony's gruffness, offering him a benevolent smile. "So every now and again, maybe twice a year, I'd overhear Mr. Parker speaking with one of his cousins. And it would always be about money, as in money leaving him and sliding over to them. After a bit of sighing, he'd ask for a pen and paper and write down their bank and account number, details like that. I think he never says no, but he'll be in some bad mood for the rest of the evening. Next day it's all forgotten, but I think he's getting tired of the free-loading. I wouldn't be a bit surprised if one day soon he up and says no to them. Oh my goodness, they'll fall off their chairs!" She broke off in peals of laughter.

Donovan waited until she composed herself. "Did you ever hear any amounts discussed?"

D-A frowned. "Once, maybe twice, I guess. I clearly heard him say 'fifteen thousand,' as if he was repeating what he'd heard over the line. And one other time, I'm sure I heard him say 'twenty thousand, and I can't send you anymore this year.' I must say, I smirked at that one, since it was January sixth: Old Christmas. I bet they were eating macaroni and cheese, come November of that year." She laughed again, and then her face took on a somber look. "These are just the instances I heard myself. There were probably lots more. Can you imagine, being asked for fifty thousand dollars a year, with no hope of getting it back? I make less than that, but I'm happy to work for it." Her gaze met Tony's, who nodded in affirmation.

It was Beth's turn to interject. "What about Riley? Does she ever go visit her relatives when she's in New York State? I realize you aren't there, so this one might be harder to answer."

Donna-Ann pondered the question. It appeared as if Beth had stumped her. In a moment, the cook responded, but the words came out slowly, as if each one had been crafted by hand and polished, before being uttered. "Well now, that's a good question. I can't recall her saying anything that refers specifically to her cousins. She probably did, since they live in the same part of New York. But no, I can't say for sure."

"Can't say what, D-A?" Riley stepped across the threshold into the kitchen. Her arms were full, with a cloth sack containing four bottles of wine in one hand, and a case of Stella Artois beer in the other. She placed them on the charcoal-granite counter and gave the room her full attention.

Beth smiled. "I was asking if you visited with your relatives during your school year in New York."

Riley struggled to keep a neutral look on her face. "Why do you need to know that? Mother died here, not there."

"There don't appear to be many suspects here, and—"

"What you're saying is, the only suspects in St. Andrews are gathered in this kitchen, plus my dad."

Beth was patient. "What I'm saying is, in order to clear the people gathered in this kitchen, it really is necessary to take in as much information as we possibly can. You want the murderer found and no mistakes about it, right?"

Riley folded her arms, her lips pursed and eyes narrowed. "I want the murderer found, yes. But I also want things...back to normal. Is that asking too much?"

Donovan spoke up. "In fact yes, it's asking too much. You're not a child. You know taking a life is pretty much the most extreme act a person can commit. Donna-Ann spent years studying how to be a good cook. Same thing for Tony becoming a groundskeeper. Do you think finding a murderer is as easy as walking out to the highway and asking the murderer to slow down as he drives past? If you want things to return to normal— and they won't, by the way, even after someone is caught—you have to give up your privacy, together with whatever information you have. The faster you accept this, the more likely this will be solved."

The cook busied herself by putting away the beer and wine, while Tony studied a spruce budworm moth trying to hide in the lower corner of the door screen. Donovan continued. "Did you take statistics at school? Yes? Eighty-seven per cent of murderers were known to their victims. Why wouldn't we ask about your cousins, or anyone else in touch with your mother? The numbers warrant this sort of questioning, as intrusive as it may seem. It's got to be done.

"And if it was someone you know, I would think you'd want to know who it is, as quickly as possible, in order to prevent them striking again. You wouldn't like what you heard, perhaps, but you'd still want to—need to—know. You and I can hope it was a stranger, but I'll be looking everywhere." He pushed his chair back. "We have to go visit Mr. Rafuse now. But if you hear anything, or if something springs into your head, please share it with us. "

Riley seemed preoccupied with preparing a sandwich, ignoring them as they prepared to leave. Beth thanked them for their time, apologising for the awkwardness of their first encounter, and they let themselves out onto the verandah.

* * * *

The couple found Harry Rafuse sitting on the second-story balcony of the guest house, a glass of Nick's scotch in one hand and a cigarette in the other. Squinting, Harry leaned over the steel and glass railing and invited them up.

"Can you believe the view? That's Minister's Island over on the right, and that water there's…well, to be honest, I don't recall what its name is, but it's clear and cold. It should be called Budweiser." He cackled, just a little and caught a drop of amber liquid with the back of his hand just before it dribbled off his stubbly chin. "Care for a drink?"

Beth put up a hand in the stop position. "A bit early for me." They introduced themselves to Rafuse as friends of Jack, John, and Peggy, explaining they were investigating the murder.

Harry wagged his head and offered a raspy sigh. "Shame, that is. I remember when they got married, her and Nick. That was awhile back, I'll tell ya. They seemed a nice couple at the time, but I guess things got complicated. I'd have forgiven her if it'd been up to me, 'cause she was a looker, back in the day." The hint of a leer appeared for a second, disappearing just as quickly.

"Anyway, what can I do you for?"

Donovan sat on the arm of a teak chair, facing Nick's summer guest. "I'm a little unclear as to why you made your way up to Canada this year. I understand this is your first visit?"

"I hadn't seen cousin Nick in a long spell, so when my house needed renovations, I decided to impose on his hospitality. I didn't want to stop my painting either, so I thought by coming here, I could kill two birds with one stone." The words flowed easily from him, as if rehearsed.

"I see. When did you get into town?"

"On the twelfth of July, almost the thirteenth. It was a long day, I tell ya. I underestimated how far it is from Montauk to New Brunswick. If St. Andrews wasn't just over the border, I'd 'a had to put up somewhere for the night. Either that or sleep in the truck." Sensing it must have made him sound like he couldn't afford a motel room, he hastened to add "Just 'cause I really wanted to get here and get settled in, you know."

Beth stopped scribbling notes and looked up. "That was just after Tricia Parker died. Well, sometime around then."

An unpleasant look came over Rafuse's face, and once again, he hid it immediately. "I suppose it was. But I was in Montauk—" He jerked a thumb toward the loft bedroom, "—packin'. Cousin Nick'll tell ya I called as I set out." His voice carried a triumphant tone, one Donovan thought sounded like a challenge.

Beth stepped in to mollify Rafuse, her voice like honey. "Of course no one has you in mind. Our hope is to gather up enough tiny bits of information to see if we can piece together a significant clue. You may have been out of town—the country, in fact—at the time, but on the other hand, you may have seen or heard something later that could come in handy down the road." She tried another tack. "Tell me a little bit about your painting. Neoclassical, modern, post-modern?" She let the question hang.

His response betrayed a flustered subject. "I, ah, well, I'd say you could call me something between an abstract guy—painter! And one of those fellas that paint simple paintings that everyone likes."

"Primitive?" Beth tried not to smile.

Relief washed over Rafuse's face. "Yeah, primitive. Dunno why I can't remember that word."

"Care to show us some of your work?"

"No, no. I never show my painting until it's done, and I left all my completed works back in the States." He threw up his hands, palms outward. "Nuthin' I can do."

"No, of course not." Beth appeared to have changed gears, as Donovan appeared to be biting his tongue. "So, how do you like the town? Pretty quiet, compared to what you're used to, I suppose. Are you able to get downtown, or is your schedule too busy?"

He cast a suspicious look before answering. "I get out. I try to take a walk in the afternoon and again after supper, for inspiration. Don't wanna get cabin fever, no sir. Yeah, this is a pretty small town, all right. I wouldn't like it here in the winter, that's for sure." He rose without excusing himself and went inside to the bar, returning in a minute with a fresh drink.

"Anything else? I wouldn't mind getting back to my painting. 'When the spirit moves you' sort of thing. You know."

"Of course. I'm just curious about one more thing. I understand the Parker clan has what some might call successful families. How do you get along with them, back in New York?" Donovan watched his face, studying how the man attempted to control his emotions.

After a moment, Rafuse spoke in a neutral manner, emotion washed away from his response. "They're all right, I suppose. Ya can't pick your relatives, but I suppose they're harmless, as far as that goes. I don't see as much of them as I should, being as how I'm a more…distant cousin. Besides, we're not much for family get-togethers, since we don't have much in common."

"Do they collect art?"

At that, Rafuse seemed to have run out of patience. "Look it here. I've been a good guy, but yer asking a lot of questions and frankly, I don't see the point. I thought you were here to ask about Tricia. Well, this here doesn't seem to be getting' us anywhere. Why don't you go and figger out better questions. Maybe you'll get better answers." He stomped back into the great room and made a show of sitting in an easy chair and snapping a newspaper to attention.

"We'll see ourselves out. Thanks for your time, Mr. Rafuse."

"Uh-huh." The paper didn't drop an inch.

Once outside and away from the balcony of the guest house, Beth glanced over at her partner. "He's a piece of work. Aside from the fake congeniality, which hot button did you hone in on? The line where he said he's here to paint when he seems not to know his arse from his elbow, or the nerve I touched when I pointed out he arrived just after the time of the murder?"

"Neither, although we'll have to look more closely at both. I found the most interesting part was the one that got us thrown out."

"The relatives dabbling in art? Yes, that was a good one, too. Why on earth wouldn't he be excited about his relatives collecting art? Whether it was so he could foist his crap off on them, or if they could get him sales through their connections, it seems to me he should be thrilled they collect art. Instead…"

He finished her thought. "Instead, he shut us down quicker than a cop collaring a teen in an unlicensed bar. I think there's a story, south of the border, and I'm going to know more about it before we go too far."

"Agreed. And I think I'd like to take a peek at his latest masterpiece. I just bet it'll be a piece, but of what, I'm not certain. I think we need to actually see if he's a painter or a faker."

The couple approached the main house and stepped onto the verandah. "Either way, I think he may be a dangerous man, murderer or not. Don't let yourself be cornered alone by him, do you hear me?"

She linked her hand into the crook of his elbow. "I can take care of myself. But yes, I hear you. Let's say goodbye to the Parkers for now and head downtown for an ice cream and a look around. By the way, we've been invited to an arts event tomorrow evening. I brought a nice cocktail dress and we'll rig you up with something, I expect. There'll be wine, cheese and hopefully lots of town gossip."

Chapter 20

St. Andrews

YEARS EARLIER, THE ESTATE OWNERS in St. Andrews had established a Friday evening get-together for the arts community, a function that continued through the years. The artists had intimate access to the moneyed set, while the estate owners got to know which artists' works spoke to them. It often led to situations where the newest piece never made it to the retail galleries. Commissions became a significant part of the income for some of the artists.

Nick Parker gave Donovan and Beth invitations to the event, called Friday Night Drinks. Earlier in the day, they'd visited the police—who reluctantly revealed Tricia's death was being investigated as a possible homicide—and chatted briefly with D-A, the housekeeper. They ate early, enjoying crabcakes at a tiny restaurant on the beach, and returned to the inn in time to dress for the cocktail party. They'd established it wasn't so much a formal event as a weekly celebration of originality in support of the arts crowd. Donovan grumbled, "I should probably wear a tie-dyed Joe Cocker shirt, and you'd better lose the bra and stop washing."

"Anything to get me out of my clothes, eh?" she teased. "Come on, it'll be fun. And we have two of the three groups we need to know more about, so that can't be bad, right? How do I look?" She twirled a jade mini-dress with matching earrings and necklace.

"A bit over-dressed. You look like we may have to be a half hour late."

She stood on tiptoes to kiss him. "Thanks for that, but I brought this little number to show off to others, and I'm wearing it, over-dressed or not. What will we be looking for, by the way?"

"It's a bit of a fishing expedition, I'm afraid. I want to know more about the estate owners: which ones are from New York and maybe which ones interact most closely with the Parkers. As for the arts crowd, I'd be curious to know if there's a heavy import-export traffic for the higher-end pieces. And are they talking about the murder? The artsy crowd hangs out with all society types. Someone may have heard something." He shrugged. "You never know."

"Well, it's half-past 'I'd like a drink.' Let's get going."

* * * *

The tiny caravan of two vehicles drove along the main street of the downtown shopping district in St. Andrews, parking between William and King Streets. Nick, Riley, John and Peggy exited the black SUV and waited by Joba's Gallery until Donovan and Beth parked their rented Impala. The sun shone along Water St. as shoppers ambled from the shops to the restaurants. With the glassy waters of the bay peeking between the waterside buildings, it could have been any one of a number of summery seaside resorts up and down the east coast of Canada or the USA.

Just before entering the gallery, Donovan took Riley aside. "So, our painter Harry didn't drive with us to this art event. Will we see him inside?"

Riley stared for a second before responding. She looked annoyed as soon as her cousin's name was mentioned.

"You and I know that man isn't a painter. If he showed his nose in this building, the real artists would reveal him as a fraud in two seconds. He's probably hiding out at home, studying a racing form and drinking all of my father's beer." She sped up to catch the door just as her father entered.

Nick led the group through the gallery doors. The shop specialized in sculptures; pottery and pieces crafted from wood and metal, and Beth raised an eyebrow when she spied the price tag on a piece of raku pottery. After a few moments of idle chitchat with the brunette sales girl behind the cash, the small group entered a door to the back of the building. A score of people milled about a capacious room, filled with golden, low-horizon sunlight that streamed in from a full wall of windows and doors. Another dozen men and women stood outside on the deck, sipping wine and beer and watching the boats idling in toward the wharf. The water was too calm and the tide too far out to hear the waves lapping, even from that brief distance. Nick led his friends over to the gallery owner to be introduced.

Riley gave Carlos Joba a brief hug, having known him for years, and sauntered over to the bar to grab a beverage and chat with one of the bartenders, a girl she knew from the college.

Carlos was a big man in his late forties, with a body of a rugby player: barrel chest and thick, sturdy legs beneath a solid frame. His face was the kind that seemed always in need of a shave, and the laugh lines around his eyes and mouth cut deep into his tanned skin. He wore a blue Hawaiian shirt above white linen pants and leather sandals. Sunglasses attached to a stylish black neck strap lay nestled in his thick ebony hair. After greeting them all and saving his most effusive compliments for Nick, he focused his attention on Beth.

"What brings you to this neck of the woods? You're not from here, are you?" Carlos made a swirling motion in the air with his finger for the bartender to defer her chat with Riley and to bring drinks all around.

"We're from the greater Toronto area, and we're here on our honeymoon, actually." She showed her dimples. "Carlos Joba. Sounds Spanish. Are you from Central America?"

The gallery owner's grin broadened. "You'd think so, with a name like mine. But no. I came here as an exchange student, from The Netherlands, of all places. My brothers and sisters still think I'm crazy, after all these years. But I love it here. I go home in February because no one in his right mind wants to live in Canada in February. But during the rest of the year, this is a most beautiful and inspiring place.

"Let me introduce you around. But before I do, I'm curious: Are you here to see some art, or see some artists?" He paused while drinks were served. His question got different answers from Beth, John, and Peggy. Donovan chose not to answer, offering instead a shrug and a smile.

Carlos introduced the group to a couple who dealt in antiquities, and when it was time to move on, John and Peggy stayed behind to chat. Beth and Donovan left them discussing the sanity of tourists who overpaid for decrepit buoys and lobster traps to tie to the roofs of their cars for the long drive home from vacation.

Near the wall of windows, they found an older gentleman with thinning gray hair and twinkling green eyes, studying the color of a glass of wine.

He held the glass so the setting sun played with the ruby liquid, sending refracted splays of rainbow down onto the worn hardwood planks. His face brightened as Carlos brought Nick, Donovan, and Beth over.

Patterson Pond shook hands with each of them in turn, adding an avuncular pat on the back to Nick. "So sorry for your loss, Nick. I know it's been ages since you and Tricia were…together, but still, it must be a strange feeling, to cross paths with your, um, ex, under these circumstances."

Nick gave him a broad grin. "Pat knows everything there is to know about this town and its inhabitants, often well before they themselves hear of it. He runs the glasswares and jewelry shop just across the street from the wharf, beside the pharmacy. While he's not technically an artist, he has supported the artisan community since before I first came here. We used to meet above his shop, but now different artists step up to host these Friday get-togethers each week. I used to host as well, but my place is boring, compared to—"

"Compared to a dusty old studio with an uneven plank floor in the back of a shop, is that what you were going to say?" Carlos winked at Beth.

Nick continued. "I was going to say, compared to a room full of art on its way to becoming valuable collectibles." He pointed to a table in the middle of the room, around which a half dozen onlookers were standing, gazing in rapt attention. The "table" was an oval, eight-foot sheet of barely tinted glass, beneath which sat, in its glory, a hand-crafted rowboat that gleamed golden. All of the hardware: fittings, socket block, sculling notch, breasthook, oarlock inserts, and front transom doubler were made from gold. The boards were a combination of teak and mahogany, and the pricetag indicated forty-nine thousand dollars.

"In fact, I was thinking of buying that, if we can agree on a price that won't put me in the poorhouse. Let's find a quiet place to chat, shall we?" The men excused themselves, leaving Donovan and Beth to be entertained by Pat.

"Is this your first time out to the east coast?"

Beth shook her head. "No. We were here last year, and I'm originally from Halifax. We love St. Andrews, though, from what little we've seen.

I'm looking forward to doing a little exploring. We're staying at the Rossmount, so that'll be our tourist headquarters."

Pat nodded in approval. "Be sure to grab a few dinners there. I believe they serve the best meals in southern New Brunswick. Perhaps in the province. Did you climb Chamcook Mountain? The inn sits in its shadow. It should probably be called Chamcook Hump, but that sounds a bit less grandiose, wouldn't you agree?" He lowered his voice. "I heard Mrs. Parker was up on the mountain the day before she died."

Donovan, who was listening to a couple of conversations at the same time, brought his full attention to Pat's comment. "Really? Who mentioned that?" The intensity of the look Donovan gave give him must have startled the shop owner, for he took a step back.

"Well, I heard it from my niece, Tanya Brookness, who is a friend of Riley. Riley told Tanya she bumped into her mother when she was attending the grad party at the Rossmount pool. Riley wanted to go for a walk during the party, to lower the sound level for a bit. She said as soon as she recognized her mother, she turned and went back down the mountain without saying a word to her."

Beth stood slightly behind the shopkeeper, her eyes wide, and mouthed a single word: What!

Donovan's voice was casual as he regained his composure. "They didn't say a word to each other?"

"So I understand. Have you heard anything more on the investigation? The town's a bit on edge, you know. We all know each other, except for the tourists."

Donovan shook his head. "No. I expect the police will turn something up shortly. Like you said, it's a small town and everyone knows a bit about everyone else. On that note, I have a question, since you know the arts community. Does a gentleman named Harry Rafuse ever come to these events? He's only been in town a week or two, but I was just curious, since he's a painter."

Pat nodded in recognition of the name and took a full mouthful of wine before proceeding. "I have actually met the man. Nick brought him by on his second day here. He was out of art supplies, and Nick was going to treat him to whatever he needed to get set up painting at the Parker estate."

Beth rolled her eyes at that, again, just out of Pat's line of vision, as he continued.

"Funny thing, though. When I asked him which brushes he needed, whether he worked on canvas or board, things like that, he was pretty vague. It was almost as if he didn't really know what he wanted. Anyway, that was the last time I saw him, except for one late evening this week. I had a yen for a big, fat, juicy burger from the pub—you know how that can happen—so I phoned ahead, just before the kitchen closed. When I picked it up, there was Rafuse, sitting in the corner with Billy MacLeod, one of the local fishermen. Their heads were together, as if they were telling dirty jokes, or maybe they were up to something.

"This isn't so unusual, as the local fishermen are a pretty friendly bunch, for the most part. But Billy, well, he's Billy."

Beth raised an eyebrow. "He's Billy? What does that mean?"

"I'm sorry. I shouldn't be telling tales out of school, but Billy's well, he's maybe a bit…harder than the rest. Nobody messes with Billy, since he has a short fuse. I just found it curious Mr. Rafuse would find a buddy so fast, only to find Billy MacLeod would be that guy. I would have thought they'd get together like cheese and chalk, as in: not at all, but they seemed to be pretty tight, that night." The shopkeeper looked embarrassed. "I shouldn't have said anything. It's not as if he's gone out and killed anyone, for goodness' sake."

"No, of course not." Beth changed the subject. She waved a finger at the people in conversation throughout the room and on the deck. "Are any of these people from the Parker neighborhood in New York?"

Pat surveyed the room, eyes narrowed in thought. "I saw you come in with John and Peggy Whiteway. As you know, since you arrived with them, John used to work in the same company as Nick. That was several years ago, but they of course are still best friends." He pointed to a stern-looking woman of a certain age, wearing an oatmeal-colored cardigan even in the summery warmth of the room.

"And there's Mavis Rockefeller, who's quick to point out she's not from 'those' Rockefellers. I understand she's from Montauk, and they sometimes chat about which galleries to visit and which ones are either too bourgeois or have nothing to offer." He did a double-check of the room, nodding in satisfaction. "Yup. Of the ones here this evening, I'd say they're the ones who know the Parker family the best from outside of the St. Andrews context. Want me to introduce you to Miss Mavis?"

"Yes, that would be nice."

On their way across the room, Beth leaned in to whisper in Donovan's ear. "My money's on Rafuse. He's no more an artist than I am."

"Riley's not looking lily-white here, either. Let's just tease out whatever we can find, and eliminate people as they alibi out."

Mavis Rockefeller introduced herself as the woman who lived two properties down from the Parkers. "In the Sea Breeze home," she added. As soon as names were exchanged, her features softened, and the trace of a smile formed. She was painfully slender, with high cheekbones and shiny black eyes set back, just a bit, exuding intelligence. The woman's hair was beautifully coiffed with soft, sandy-brown waves that floated above her frail shoulders. She leaned on a beautifully crafted cane, and both her hands and the cane were burnished walnut. As Pat turned to leave, Mavis caught his arm. "Can I bother you for a wee dram?"

"Absolutely, Mavis. What'll it be?"

The smile widened. "Single malt scotch?"

"Peaty or no?"

"Not, thank you."

"One Balvenie on stones, coming up." His green eyes twinkled.

Her handshake was of the no-nonsense variety. "I understand you're staying at the Parker residence? I haven't seen you walking the beach."

Beth shook her head. "Actually, we're not. My husband and I are staying at the Rossmount. But we are friends of the Parkers. Their guest house is currently occupied by Mr. Harry Rafuse, so we're at the inn, which is gorgeous. Harry's a painter; have you heard of him?" Her eyes offered nothing but innocence.

Mavis sniffed. "The man claims to be a painter, does he? I've seen no evidence of it, neither here nor back home in New York, and I've known him for years. We're neighbors there, you know." She leaned in, as if to share a confidentiality. "Not that I shout it from the rooftops. He's not much of a…well, he's not much of an anything, really." Her dark eyes glittered, as if defying someone to challenge her statement.

"Might he be new at painting, do you think?"

"To be honest, if he lifted a finger to accomplish anything, that would be new." She chuckled, an act that took years from her perceived age. "He won't even get his house painted. Imagine that! Someone—" she nodded toward Nick, "—gives him enough money to buy a decent home in Montauk, and he doesn't even have the pride of ownership to maintain it. Shameful."

She continued, appearing to latch onto a subject. "I'll tell you what he is, though. Lucky." Her eyes pierced Beth. "You know the kind—lucky at line-up queues, scratch lottery tickets, having distant relatives who are generous. Green lights and such. Here's the thing. That kind of shit runs out, and he'll be caught up, one day." She continued to glare, causing Beth to work hard at stifling a smile at her words.

Mavis paused, a frown gathering up around her thoughts. She took in a deep breath, seeming to consider diving into the bay outside the window. "You two are trouble." A trace of a grin formed, softening her words. "From the moment you walked up to me, I've been spouting ill will toward my fellow man. Now, we must put a stop to all of that." She placed a hand on Donovan's forearm, seeking support. Donovan, however, wasn't certain whether she was leaning on him for balance, or securing some small measure of intimacy. "So tell me, what are you doing in small-town Canada, truly?"

Donovan rushed in before Beth could speak. "We're on our honeymoon. We got married on short notice, and this is a stopping point to meet with friends. We'll stick here for a bit, and then we're off to Nova Scotia to meet Beth's mother." Without changing his tone of voice away from conversational, he changed the subject. "And you? What do you do when you're not summering in St. Andrews?"

Mavis became animated. "I am—I was—the curator for an art gallery in Greenwich Village. Village Art, on Bleecker. I'm retired now, but my former co-owner, Anne Coffey, calls me in as a…as a consultant, I suppose, to curate installations. I still love it. The gallery is sandwiched between a film school and a ballet school, so it's a very vibrant community, with energy and creativity oozing through the walls and from every door and window.

"Did you know, I was once on a team that helped authenticate a Klimpt found beneath a stack of worthless paintings repatriated from the Austrian government? They'd been stolen from Jewish families after 1939, eventually ending up in the hands of the Austrians, years after the war." She paused, a modest look on her face. "It wasn't the famous *Adele Bloch-Bauer I* painting, but still, a thrilling moment in my career."

"So, you're pretty familiar with the New York art scene?" It was Donovan's turn to flash glinting eyes. No one noticed Beth's imperceptible poke in the ribs.

Mavis threw her hands up, shrugging. "Who can truly know the New York art scene? Five minutes after you think you've got it all figured out… pfft, it's all changed. Any scene that can be described using words like Neo, Contemporary, Post-post Metamodern Regionalism, SoFloSuperflat, and the Avant-Garde movement is a scene to keep one on one's toes." She laughed with a dry cackle and shook the stones in the bottom of her scotch glass. The bartender caught the gesture and reached for the scotch bottle.

Donovan casually asked again about Rafuse.

"Trouble." She looked as if she wanted to spit on the floor. "No matter what question people ask me about that man, that's the answer I want to give. Nick wouldn't say it, but Mr. Rafuse and I have had run-ins in the past. He once tried to sell me a stolen piece of art. It was a very obscure piece, so I suspect he thought no one would catch it." She wagged a bony finger. "I certainly haven't trusted him since. And most of his relatives are similarly—" she leaned in, "—honorable, although he might be the worst of a bad lot." It sounded like a curse word, the way she spoke it. Her upper lip curled up in an unattractive manner. "Certainly they have artwork, inherited and not-yet sold off. I'm afraid they appreciate it more for its cash surrender value than anything intrinsic.

"And the pieces keep disappearing from their family collections, year over year. And I don't mean him." She wagged a finger vaguely in the direction of Nick. "Here's an interesting fact. Fifty per cent of inherited money is lost within one generation. And ninety per cent of inherited money is gone in three generations." She sniffed. "Someone isn't bringing their children up right, I think. Again, Nick being the exception, of course." Mavis sent the slightest of glances over to Riley, who was still chatting with the bartender. "That one is bright. She'll do her father proud. Now, please forgive me, but these old legs are getting weary, and I have to tug on someone's sleeve about an errand this weekend. I have a nice bottle of scotch and a scandalous cellar full of red wine, should you decide to visit me. I'll leave you to your, ahem, honeymoon. Can you excuse me?" Without waiting for an answer, the old woman walked, stately, slowly, and with grace to a chair with its back to the setting sun, to await her next audience.

"She is so sweet, even if she is onto us." Beth took Donovan's now free arm. "Do you remember the time in London when we were talking about suspects, and you said you'd stare down your own grandmother until she came up with an alibi? Well, what about our Mavis? Not her, surely!"

"He grinned. "Depends. Have you seen her alibi?"

Beth's smile slipped away. "Moving on to the next subject, what the hell are you thinking, asking about Manhattan art galleries? Is this Arles all over again? Are you looking for a case in the middle of a case? Because, as I once heard a New York City cop say, 'Ain't nobody got time fo' dat.' Let's stick to the matter at hand, okay?"

Donovan waited a moment, ensuring no one was eavesdropping. "Here's what I know. Nothing is linear. This case, like every gig I've ever known, will not go from A to B to C. We thought it was all about Person A murdering Tricia. We come to find out she's American, in town just one day before she gets offed. That's a narrow window of opportunity to piss someone off to the point of murder. We've got to suspect she brought her trouble with her." He raised a hand to quell her protest. "I know. Nick and

Riley are right here. And it might be as simple as Nick still hated her and wanted her dead. But why is Riley lying? Why is Rafuse not telling the truth? Oh." He grinned. "Speaking of our Harry, while you were chatting with D-A, I went to visit his place."

"I thought you'd gone to the bathroom!"

"Umm, no. I wanted to see if he could paint. And. . .no. It was a piece of shit. He's lying about his reason for being here.

"And speaking of lying, people lie to hide things...maybe things relating to Tricia's murder, maybe things completely off-topic. We need to sort through all the bullshit, setting aside all of the mess we accidentally uncover. I wish Montauk, New York was as close as St. Stephen. We could go get some information and be back by suppertime. But that isn't going to happen. We may have to fly down."

Beth frowned. "I promised Mom we'd be there in a week. Two at the most. How are we going to fit everything in? You may recall we didn't even invite her to the wedding. I know why, but still."

"That's right. We didn't invite anyone to the wedding, not even your boss the ambassador and his wife. Look, worst case scenario, you head on to Nova Scotia to see your mom, and I'll scoot south and be back in time to visit with her as well. Could that work?"

Beth's look suggested she was still unhappy. "Let me think about it." She started to say something else, but interrupted herself, pointing to the door. Over Donovan's shoulder, she could see Nick speaking with a pair of RCMP constables. Riley crossed the floor, half-walking, half-loping to be by her father's side.

"Looks like we have a new development. Let's go eavesdr—" but Donovan was already on the move.

* * * *

Nick and Riley rode in the back of the white cruiser sporting the RCMP logo on the doors, with Donovan and Beth following as close behind as they dared. On their way out of town, they passed The Rossmount Inn and then headed across the causeway that separated Chamcook Lake from Passamaquoddy Bay. As they approached Bocabec Cove, the cruiser slowed, pulling into an unmarked road that was little more than a cow path.

Beth pointed to blue and red lights flashing through the dense undergrowth. Twenty yards ahead, the tiny caravan pulled up behind a second, unmanned police cruiser and stopped dead.

Donovan and Beth got out and waited for the officer to open the back doors for the Parkers. The six trooped single file down, down, down a contiguous stairwell of treated lumber until they descended past four landings and ultimately out onto a beach a hundred feet below their vehicles. The cove, little more than an inlet, was walled on three sides by sandstone cliffs. The beach floor was comprised of wet, brown sand from stairs to shoreline. Bits of driftwood defined the east side of the beach at the low tide mark. One officer stood over what appeared to be a pile of clothing as the second officer walked away from his partner to join the newcomers.

"Gentlemen. Ladies. We have a body: male, no deterioration from water, so it doesn't appear to have anything to do with drowning. Based on the tides and the condition of the body, we estimate this event to have taken place within the past few hours. I'm sorry, Mr. Parker, we have reason to believe you know this man. Can you come identify the body? If this is too extreme, we could take the remains to the morgue and make him more presentable. I'm afraid he appears to have been…assaulted."

Nick Parker looked distressed, the lines of worry crossing his forehead. "No, that's fine. I can do this." He took a deep breath, and Donovan felt he was attempting to convince himself. He started toward the shoreline, with Riley following.

Beth called out to Riley. "Want me to come with you, Sweetie?"

"I need to be with Daddy."

Beth and Donovan exchanged glances, waiting with the officers who had escorted them down to the beach. It took but a few seconds before Nick waved them over. "It's Harry, Sean. I've lost another one." While his words sounded desperate, Nick's tone was closer to the melancholy of despair. He clung to Riley, who appeared to want to be anywhere but in front of the mangled, distorted corpse of a relative at her feet.

"Who could have done this? It's barbaric."

Harry Rafuse lay on his back, one sightless eye staring up at the darkening evening sky. The second eye was missing, perhaps having been explored by a seagull or osprey. One arm had been wrenched from its socket and lay at an unnatural angle, contorted away from Rafuse's side. Similarly, the right leg canted straight outward from the body, at the knee. An officer sidled up to Donovan, noting in a low voice that the ribs along one side appeared to have been beaten in as well. "This gentleman was worked over good, probably before he was killed."

Beth glanced at the area immediately around the body. Not seeing anything out of the ordinary, she turned and headed back up the beach. Donovan asked the officer who had whispered to him if any evidence had been found, other than the body.

"We found a shovel, over there." He pointed to a cliff crevice sprouting puny spruce shrubs. "The mouth of the shovel was wet, but the crevice itself is very damp, so we can't infer too much from that. For example, there was barely enough blood on it to cause us to suspect it was the weapon. It could have been washed off in the water. Forensics will tell us more." This time he pointed to the change in tide, carrying the water up the beach.

The lead officer spoke up for everyone's benefit. "If EMT doesn't get here soon, we'll have to pull the remains up beside the stairs. Mr. and Ms. Parker, why don't you head back to town with your company?" He pointed to the Donovans. "We'll have a full report drawn up by ten tomorrow, and I'll be pleased to go over it with you. Thank you for the identification, that part is never easy. Do you have any questions before you leave?" The Parkers shook their heads in unison.

Donovan looked at the isolated cove and then looked back at the officer in charge of the scene. "Who told you the body was here?"

"The Donaldsons, an American couple who live down the shore at Ovenhead, were sailing by when Mr. Rafuse's jacket caught Mrs. Donaldson's eye. They phoned it in from their boat. We'll be speaking with them again tomorrow. I'm asking you to refrain from contacting them, please." It didn't sound like a request, as much as an order.

Donovan and Beth drove Nick and Riley home, with none of them exchanging even a word, other than Donovan asking if they could walk through Rafuse's apartment without touching anything. He mentioned, as they left, the RCMP would cordon off the guest house, possibly as early as this evening. Nick was reluctant to allow it, so Donovan didn't press the issue.

The moment the car turned in the driveway and headed off the Parker estate, Beth exploded. "What the hell? Our very best suspect…murdered. I almost want to say twice as dead as most folks are when they're dead. It's the damndest thing. It's so far away from what I expected, I almost feel betrayed."

"You'll get over it. That's the thing about murder—there's almost always another suspect to come along." He paused, thinking. "The thing for me is, this is getting really dangerous. For a second murder to happen in a quiet little town like this—and keep in mind, we're seeing two Americans arriving here for an insanely brief period of time before they were brutally killed—I have to think the danger quotient has gone up a notch or three. And I think Nick, Riley, you and I shouldn't be strolling down dark alleyways anytime soon.'"

"Us by association with the Bad Luck Parkers, I take it?"

He nodded in the dark. "Look who's been hit. Nick's ex-wife and then the only cousin he has in town. Her popping up out of nowhere was sketchy, after seventeen years. And now that we've just seen Harry, the case is officially nuts."

Beth nodded. "I know, right? Some painter, by the way." she scoffed. "He's been here for more than a week and all you saw was some kiddy drawing on a single canvas board. None of the remainder of the supplies was even opened. I have to ask, why is he here, if not to paint? He could have just asked with no explanation and Nick would let him stay for the summer."

It was Donovan's turn to nod. "I think one of us needs to chat with that bad boy fisherman." Beth got the final nod in as they pulled into the long, ascending driveway of the Rossmount Inn.

Chapter 21

Niagara-On-The-Lake

Ex-Detective Jack Miller's own snoring awakened him in familiar surroundings at five fifty-five in the morning at the Plenitude Wine Estate. Half awake, he noted the view outside his window, sank farther into the decadent comfort of his bed, and rolled over onto his right shoulder. This caused him to roll right back to his original position with a wince. The bullet wound from nine months ago still reminded him, every time he tried to sleep on his right side, that healing takes time. Still, he smiled.

After leaving the RCMP, Jack had wondered what he'd do with himself. The last case he had worked on prior to retirement left him in a Romanian hospital, full of bullet holes. Waking up in a most excellent bed with vineyards outside as far as the eye could see was a vast improvement over the death and danger he'd witnessed throughout his career. And his unofficial assistant on this case, a fetching, intelligent French lass one-third his age and with a nose for wine, was a joy to work with.

Concern for his new acquaintances, Nick and Riley, placed a new crease on his forehead. But they were in good hands. Donovan and Beth were there in St. Andrews, and he was here in Niagara. *It's as simple as that. Bitching and moaning won't reverse it, so I may as well get out of bed and go to work.* He rolled over and placed warm feet on the floor, noting the potential for a sun-shiny day and taking care not to evoke further complaint from his shoulder.

Once dressed, Jack picked up a murder mystery novel he'd started on the plane back to Niagara. He read until seven thirty, and then ambled over to the kitchen for coffee and to see who was about. Claire waved from a table in the corner. She was facing the vines, the heel of one boot up on the edge of her chair and a copy of *La Journal de Montreal* spread out before her. She wore faded jeans and a cream chambray shirt, her everyday uniform. Another daily habit, a *pain au chocolat* croissant sat in front of her, keeping company with an empty coffee cup.

Jack beamed at his favorite person. "Good morning, Missy. Here we go traipsing into another day in Wine World."

She returned his smile. *"Bonjour, toi.* Everything is going good with you?"

He nodded, pulling out a chair. "You bet. With a missed flight and no one to talk to when I got in yesterday, I missed a day's work. But you'll get me caught up, right?"

The youthful lack of concern slid away, replaced by the burden she'd been carrying for almost a week. He noticed her hand trembled, just a little, as she folded the paper and put it aside. He remembered watching her pouring must and reagents from beaker to beaker in the lab. There was nothing resembling a tremor in those tiny, youthful hands at that time. "Missy, you do remember this is not life and death, right? You can't let it consume you. Let me carry the burden, while you continue to make good wine."

"I do confess it's nice to have you back, Jack. I feel like I've stopped sleeping, or maybe that I cannot wake up, as if I'm in a dream. Do you know what I mean? I wonder if I've missed something, or if there was something I was supposed to have locked, or secured or whatever. It's making me crazy. But, you know, Beth and I were talking just before she left. She reminded me you spent a lot of time solving cases like this. She trusts you so much, Jack, so of course I do, too.

"Did she tell you how we met? Donovan did? Yes, they came to my place because they had heard on the news about a cask of wine disappearing from our farmhouse. Beth reminded me about it. About how, by just asking a few questions, he knew—he just knew—the wine hadn't been taken, merely hidden. So we looked around and *la*! it was cached! Hidden inside a hogshead barrel, in with the old farm equipment, in a shed." She paused a minute, recollecting the events of that day a year earlier, and began again.

"Did Beth tell you of a private conversation she and I had in the wine cellar? No? Well, Monsieur Donovan quickly found the wine. But when we were alone in the cellar, Beth asked me a few questions and I found myself telling her who the thief was. I shocked myself with my own words, because I didn't know who it was until that very moment. And I made Mademoiselle Beth vow to keep my words a secret. Until now. I'm going to tell you, because I think we can use it."

Jack was intrigued and forgot the coffee that had arrived while she was speaking. He leaned in, all of his attention on her words.

"It was my cousin, the same age as my father and his very best friend and companion all of his life. I was so shocked, to this day I cannot reveal this betrayal to my father. It would break his heart."

Jack knew where this was going, and his heart beat just a little faster. *An inside job. A trusted employee. A classic betrayal, all wrapped up in a family secret. Shit.* He sat back, rubbing his chin and pushing his hair back with the palms of his hands.

"What? You don't think so?" Claire waited for a verdict.

"*Au contraire*. Of course I'm thinking along those lines. I can't just dismiss other possibilities, but you and I are on the same page. You haven't seen the size of the payroll, but I have, and even if you dismiss the contractors, the shipping drivers, summer staff, all of the contracted-out work, you still have almost sixty people depending on Plenitude. That's sixty alibis, back stories, relationships, real or imagined grievances. Misunderstandings. Ah!" He moaned so loudly, heads five tables away turned from the clerk at the cash.

Claire looked startled, but Jack broke into a grin. "Missy, let's say we're looking for a needle in a haystack. Our chances are bad, right? Especially if there's a clock ticking. What if someone cut the haystack into two halves and said the needle's in the hay on the left? That's still bad, but better, right? Well, you just cut our haystack in two, and I'm very happy. Thank you." He patted the corner of the table in front of her. "Now, let's go take a look around while you tell me what you've been up to, and then I'm going to go to the payroll records and see if any stories emerge from the names and numbers."

By mid-morning and in Beth's absence, Claire had received an update from Jimmy, who'd been compiling a list of visitors to places in the winery they wouldn't normally have frequented. She copied his information to share with Jack later that day. In addition, she'd compiled a list of staff having a reason to visit the lab and compared it to her list of staff actually seen visiting the lab. After double-checking with Dieter and then Jimmy, she located Jack in his tiny office in the lower level just past the boardrooms.

"Jack, I found a couple of names." She held a notebook with numerous inscriptions filling the pages.

"Is one of them Claire?" The older man's eyes twinkled.

"Be serious." She sat down, uninvited, and placed two lists on the desk in front of the head of security. "I made a list of people who I should see in the lab, and a list of people I wouldn't expect to see in the lab. Jimmy did the same thing for some of the areas he's familiar with, like the lower level and the kitchen and the tasting counter. On both of the 'I shouldn't see this name here' lists are a couple of staff members, and I was just wondering if there is a reason they might have needed to be there. It's probably nothing, but both of these girls work in the wine tasting station area. Should I ask them a few questions, or perhaps you could?" Relief flooded her face when Jack pointed to his chest.

"I'll be interested to see who they are, as well. I've been going through payroll and hiring records and very little is waving at me. I am curious, I suppose, as to why Dieter and Anna's son, Kurt, is being paid a wage, since he doesn't work here. In fact, he hasn't for two years, yet he's still receiving a hundred a week. For what?" Noting her look, he continued. "I know, this is the boss's son. But what I don't understand is, why is he being paid by the vineyard? There are accounts payable and maybe that's where this kind of expenditure belongs, if anywhere. I don't begrudge him the money, hell, it's none of my business. And since it's such a small amount, I feel funny even questioning it, so let's forget about Kurt for a while." Claire wasn't sure whether he was trying to convince herself, or him.

"Tell me a little about these two girls." His thick finger jabbed the paper resting between them.

Claire frowned in concentration, her pen doodling circles around the two names. "The first person is Lisa Cotton. Lisa finished school in May and wants to take a year off, so she's applied to work here through the winter. I don't know her family, but the car she drives is terrible. There is always something falling off it, and I can't tell you how many times Jimmy has been asked to help get it started so she can drive home. I don't know if he's getting tired of helping, but of course, you know Jimmy. He wouldn't say a negative thing to anybody about anything." Jack raised an eyebrow at this personal revelation about Jimmy, and he nodded for her to continue.

"The second girl is Jenna Thrush, which doesn't sound like any name I've ever heard in France or here in Canada. Is Thrush a common name?" Jack shrugged, and she continued. "Anyway, I know a little bit more about Jenna than Lisa." She burrowed into her notebook. "She is…twenty one, has taken the bartender's course and has her licence to serve alcohol. She started work here last year, there haven't been any problems that I could find, and…she's friends with Kurt, the owner's son." Claire looked up, as if anticipating praise for her diligence.

"How did you find that out?"

"About her and Kurt? He told me."

"Ah. So, you know him."

"Yes." Her voice was matter-of-fact, and she leaned forward, her body language revealing to Jack that she was being open and engaged. "I met him soon after I arrived. I told Anna I was a bit lonely—this was before you arrived—so she took me to visit Kurt in the rehab center. He was, ah, inside of himself…"

"Introverted?"

"Exactly. But I assumed it was because of his illness and his long… convalescence? Is that the word?"

"Absolutely. And how is his convalescence going?"

"It's been slow, I think. He's able to get out of his bed, and he can walk across the room before having to return to a chair or his bed. He gets very tired. But, he's much better than when I first started visiting him four months ago. He's supposed to come home soon. In two weeks, I think. I don't believe he can resume his studies until January. His body is recovering, but his attitude hasn't fixed, yet."

"What do you mean by that?"

Claire looked embarrassed, perhaps feeling she'd betrayed a confidence. "When we would drive over to see Kurt, Anna would tell me what fun he was to be around. He was very sociable, always seeing the sunny side of the situation... *avec les lunettes roses?*"

"Wearing rose-colored glasses. I know a few folks like that."

"*Oui*. Anyway, that was not the person I met, some months ago. He was very negative, suspicious of people's intents, and he often saw the bad side of things. But, I felt if I was going to be loyal to Anna, who has been so good to me, I would have to oversee..."

"Overlook." Jack offered a gentle smile, his eyes questioning.

"Yes. I have to overlook his attitude and be encouraging."

Jack took a moment. "Do you think Kurt limits his negativity to his illness and his...new physical limitations?"

Claire thought about it for a moment. "No. Not at all. You see, this is the problem. His illness seems to have affected his complete outlook on life. I swear, if you tell him it's Wednesday, he will reply 'Oh, but that is so far away from the weekend.' He is very discouraged. No, not discouraged. More like, negative. Ah!" She brightened, having found a better word, and offered it: "Resentful."

Jack nodded. "I understand that word: 'resentful.' Sometimes it's used to direct resentment toward a circumstance. But sometimes..." Jack paused, debating with himself whether to continue. "Sometimes, this resentment is directed toward someone. I'm also thinking of another word. 'Blame.' Someone once told me resentment is never without a reason, but seldom with a good reason. So. Who does Kurt resent, for his current circumstances? Does he lash out at anyone in particular? His mother?"

Claire looked doubtful. "Certainly not his mother," she said in a clear tone. "He worships her. He may have some resentment for his father. Dieter was obliged to bring him home from the United States as soon as he was able to travel. It was so expensive, every single day in the hospital and then in the clinic. But Kurt, well, he wanted to stay. At first, he blamed his father for losing the winery—these are his words. I'm sure he now understands the change in ownership was beyond his father's control and was actually used to help Kurt in his time of financial need. His feelings for his father are much better now."

"Do his parents or you take him out on jaunts? Day trips?"

"He wasn't strong enough, until now. I think his mother might take him to visit her sister. It's not far from the clinic, and it will be a good first step, according to Anna. Then, he might come to Plenitude next month to complete his recovery before returning to school. At least, that is what I heard."

"He doesn't seem up to lifting a dozen vines, roots and all, does he?" Jack's voice was dry, finality washing through it. Claire nodded in agreement with his sentiment, without actually ascertaining how serious Jack was. "No, not at all. Well, I'll check out those two girls and get us back to square one." Jack broke away from studying his spreadsheet. "Uh, are you eating here tonight, or going off-site?"

"Jimmy asked me to go out with him for dinner. We're going to Johnny Fresco's Restaurant, in Niagara Falls. It's Italian food. Would you like me to bring you some back?"

"No, thank you. I'm eating with Dieter and Anna. I just wanted to make sure you're getting out from time to time. 'Too much work and not enough play makes Claire'...a person who works too hard." Claire had never heard the original expression, so the humor was lost on her. She waved as she left the room, offering a little *'à tantôt'* farewell as she left. Jack put his nose back into the payroll records.

Chapter 22

St. Andrews

"Ronnie! Another tray, buddie." The bartender at the Red Seal laid out another six draft glasses and began pulling beer for the three fishermen sitting in the corner. It was Thursday evening, an hour before last call and the room was all but empty. The men were still dressed in their work clothes: work boots, Spartan Industrial Marine ball caps, worn long-sleeve tee shirts, and bib overalls with tar-stained orange rubber gloves tucked in the back pocket. Two lunch pails sat on the floor beside the pair of workers facing Billy MacLeod.

"Last one, and then I gotta get home. It's gonna be a long day tomorrow, and today was extra long, what with having to swab the boat after coming in." James Orr picked up his lunch pail and set it on the table beside the fresh tray of beer.

"Pussy. Anyone can work a Friday, for God's sake. It's just one day and you can sleep all weekend. You got paid for the extra hours, didn't ya?"

"Maybe you can sleep the weekends away, Billy, but I've got kids keepin' me up all night." James's voice took on a plaintive, whining tone. "One fell out of bed last night and kept me up for two hours."

"What was Amy doing? Her nails?" Billy smiled a wolfish leer, thinking about her breasts and hips, thinking about a time in the past when he and Amy knew each other better. "That's all right, my boy Devin and I can handle it from here." He picked up the pair of draft sitting in front of James and placed one in front of Devin, drinking the other in three gulps before setting it down on the table.

James stared at the empty glass. "Sometimes you're an asshole, MacLeod. I just said I hafta get home soon. We'll all be thrown outta here soon, either way."

The boat captain laughed. "I *am* an asshole, aren't I? Let me get you another. Ronnie!" The bartender who had been pretending not to listen poured a single glass and carried it over to James, who was mollified somewhat.

Devin changed the subject. "What do we have coming up for work? Any tourism shit?" Devin was a worker and, unlike James, he was always on the hunt for more hours.

Billy leaned his chair back on its rear legs. "Maybe yes, and maybe no. I've got a little job coming up, but I think I can do it alone. I'm waiting on word back from the artists group. They want a weekend day when the water's dead calm, so they can go out and paint the whales breaching. Now, I have a personal opinion the whales don't like breaching when the water's dead calm, but saying something interferes with a possible payday. So, if the water's calm on Sunday, I'll go out with one of you." His eyes glinted, and a cold grin formed. "How about you, James? You want to come with me?" He knew James loathed working on the weekends, as much as he knew Devin was desperate for more hours. *Gotta keep everyone on edge. Can't let them get too complacent, can I?*

Devin, who'd known him longer, took a sip of beer, waiting. James shook his head slowly, trying to frame a response. "Carly's gettin' baptised on Sunday. I-I can't get away this weekend."

Billy opened his arms in an expansive gesture. "Good one, Jimmy-James. I knew you'd find a way to skive your way out of working. And Devin here would sell his mother for an hour's pay, so I guess I'm stuck with one bastard over the other bastard." His harsh laugh reached every corner of the empty pub, as the bartender reached under the bar for an imaginary utensil, in order to avoid eye contact.

"Prick." Billy missed James' slur, as he watched Devin finish his last beer and stand up.

"I'll do out these jobs with you, Billy, but I'm moving on after that. I'll be on another boat come next season." He put the glass down and reached below the table for his lunch pail. Out of eyesight of Billy, James' eye shone with admiration.

MacLeod laughed again. "Come on, Dev. Can't you take a joke? Stick with me, it'll be fun."

Devin headed for the door. "After this season, Billy, all I want to see from you are taillights going down the driveway." He strode through the door and onto Water Street, with MacLeod still laughing in the almost-empty room. A minute later, James followed.

It was after midnight when Billy left, alone. He heard but ignored the pub door lock behind him and stared first left and then right at the empty street. His was the only vehicle from one end to the other, and he thought for a moment there was no one about, either. But he saw movement from a dim-lit park bench in front of the Candy Emporium. Without a word, the apparition stood, motioning him closer and then returned to the invisibility of the darkened bench.

Billy recognized the cane hooked over the seat back, recalling a conversation he'd had with the recently departed Harry Rafuse. A Frenchman with a cane had tried to approach MacLeod a few days back, but they'd missed each other. Rafuse knew him, though. He sauntered over, a bemused smile on his face. He approached the bench, pausing to study the darkened windows of the apartments above the shops and across the street from the bench. MacLeod sat down beside the stranger, staring straight across the darkened street but not mincing words. "I don't know you from shit."

In response, the man lit a cigarette, the flame from the lighter revealing the man's face. "No, you don't. But you can call me money, because that is what I will soon mean to you. When you think of me, you're going to think of better times."

MacLeod leaned forward, placing his elbows on his knees. "I do like money. What makes you think I need better times?"

"Don't be an asshole. More money means better times, and anyone, including you, can benefit from more money."

"Get to the point. What do you want, and how much is it going to cost me?"

This comment elicited a low chuckle. "Oh, no, my friend. I'm here to give you money, a lot of money. Have you ever heard of an American named Rafuse?"

Silence.

"Harry Rafuse passed away recently. It was from an unfortunate accident, so I heard. That's not important. What is important, the important part, is this man had unfinished business here. With me."

"You don't say."

"I do say. That business will be taken up by someone, and soon. People like you and I can stand by and watch someone else make a pretty penny, or we can roll up our sleeves and take it for ourselves." The man turned his head to stare at MacLeod, who didn't move.

"What do I have to do? And am I a hired man, or a partner?"

"What do you want to be?"

"What'll make me more money?" The fisherman finally looked up to face the stranger. "What's your name, anyway?"

"Palu. I'm an art collector. What's more important to you is I also move art into the hands of other collectors. I happen to know the approximate location of a modest collection. It's nearby—"

MacLeod interrupted him, deciding to take a chance by revealing more information than he typically would. "It's in Eastport. With Rafuse gone off to hell, I was going to go grab it myself, but I hadn't worked out the details around what to do with it afterward."

He heard another soft chuckle in the darkness. "Do you not see an opportunity unfolding? You know where it is and have the resources to go get it. And I have the resources to broker it for top dollar, once we have it on Canadian soil. Now do you see where I am going with this little chat?"

The fisherman smiled. "I believe I do. This is shaping up to be a fine partnership. It'll be a fifty-fifty thing, right?"

"Of course." Palu's voice was oily smooth, his tone unreadable. "When can you go over to Maine to pick up the goods?"

There was a lengthy pause. "That's going to require a bit of figuring. I ain't going across in moonlight, and I want the tides working with me. I also want the fishing season working in my favour. Do I want to be out there on crowded water, or empty seas? Do I want to scoot over just before dawn, or is two in the morning better? And then there's the fog. I have lots to think about, and I'm the guy that figures through all the details before I jump." He made it sound almost accusatory. "If something goes wrong, it won't be because of me, know what I'm sayin'?"

"I do. Let me know what you decide. With these sorts of things, it's better if we keep each other up to date on everything. *Everything*, got it?"

"Fuck off. I'll do my part, which requires you trusting me. Then, you'll do your part, which requires you staying the fuck away from me. You don't need to be in my shirt pocket, watching. Just keep your pants on, give me your cell number and I'll call you when you're needed."

"You're a tough guy. I like that." Palu handed the man a business card, and there was wary admiration in his voice. "It is clear you could beat the shit out of me, if I screwed you over." He paused, watching tendrils of mist inching up the street. "As for me, I'm more of a 'knife you in your bed and you wake up dead' kind of guy. We'd make a good pair, don't worry about it."

MacLeod studied the man beside him, reading nothing. He pretended to yawn. "Well, that's a great bedtime story, and I gotta go to work in four hours, so I'll be off. Smell ya later, man." He rose from the bench and headed for his truck. A minute later, Palu limped up the street in the opposite direction.

From a darkened alley, twenty feet away, a man pulled his face away from the rough brick outer wall. He uttered a single word as he drifted down the alley toward his pickup.

"Prick."

Chapter 23

St. Andrews

RILEY PARKER WAS IN A mood, and it wasn't a pretty one. Storm clouds had gathered above her, and she paced across the bedroom, her steps audible. *How is it even possible my father is a suspect in my mother's murder? Is this even slightly possible? And if it wasn't him, then who? Harry was a possibility, even if he said he only arrived a day late. But with him dead...* A mild curse escaped. She paused in front of the window, staring hard at Minister's Island and, between the beach and the land mass, the underwater road.

She couldn't pass that window anymore without her eyes being drawn to the spot at which Tricia had been found. Intellectually, she could still see the beauty of the beach, the water and the sky, but on some level, it was now tainted. She cursed again, grabbed a faded denim jacket and a compact umbrella and headed out of the house, calling to cook to not make supper for her.

Riley's first stop was the pharmacy to pick up some lip gloss. She purchased two, the second one for Thalie, a part-time bartender and very good friend. A quick message was returned immediately; Thalie could be found behind a fat-bowled cup of fair trade coffee at the Down Easter café. Riley crossed the street to the café and, ignoring the chair opposite her, slipped into the banquette seat to link arms with her friend.

Thalie patted Riley's arm. "I'm really sorry about your mom. How are you doing?"

"I'm feeling a bit better. It's not like she was in my life anymore, but, still, she was my mother." This got her another sympathetic squeeze. "How's the course going?" Thalie was taking a combination Reiki-and-

Massotherapy course in nearby Saint John on Tuesdays and Thursdays and tending bar as many evenings as she could.

"Getting by. On the mornings after a late night, it's a bit tough waking up, but a girl's gotta do what a girl's gotta do. I'm a little worried about my car. It's been acting up, but it only has to last one more week, four days, really. I got a line on another one. Darren from the big hotel is getting a new one next month, so he promised to let me buy his old one. That'll fix me up." Thalie moved just a bit to make room for coffee sips and elbows.

Riley frowned. "That's two weeks of maybe breaking down on the highway. Why don't we trade cars until then? You can drive mine over to Saint John, and I can scoot around town in yours. And if yours is really fried, I can always use the grounds truck. It sits around most of the day." Her frown softened as Thalie considered this request.

"It would take me a bit to pay you back, Ri." This earned her a punch in the arm.

"It's just a car. Here. You can drive me home and keep it. Drop it off when you're done, the tank's full." She dropped the keys to the Beamer on the counter.

Thalie finished a last sip of coffee and Riley finished off her friend's ginger-molasses cookie. After a moment of pondering the pattern on the table, Thalie asked if any progress had been made in finding the persons who had killed Tricia or Harry.

"No. And there are no clues." She turned to face her friend. "You know this town. Everybody knows everything. I swear, if I lip-synched a hymn in church, Nick would hear about it at supper. So why is this so difficult to figure out? All we know for sure is both of the victims are Americans who had just got into town. Oh! Here comes Beth. Don't make eye contact! I don't want to talk with her. She's some kind of detective or something."

A second later, they heard a tap on the café window and Beth motioned permission to come in. She ordered three coffees and a single, gigantic molasses ginger cookie for the table and sat across from Thalie. "I saw you at the arts get-together last Friday. You were working."

The young lady nodded. "That's right. I'm a student in Saint John, and bar gigs pay the bills. Are you from New York? Ri says you're a detective." Thalie smiled, her face awash in curiosity, while Riley squirmed.

Beth chose a mug. "Actually, I'm not. I'm a director of Communications at the Canadian embassy in London, England. I'm in town to help a friend and, by extension, Riley and Nick. But yes, I'm trying to get to the bottom of the two murders."

"How's that working for you?" Sarcasm dripped from Riley's voice, but Beth seemed unperturbed.

"It works like this: I hear something, I learn something else, somebody shares something, and at a certain point, a picture forms. I believe a picture is forming now."

"Are you picturing more murders, because the population of New Yorkers in this town is going down fast."

Beth offered a sympathetic smile. "I know how hard this must be for you, Riley. But information is being gathered by police, by Sean and myself. And also by you, I'm sure. Patterns are forming, and here's the thing: this is a small place. A *very* small place. People see things, they hear things and eventually, we'll sew the pattern together. Until then, Riley, you have family watching over you."

"It didn't help my mother much, did it?"

"To be honest, your mother wasn't really a part of the family at the time of her death. And no one was watching over her. I mean, in the way that your father and his friends are watching over you."

Thalie's eyes widened at this, but Riley pursed her lips before speaking. "It didn't help Harry."

Beth furrowed her brows. "We have reason to believe Harry might not have been as…forthcoming with information—truth, really—as we originally thought. For example, he's not a painter at all."

Riley's eyes narrowed. "But the supplies Dad bought him. I knew they weren't for painting. What was that all about?"

"Mr. Rafuse—Harry—was obviously up to something. We haven't put everything together, but it's clear he was duping everyone about his reasons for being here. I think Nick might have some answers, but where they'll lead…" She left the thought to dangle and swirl around them.

"I suppose you think Father is behind all this, like some sort of New York Mafioso type." Riley studied the coffee mug, her normally full lips a thin line.

Beth leaned across the table, placing both hands on the young lady's forearm. "Oh no, Sweetie. I think he's a kind, generous man who's been taken advantage of. I'd bet anything he has nothing to do with this mess. But that doesn't mean he doesn't unwittingly carry information in his memory that might prove useful, do you know what I mean?"

Riley nodded, as Thalie hung on every word. "All day, every day I think back to each of the events. And I wonder what I'm not seeing. Yesterday, I tried to think of what the two…deaths had in common. It was quite a bit, actually." She counted off a litany of commonalities. "Tricia and Harry were Americans. They were new to St. Andrews. They both carried secrets. They were both, um, sketchy. I may as well say it as think it." Riley looked self-conscious at her own familial betrayal.

Thalie interrupted the shopping list of commonalities. "And they both died on or in the water." She broke off a piece of the communal cookie and nibbled.

The table went silent. Both women stopped to stare at Thalie, who was focused on the cookie, oblivious to the significance of what she'd said.

"Shit." Beth sat back in her chair, absorbing the statement. After a minute, she repeated the word. "If that doesn't belong on the 'not-a-coincidence' list, I don't know what does. Whether it means they were killed the same way or not, it suggests some sort of M.O." She sat back. "Which reminds me, Riley, this is still a multiple murder investigation, so you should have someone accompany you wherever you go. Would you consider doing that?"

Riley tried to put on a brave face, but she was clearly shaken. "Is that really necessary? This is a small town. As long as I don't wander home at two—"

"Let's ask Harry what he thinks." Beth caught herself, remorseful. "Oh, Riley, I'm sorry I was being flippant about this. Sarcasm is the last thing you need. Frankly, hiding under your bed at a time like this would not be over-reacting, Sweetie. Seriously, you have to lay low.

"Sean and I will be nearby, as well as John and Peggy. If you need company and Thalie and your other friends aren't available, give us a call. I know we're lame, but at least you'll live to tell folks how lame we are. Okay?"

Riley nodded, not daring to speak.

"I have to get hold of your dad. Where can I find him at this time of day?"

Without saying a word, the young lady pulled out her cell phone, pulled up his number and pointed it toward Beth, who in turn keyed it into her own phone. A moment later Beth was out on the sidewalk, messaging Donovan. She then called the newest number in her directory. Nick answered on one ring and suggested they meet at the Colonial Inn verandah for a drink. Beth agreed and in five minutes was seated down the street in the shade of the inn, a glass of Shiraz in her hand.

* * * *

Donovan stepped up the broad wooden steps of the Colonial Inn, spied Beth and sat down behind a Picaroons Dooryard ale. "Thanks, Hon." He tapped the glass with a fingertip.

They got caught up, with Beth offering her most recent revelation, while Donovan told her he'd just bought a single airline ticket to New York. There was barely enough time for her to close her mouth and glare before Nick strode up.

"Has there been a break?"

"No." Donovan shook his head as Nick's drink arrived. "Beth came up with something that needs to be explored. She had a little help from Riley, so, thanks to her. But I keep thinking Rafuse and your ex-wife brought their troubles with them. I need to know the story of the Parkers, including Tricia's role. And the Rafuse clan as well, for that matter. We're being intrusive, I know. I don't care. If you want to get to the bottom of all this crap, you need to tell us the good, the bad and the really ugly about your family."

"And you're convinced these murders both started back home?" Nick didn't sound convinced.

"I am." Donovan tried another tack. "Let me remind you about the details surrounding the two victims. They're American, and they had no ties to St. Andrews, or Canada for that matter, outside of you and Riley. They weren't here long enough to establish a relationship with anyone, yet they died soon after their arrival. It sounds to me like they brought the elements of their demise with them. Do you think I'm wrong?"

Nick shook his head, and Donovan continued. "Tell me your story." He sat back, waiting.

"All right. I am what you'd call an industrialist, like my father before me. We specialize in architecture and design, and there's a construction arm to the company as well. My father and uncle set up the business and the operation took hold. When other cousins came along, they were encouraged to go into the business as well. There ended up being five, including me who learned the ropes and three who chose other paths.

"Only one chose not to get into the business. He became a doctor, found his God and went to Africa to practice medicine for a missionary organisation. Mark got into a disagreement with the local shaman and was beheaded one night. The rest of the cousins went into the business, with myself arriving last and late to the party. Jeb and Jeff found their niche early, but I soon acquired the sense I needed more education.

"Of the cousins who went into our parents' business, I was the only one who chose business school after university. Later, when I joined the company, I arrived without an actual position to fill, so I went to work as an architect, essentially for Jeb and Jeff. It was at that time that I met John Whiteway, a fellow architect and good man. We've been best friends since. As for my four cousins, they settled in with varying degrees of satisfaction, I suppose. Erin, quite a bit older than the rest of us, married a nasty man named Ike Tannen and rose to become manager of finance and marketing. When asked if she wanted to be a director, she refused, putting her family first. She's still married to him, but hasn't seen him in years, ever since she had him legally and financially cut off. Pete worked for a while, got interested in boat making, and retired early to design small boat craft. That caused a divorce and he's never been happier since he shed himself of the wife and the family business.

"That leaves two cousins: Jeb and Jeff Parker. The brothers were running the factory when I finished school and I began to—I guess you'd say, show a talent for turning things around. In time, my father and uncle accepted my ideas to modernize the operation, change the pay scale and working conditions to make the workers more satisfied. Most significantly, my ideas led to increased profits.

"You'd think that was a good thing, but the more I did, the less happy Jeb and Jeff were. They plotted to get rid of me and it came down to whom the board wanted. My father and uncle supported me with the board, and Jeb and Jeff were paid handsomely to leave. Jeb hasn't spoken to me since, and none of his children have reached out to Riley or me, either. My uncle passed away shortly after that, from a heart attack. Stress, they say. And my father died five years later, of the same thing. That was quite some time ago.

"A few years ago, Jeff made an attempt at mending fences, spurred on, I think, by Riley, and by Jeff's daughter, Kate. It was awkward at first, and we never quite got on an even keel. Kate and Riley go out on the town when Ri is in New York, but Jeff has been...cool. I get a smile and a firm collegial handshake when we meet at social events, and there never seems to be a follow-up to our chance meetings."

Donovan assessed Nick while he sipped his drink. "Jealousy, pettiness, envy?"

Nick shrugged. "I suppose so. You can tick all those boxes."

"So, you are left having family connections only with your cousin Erin, boatmaker Pete, and Jeff's daughter, Kate. That's it?"

"That's it. I guess you could say we're a messed-up family, including me. The Tricia marriage wasn't my finest hour, and Riley didn't have much of a family connection when she was younger. I kept close with Erin over the years. Her husband Ike—a terrible man, as I said—took Erin to the cleaners and disappeared one night. I don't know if he's still alive. She was left with a massive debt, with a huge mortgage on the house, and bills from here to the street. We used the company to straighten the mess, erase the debt load. I redecorated her home with new furniture and appliances. In fact, I dropped off some of my own artwork, and whenever I see something I think she may be interested in, I'll buy it and place it with her, on an extended loan. She protests, but it's an indulgence for me, you know? I get to buy items that make me happy, and she gets to enjoy it. I fully expect Erin to get back on her feet one day, and she'll be fine."

"Is your artwork still with Erin?" In instances like that, Beth would offer up a glare or a kick under the table to keep Donovan on track and focused, but in this instance, she merely appeared interested in Nick's response.

"I suppose so. I consider the pieces to be more like loans I won't ask for, except for maybe one or two of the nicest ones. She was traumatized when her husband stole everything. It's taken her years to get to the point where she doesn't feel the need to pinch pennies."

"How does Harry Rafuse fit in to the picture?"

"Ah. Poor Harry. He's more of a distant cousin. He was always around Erin's home after Ike left, fixing things, helping her to choose various art pieces before she lost everything. Honestly, I could never tell if he was leeching off my cousin, or if he genuinely tried to help out, you know, to make up for his, ah, uneven behavior."

"Did you know he wasn't an artist?"

Nick sighed. "I suspected as much. In all the time I've known him, I didn't see any evidence of his artistic side. Other than choosing art. The man knew a bit about valuable pieces."

"Oh?"

Nick nodded, taking a sip. "Yeah, this is where the 'uneven behavior' part comes in. At times he'd be helpful to Erin, and at other times, he'd be just barely skirting the law. I could never figure out if he was a good guy, trying to be bad, or a bad guy, trying to be good. Somehow he learned his way around art and collectibles. The funny thing is, Harry wasn't educated by any stretch of the imagination, yet he taught himself how to recognize which art pieces were valuable. What a bone-lazy man! He could have made a career for himself, if there'd only been an effort. It was kind of a waste, if you think about it."

Beth leaned in to join the conversation. "Sean will be going down to New York shortly, and I'll be staying here. We've decided to take two different approaches to this case, so while I'll be looking at the actual murders from this end, Sean will be trying to figure out what caused the trouble to be shipped north. He wouldn't ask for it—" Donovan's eyes narrowed at that "— but perhaps a phone call to Erin might be helpful, just to smooth the way?"

"Of course. She phones me regularly, so I'll mention Sean's visit when she calls me this evening. When do you get there?"

"Tomorrow. Beth is driving me up to Fredericton in the morning. Nick, I have to mention one other thing. Two people have been murdered in town, and they both connect to you. If I were you, I'd consider not going anywhere alone. Same for your daughter. This sounds obvious, but I'd feel bad if I didn't say it and…"

"I understand. Should I hire someone to watch over Riley?"

"Beth will be here."

Beth spoke up. "My impression is your daughter thinks I am an intruding outsider. I'm working on gaining her trust, but there's something bothering her. I think she knows something that she feels it isn't time to share. I'm okay with it, because when the time comes, she'll know what to do. If that time comes and she opens up to you, I hope you won't dismiss whatever she tells you. It may be nothing, or it may be the most important thing, and we won't know until we hear it." She paused to let an older couple ease past their table. "In the meantime, I'll keep an eye on her."

Nick stared into his coffee, his lips pursed. "Could we be exaggerating, here? What I mean is, if Harry and Tricia brought trouble up from New York, isn't it possible the trouble is finished? You know…Riley and I are nice people, believe it or not, and we might not be mixed up in this at all. What if whoever caused this mess is finished and long gone back to New York, or wherever? Why can't that be the case?"

"It's possible." Donovan's words belied his tone. "But is that a gamble you want to bet your daughter on?"

"No. Of course not."

"Then, we're on the same page. Please keep Beth informed on anything you think she needs to know."

Beth nodded. "I'll do the same for you, Nick."

Nick left a few moments later, leaving the newly married couple to sit for a minute. Beth broke the silence. "So, you're going to leave me in a lawless town with mass murderers on every corner."

"You bet. They'd better watch out—you're a terrible bunch."

"Sean, do you know anything about teens and young adults?"

He shook his head. "Not a damn thing."

"Whenever anyone offers them a suggestion, they want to do the opposite. They can't help it, it's imprinted in their DNA. I'm going to have my hands full, keeping an eye on that girl. She's willful and intelligent, which is a bad combination. Worse, she's hiding something. For that matter, Nick's also hiding something. I don't know if it's a worry they don't want to share, or something more tangible, but they both know something I wish I knew. And I don't even know if this thing they've got hidden from us is the same thing with each other, but I'm going to make it my business to suss it out. When are you back, by the way?"

Donovan shrugged. "Who knows? I could say two days to a week, but I'd be guessing."

Beth smiled. "I vote for you staying away a maximum of two days. In the meantime, let's go out with a bang. How about a walk out to the end of the wharf, dinner at the Rossmount and get to bed at a reasonable hour? Is that wild enough for you?"

"Sounds exactly wild enough. Except, I have to go to St. Stephen to visit Customs. I want to know a bit about tracking Americans in Canada. I might get somewhere or not, but I have to at least ask. Want to come with me?"

She declined with a quick shake of her head. "If I'm going to take this Riley thing seriously, I think I have to track her down and see if we can become more trusting."

"Didn't you already try that?"

"Not alone. There was always someone around. I want to corner her and provoke a decision. It could backfire…"

He completed the thought. "But you have to try." She nodded, slipping some money just under her glass. He walked her to the car, and she drove him to a car rental agency.

* * * *

Sean Donovan exited the Canadian Customs office on Milltown Boulevard in St. Stephen. *That was a huge bust.* Officials were completely uncooperative, refusing to answer even the simplest of requests for information. Citing national security, the Canada Border Security officer wouldn't discuss how the Canadian and American databases were synched up. They wouldn't speak about how specific Americans could be tracked after entering Canada and certainly had nothing to say about whether the RCMP had approached them regarding the murder cases in St. Andrews. Disconsolate, Donovan left the Canadian Customs building. His objective was to head down Milltown Blvd. to the RCMP detachment, but he spied a coffee shop on his right.

World's Best Coffee was a long, narrow shop on the river side. A pretty young woman with bright red lips, ebony bangs that grazed the tops of over-sized glasses, and a preoccupied look on her face stood near the cash register at the front. Beside her, an array of air pots of varying coffee strengths stood guard, followed by a narrow corridor lined with tables for two. The end of the corridor opened up to a warm, rectangular room with a bank of windows facing the St. Croix River on one side and a fireplace with leather club chairs on the other. Books lined the shelves of the room as well as the corridor. Donovan purchased coffee to go, but wandered down the hallway to peek at the room with the LIBRARY sign above the door.

He was almost through the door when he spied a familiar face whose nose was in a book. Backing out in one smooth motion, Donovan hurried back out onto the sidewalk and over to his car. He sat behind the wheel, eyes on the entrance to the coffee shop, his breathing elevated.

Yves Palu.

Donovan thought of Bogart's line about all the gin joints in the world and wondered what sort of odds it would take to come across that bastard in this small town. Was it a coincidence? Shaking his head, he remained unconvinced. His next thought was equally simple. *What do I do about him? Ignore him, kill him, or something in between?* After a moment, it became clear. Donovan had to find out what Palu was doing here. He scrunched down into the car seat, and waited.

Twenty minutes passed with no sign of his prey. I need to know, and I'm out of the country as of tomorrow. Exiting the car, he entered the café and strode to the rear of the coffee shop. No Palu. The washroom was unoccupied and there were no stairs that would lead to a second floor. Disappointed, he returned to the front, and caught the attention of the young lady with the red lips.

"Excuse me. I noticed an acquaintance sitting in the back of the shop, by the fireplace, reading a book. I was wondering where he went."

The young lady's forehead furrowed. "Which one? I see a lot of people coming and going in the run of a day. Can you describe him?" She continued to rinse out one of the insulated air pots, in preparation for the next batch of fresh coffee.

"Of course. He's around thirty, long black hair and wire-rimmed glasses. Good looking. And he's French."

Her face brightened. "Ah. The Frenchman. Is he from Quebec or France, by the way? I can't tell. He's got a great accent, though."

Donovan forced a smile. "So, you've seen him before?"

"Absolutely. He comes in here every day, not always at the same time. He's been a customer for just over a week, but he's already a regular. He grabs a coffee, heads to the back, and sticks his nose either in his smart phone or a book. The regulars have taken to asking him to join them, he's here so often. But he always refuses, in a charming way." She tossed dark, wavy hair back over one shoulder. "Actually, you just missed him."

"I didn't see him come out." He studied her face, waiting for a response.

"Yeah. He always enters through the front entrance, and leaves through the back. I know; bad luck to leave by a different door than the way you came in, right? Anyway, when he arrives, he comes along Milltown Boulevard, but when he leaves, he walks along the river path after he leaves here. Um, may I ask you a personal question?"

"Yes. Not sure if I'll answer it, but go ahead."

"He has a terrible limp and uses a cane. Did he get hurt in an accident?"

Donovan recalled the punishment Palu endured for having threatened him and his sister, Madeleine. The notion of justice meted out by one bad person toward another bad person made him smile. "Oh, that. Sometimes young people make bad decisions and karma helps them to understand their folly. He hurt himself doing something rash."

Puzzled, she nevertheless nodded in understanding. "Uh, okay. So, would you like me to tell him you dropped by? He should be back again tomorrow."

Donovan offered her a smile, it may have been sincere. "Please, I wish you wouldn't. I'd love to surprise him. We didn't expect to run into each other so soon."

"That sounds fine. You haven't touched your takeout coffee. Would you like a fresh cup? I've just put a new pot on." Her look suggested she'd be interested in learning a bit more about him.

He demurred. "No, thank you. I'm just about to go to dinner. But it does smell fantastic. I'll come back and try it again soon." The young lady replied that coming back soon was an excellent idea. He left, started the car, and headed for the highway back to St. Andrews.

Chapter 24

New Jersey to New York

DONOVAN RENTED A NONDESCRIPT GRAY compact at the airport and headed directly out of New Jersey, toward Montauk. The late-morning drive down the shore, with the morning sunlight and salt-tinged air was good for his soul, and he felt at home with his thoughts. After listening to Ron Sexsmith and Royal Wood tunes, he turned off the music, opening the windows wider to feel the breeze swirling around him. It calmed his body, but his mind kept churning. What the hell was Palu doing in a small New Brunswick border town? Was Beth going to be all right, given she was sharing the streets of a small town with a murderer? And then there was the matter of Riley, the willful young lady. Which side of the law was she on? Or her father, for that matter? His sigh flew out the open window, fluttering along behind him, as he headed for the Montauk Highway.

While his inclination was to avoid the beach crowds, Donovan made it a habit to know his neighborhood: the real estate, the residents, the feel of the place. He continued until he arrived a few blocks away from the Montauk Point Lighthouse, which signaled the end of the road, and then turned to double back.

He chose a clam shack a few blocks away from the beach, and sat in the car eating breaded seafood and enjoying the sun through the moonroof. Tourism operators, wealthy estates, and the smell of money dominated the landscape. Food in his belly, Donovan programmed his GPS and headed back toward a row of estates lining Montauk Downs. He'd phoned Erin Parker after leaving the airport, thus wasn't surprised when the gate swung open. He entered the property and parked in the circular driveway.

Erin Parker lived alone in an angular estate house evocative of some sort of tiny palace. There were gables, a widow's walk, sheets of clerestory windows lining the fourth floor, and a grand entrance under a balcony large enough to shelter a football team. She must have been waiting for him because the door opened immediately. A quick glance as he entered suggested the estate could have benefitted from a sprucing up.

They made their way to the library—sparsely furnished, yielding only the occasional tchotchke. They seemed strewn, as opposed to having been placed across the shelves, which were bereft of any books, or seemingly anything of real value. She noticed her guest studying the room. "I could never sit down with a book. At first I thought they ate up all my 'good living' time, but later in life, I realized I just don't have much in the way of powers of concentration. Which is ridiculous, since I was always good with company books, numbers-based reports, that sort of thing." She combed tight gray curls with the fingers of her left hand. Each lock returned to the exact place they'd been parked before her gesture.

Donovan turned his attention to the hostess. She had cool blue eyes, the family chin she shared with Nick and Riley. All of her other facial features appeared to have been honed with a chisel. Tall and extremely thin, she walked with an awkward gait, and even in repose, looked as if she'd tip over and fall from whichever piece of furniture she perched upon. But there was a smartness to those cool blue eyes, and she seemed loathe to reveal any important words, thoughts, or intentions. Nevertheless, Donovan felt, if he had time, he could tease perhaps a few opinions from this austere, serious woman.

"You haven't always lived here, I take it?"

"No. First there was the family home in White Plains, New York. Then the family moved to Manhattan, I went away to school, came back and bought a home—an apartment, really—on Bleeker in the Village, followed by a larger apartment in SoHo. But I've lived here for years. Tea?"

"No, thanks. Was it the beach that persuaded you to move out of the city?"

This elicited a dry laugh. "My ex-husband wanted a place by the beach, so he dragged me kicking and screaming out of Manhattan. And now he's gone, but the beach remains." She opened her arms, as if to invite the universe to laugh along. "The first few years, you go to the beach every day. You cannot get enough of it. After a bit, you find yourself visiting the beach for events, like fireworks, or some family get-together. Finally, you end up getting dragged there only after being bullied by distant relatives who've come to see you from non-beach places." She wagged a finger from side to side. "Ostensibly to see you, but really, it's clear you're playing the part of the innkeeper. Now, I have a question for you."

"Fire away."

She leaned forward, and again, Donovan had the eerie sense she was about to tip over onto the lush carpet. "Harry Rafuse. How did he die, and who did it?" The look she gave was curious, as if she wanted to know but…didn't.

He took a moment to reply. Of course she would ask this, whether she knew the answer or not. And of course she'd be more curious about her cousin Harry than Nick's ex-wife, who'd long-since been booted from the Parker universe. But wouldn't it have been the better question to ask why two associated individuals from here would have been attacked and killed so far away and within a fortnight of each other? Curious.

"Harry was murdered. On the beach. It was a particularly violent crime, almost as if there was some, ah, emotion invested in it. There are no persons of interest actively being pursued at this minute. But it's a small town. Like the song says: voices carry."

Erin sat back on the chair. "Oh." After a pause of some length, she added "I see."

"Do you have any thoughts on the matter? Was Harry, or even Tricia, for that matter, involved in anything suspicious around here, just before they visited St. Andrews?"

"I believe you know we haven't had any discourse with Tricia—" she sniffed, "—so it was a complete surprise to everyone when she showed up in St. Andrews, unexpected and uninvited. Harry, on the other hand, had mentioned to the family he was going to Canada to visit with Nick for a bit. We all loved Harry. He was a scoundrel, but he always found a way to endear himself to each of us. He didn't have an unkind bone in his body. This is such a shame." She tsked. "In recent years, he'd fallen on hard times and even though he had his own home, he used to visit me, sometimes for a week at a time. He'd putter about, re-painting this and repairing that. He made himself so useful. So it was easy to forgive any little…slips he might make, from time to time."

"Slips?"

Erin squirmed, just a bit. "He was investigated, on a couple of occasions, for something to do with art. Totally fabricated, I am sure of it. No charges were laid, and I believe it to be a conspiracy of some sort." She shook her head. "Or a personal vendetta, at the very least."

"What did Harry do for a living?"

She waved an arm, almost as if to mitigate anything she was about to reveal. "Oh, a little of this, a little of that. He didn't have much in the way of a job or a steady source of income, but he always managed to get by. I don't recall him actually having anything as formal as a job *per-se*, but he was always busy. After my husband took advantage of my hard-earned finances and left me bereft, Harry was always there to take care of things. He was a real comfort, I must say."

"I'm sorry to interrupt, Ms. Parker, but I was under the impression it was Nick who got you back on your feet, financially speaking. I don't mean to pry, but as you know, when investigating a murder, you have to, well, ask personal questions."

"I understand." The look on Erin's face suggested she didn't quite understand. "Well, certainly, Nick was helpful, in his way. But it was Harry who arrived every day and rolled up his sleeves, so to speak." Her face remained void of emotion, but Donovan thought he detected a challenge behind those cool blue eyes. She opened her mouth to speak, but a telephone rang some distance away. "Would you please excuse me? I have no help on weekdays." Donovan rose, nodding as she took her leave.

It might be time to look around. He went to the hall, noting the direction of Erin's voice at the back of the house and headed in the opposite direction. Donovan slipped up the stairs, glancing to the right and left as he stepped onto the open corridor that flanked the balcony. The rugs were worn, but had been handsome in their day. There were several doors off the balcony, and he dared to peek into two of them before hurrying back downstairs with a pocketful of first impressions.

Erin returned to see Donovan standing by the library window, looking out at the unsightly, neglected lawn. "I beg your pardon for the intrusion of the call. I was expecting confirmation of a service call and didn't want to miss it. Was there anything else, Mr. Donovan?"

"Just another question or two. You stated the former Mrs. Parker—Tricia—hadn't been in touch for years. But can you possibly think of any reason, however unlikely, that would take her to Nick's neighborhood?"

Erin shook her head. "No. No reason whatever." But as she spoke, Erin turned as if to look out the window, thereby obscuring her eyes from his intent stare.

He let it go, but filed it for future scrutiny. "All right. One last question. I notice you have no art—*objets d'art* or paintings—to speak of in the area between the front door and here. I didn't see any on the landing upstairs, either. I understood you to have quite a collection of pieces. The reason I'm asking is because Nick collects art, Harry seemed very interested in art, based on those occasions when I was chatting with him, and I was curious as to whether you were also an art collector."

Although she was quick to recover, Donovan did catch a look of absolute loathing from his hostess. She was quick to assume an aspect of nonchalance and even tried a smile, but her eyes weren't able to join the recovery effort. Her head dipped, just a bit, to mask them, and then she responded. "I have, um, been doing some renovations recently, so I've placed the better works in storage. It just seemed the right thing to do, for security reasons. Now, if you'll excuse me, I must begin preparations for dinner. A good friend is coming over." She rose, staring pointedly at her guest.

"You've been very generous with your time." He saw himself out.

* * * *

Donovan had an early dinner in a high-end restaurant. It was a seafood bistro, not so fancy that a reservation couldn't be had, but nice enough that linens accompanied the silverware. He ordered the crabcakes and latkes with a lime aioli dipping sauce. The meal came with a wedge salad, which he toyed with while awaiting the crab cakes.

What was to be made of Nick's cousin, Erin? She was a contradiction, of that there was no doubt. Although much of her story rang true, there were gaps, together with what seemed like outright misrepresentations. And her story sounded familiar: under renovations, art in storage. It sure sounded like Harry's explanation of how he landed in St. Andrews.

Why, for instance, did she avert her eyes when responding to his question about Tricia? And what about Harry? Was he a mischievous scamp? Not a chance. Had Nick exaggerated his role in preventing his cousin's financial ruin? Possibly. And then there was the estate. It was down at heel, yet worth a couple of million based on location alone. Donovan noticed several obvious spots where paintings had been previously hung. Were they, in fact, being stored off-site? If yes, why was there no evidence of a renovation taking place? Packing stuff away in a commercial facility is almost as expensive as engaging the tradespeople; one would typically wish to minimize the time spent eating up money on high-end, secured storage. And squeezing each and every penny while the dollars took care of themselves was the mark of rich people. *Penny-wise*, Donovan thought.

Or had all the art been sold, in order to pay the taxes and put bread on the table? It was obvious the staff had been pared down to almost none. *Miss Erin's financial state needs to be audited, methinks*. His main course arrived, a porcelain boat with a cauliflower puree lining the bottom, lacy browned latkes were braided in a narrow path the length of the plate and all of this was topped with a half-dozen crab cakes shaped like stubby fat cigars. A lime aioli drizzle criss-crossed the crab cakes, promising complex flavours. The server poured a flute of dry champagne, received acknowledgement that nothing was wanting, and disappeared.

As he ate, Donovan pondered his next visit, an unannounced stop at the home of Riley's cousin, Kate Parker and her father, Jeff. He wasn't certain of the welcome he'd receive, but it wasn't the first time Donovan had entered a home, counter to the explicit wishes of the owner. The rest of the meal passed uneventfully, and he soon found himself coasting along the highway back toward the mainland and his next visit.

Once again, the estate was a toast to excess. Built along the lines of a Cape Cod on steroids, the main building boasted seven dormers across the front, and the carriage house was crowned with another four. The entire front courtyard was affixed with pavers, making the front appear flawless, sterile, and inorganic. The perimeter walls were brick, with exotic trees lining the inside and tall ornamental grasses framing the lower trunks, like hula dancer skirts. The security system at the gate had an audio system, supplemented by cameras pointing at the grille and trunk of his rental. He smiled at the canned music being piped out to him as he waited. After a moment, the gates opened without unnecessary argument, and Donovan's car eased through.

Jeff Parker opened the door and shook Donovan's hand, although there was little warmth in his face. "Nick told me you were coming." He turned without further comment and headed to a nearby office, followed by his guest.

Donovan noted before they completed passage through the foyer that this arm of the Parker empire enjoyed a different economic stratosphere than Jeff's sister, Erin. A glance to his left revealed at least two million-dollar paintings, and his guess at the price range of the statuary suggested he keep his elbows in when approaching anything that could tip over.

The office was old world affluent, with South American wood furniture and walls, jade-infused marble floors and columns, and Corinthian leather chairs and sofas. As old habits die hard, the security expert in him noted the windows were glazed to be clear from the inside, yet obscured from the outside. He spied a discreet cable on two windows and knew they were alarmed as well.

Jeff seemed to be waiting for something and, since drinks weren't offered, Donovan assumed the pause wasn't to silently convey the enjoyment of each other's company. In a short minute, a young lady walked in without knocking and strode over to introduce herself and shake his hand. "I'm Jeff's daughter, Kate. I understand you're a friend of Riley."

Jeff took over. "So, Mr. Donovan, lots of deaths where you come from." Donovan thought to offer the retort that the murders would seem to have been imported from New York, but asked himself what that would gain. Instead, he smiled. "It would seem so."

"Nick's ex-wife and the always underfoot Harry? Of course, not so much underfoot now." One eyebrow raised in question, as Kate protested his unkind words in a small voice.

"Unfortunately, yes. That's why I'm here."

Jeff smiled without humor. "You're here because folks keep getting murdered in another country? Interesting."

It was Donovan's turn to smile, and a gentle rebuke seemed in order, since Jeff wouldn't let it go. "It's certainly interesting how entertained you are that your relatives are getting picked off at an alarming rate, yet you can't seem to make the connection between Tricia and Harry lying there— he pointed north—and Kate standing here." He waited, expecting to either be ushered out or to re-start the conversation. Fascinated, Kate watched the tableau, as if studying a tennis match.

The smirk left Jeff's face, and he at last invited Donovan to sit on a nearby sofa. "How about I begin again? What brings you here, Mr. Donovan?"

"To be blunt, the extended Parker clan seems to be targeted for murder. It's possible all the damage to be done has been done, and it's equally possible there is more to come."

Kate's jaw dropped, and she crossed the room to sit beside her father, who'd chosen an upholstered chair across from his guest.

Donovan continued. "There's this tiny town on the eastern seaboard of Canada called St. Andrews By-The-Sea. Charming as can be, and deadly dull, in its charming way. Nick Parker and his father before him have been spending pleasant, uneventful summers there for—how many years, would you say? Fifty years without incident? This year, however, Nick's ex-wife appears, unannounced and uninvited, at least not by Nick or Riley. One day later…dead. "About the same time, cousin Harry decides to invite himself, posing as a painter. Within a fortnight…equally dead, but in a completely different manner. One by drowning, one by blunt-force trauma, specifically a shovel to the side of the head, followed by numerous blows, well, everywhere. It was as brutal as the first murder was subtle. What did they have in common? Salt water and the Parker name."

Donovan leaned forward, his voice becoming confidential. "So. St. Andrews saunters from summer to summer without incident, for years. Insert two additional Parker-types, and a tourist town becomes Dodge City. Can you explain to me why I shouldn't be looking at the extended Parker clan for clues, or even for future victims?" He sat back, waiting, but nothing was forthcoming from father or daughter.

"See? That's what I thought. My next question will probably be as welcome as my presence coming up the driveway. Okay, here we go. Are you willing to help me get to the bottom of this, given the murderer may or may not be finished?"

Jeff Parker's eyes narrowed. "That sounds a bit provocative, sir. It presupposes, to me, that you can solve the crimes and that you're better than the police. Don't the RCMP guys always get their man?"

"I'll respond to the last question first. No. They don't. And when they do, which I admit is often, it's not always before more murders happen. How would you like to be correct, 'give or take one more Parker murder?'"

Kate shuddered.

"I see." It sounded as if Jeff really did not wish to see. "What kind of questions do you have for us?"

Donovan decided he'd take the long way around, saving his more intrusive questions for the end of the conversation. "Let's begin with cousin Harry. Nice man?"

Donovan almost smiled at the reaction. Jeff replied "Nice enough." His eyes remained neutral, even as Kate shook her head in a clear indictment.

Donovan directed his attention to the daughter. "Harry wasn't a very nice man, was he? What was he? Was he a crook, a thief, a con artist?

This time, Kate gave her head a decisive nod. "Yes. He was all of those things, plus a bit of a perv. I didn't like him as a child, and I'm a bit glad I don't have to meet him again in this world."

"Kate!" Her father glared, his features reproving. "That is not the way you were brought up to speak of the dead, or...relatives." His earlier unkind comment seemed to have been forgotten in the moment.

"I know." She sighed. "Don't tell the truth about family, no matter how awful the truth becomes. Well, I'm sick of it. That man was awful, I'll tell you what. By the time I turned twenty, I thanked my lucky stars he never cornered me in the barn when I was younger." She placed a forearm over her breasts and frowned. "What's worse than the black sheep of the family? Whatever it is, that would be him." Once again, she shuddered.

Jeff looked embarrassed. Clearly, he'd invited his daughter to sit in and was now having second thoughts. It was evident he was unable to govern her comments. To mitigate the seeds of damage already sown by his daughter, he picked up the explanation. "Let me explain. Harry was always looking for the easy way to get what he wanted. As he grew up, it was clear this approach didn't...reconcile itself with the law. So, there were disagreements with the police, and Harry—didn't always...win those disagreements. He needed to be bailed out, from time to time. Sometimes the bail out was figurative, but at other times...he was literally given bail. I don't know that he actually served time, but the family...knew Harry very well." He sighed.

Kate nodded in affirmation. "Riley told me Harry had gone to see Nick on many occasions to get a loan. I've never heard of him actually paying it back. Dad, you've bought him off, too, right?"

Jeff looked at the rug covering the hardwood floor. "That's not the phrase I'd use, darling. Nobody bought anybody off. I have loaned him money in the past, for projects. Yes, I've done that."

Kate sat back with lips pursed, saying nothing but carrying a knowing expression. Donovan made a mental note to speak with her later. Alone.

"What did Harry have to do with the art scene?"

Jeff waved a hand in a vague gesture. "He bought and sold pieces, usually to small galleries and art houses. He told me this was usually on a commission basis, but I don't know that for sure."

Kate interrupted. "Wasn't it because of art that he got in trouble that time? He couldn't prove he'd bought a painting he was trying to sell?" Her voice lowered, becoming confidential. "It turns out it was stolen. Dad had to use his lawyer to keep him out of jail."

"Honey, that contention was never proved. All I did was permit him the use of the family law firm to clear up some misunderstandings." He loosened his tie, a slight flush creeping up his neck, and chose that moment to glare at her. Once again, Donovan stifled a smile.

"Any idea what Harry was up to just before he left for Canada?"

Jeff shook his head. Firmly. "Not a clue. I hadn't seen him for a month before he left for Canada."

Donovan looked at Kate, who appeared just a bit nervous. She swallowed, glancing at her father, and then refocusing on the houseguest. She took a deep breath. "Just about a week before Harry left, I was over visiting Aunt Erin. She'd asked me to come look at some Civil War documents she was trying to protect. She knew I worked summers with a conservator for an art gallery on Bleeker St, in Manhattan. She never liked to pay for things she could get for free—" this earned her a swat on the outside of her thigh from her father "—so she'd call me over, every now and again. Actually, she'd call anyone who'd work for free. I think it stems from when her ex cleaned her out. Or maybe she was always that way. I've only known her for about twenty years." She grinned at this small joke.

"Jesus." Jeff muttered an epithet under his breath.

Kate continued as if she hadn't heard anything. "I had my white gloves on, a stack of acid-free translucents at the ready, when I heard footsteps coming toward the kitchen, where I was working. A man called out 'I got the upstairs boxed. What's next?' and in waltzes cousin Harry. I swear, he looked like he was going to poop his pants when he saw me. I had to laugh.

"Anyway, he concocts this fabulous pile of BS for me. I nodded as if it was the most sensible story I'd ever heard, but it sounded like crap to me. That could be because we learned from 'way back not to believe anything Harry said, nor to challenge him. He sometimes had a temper."

Donovan filed this latest insight to memory for later reference. "What was Erin's reaction?"

Kate took a moment to recollect. "It was very weird. She looked at first as if she'd seen a ghost or something, as if she didn't expect him to pop out of the woodwork like that. Then her face, um, closed off—" She passed a hand over her face as if to erase everything. "—and all the while Harry was feeding me a line, she looked like...nothing was happening whatsoever. It was so strange."

"Mr. Parker, when was the last time you've been to Erin's residence? You said it was over a month?"

"Yes" He nodded, reinforcing his statement. "She and I were never really close. I was there at Easter. I had to pick up her income tax papers. My accountant was going to do her taxes for her. That was the last time." Kate flounced back in the chair, her face betraying satisfaction at this latest evidence of Erin's thrifty ways.

"What did you think of her house, specifically, its condition?"

Jeff frowned. "I'm trying to recollect. There was some snow around the house, and I didn't go much past the door, since all I was there for was to collect a package of papers."

"I can tell you." Kate spoke up. "For the past year, every time I've gone there, it seemed like the rooms were getting bigger. I wondered about that, and it occurred to me the rooms weren't getting bigger, they were getting emptier. I asked her about it and she replied that she was going to do some renovations and didn't want to damage any of the artwork. But that was months and months ago. She hasn't got any renos started, so I don't know why she'd take down her art and leave the rooms looking like they'd been ransacked."

"What was her art like?" Donovan elaborated. "Some people acquire specific pieces of art to enhance the look of a room. It could be Ikea, or something equally affordable. Others collect pieces as an investment, or they at least don't care much about the sticker price. Where would you say Erin fit into this spectrum of art fans?"

Kate jumped in, ignoring her father's open mouth as he tried to get a word in. "Oh, it's good stuff. As I mentioned, I used to work at an art gallery, and I learned a lot." She tossed back a mass of very blonde tresses. "Half of her works have been on the walls as long as I can remember, but she lost a lot when her ex took off. Uncle Nick used to buy her a piece every holiday and these ended up being the nice works, in my humble opinion. He didn't give her anything under fifty."

"Fifty grand?"

She nodded, her face revealing disappointment that he would even have to clarify it. "Some were pricier, but Riley told me those ones were loaners. Nick would let her keep some of his really good ones on an extended loan." She paused. "Uncle Nick has a good eye for art. A very good eye. I wonder where they're stored. Daddy, do you know?"

Jeff shook his head. "Somewhere safe, I'm sure." He turned his attention back to Donovan. "I'm sorry, but what does all this have to do with the deaths?"

Donovan thought for a moment, concluding it was premature to lay his cards on the table. "I'll be honest, Mr. Parker. I'm fishing. Harry was involved in art, and Harry's dead. I have to prove it was just a coincidence. Circumstances seem to be changing in Erin's house, so I ask uncomfortable questions about that. This all brings me to my next set of uncomfortable questions, and you'll forgive me for asking, but I'm clearly just taking shots in the dark, so no offense should be taken." He paused to receive a glass of lemonade from a servant, aware of them watching him take the first sip.

"Mr. Parker, you left the family firm under circumstances that weren't, um, entirely comfortable between you, your brother Jeb, and Nick. What happened?"

Jeff's mouth twisted, as if he'd just tasted something astringent. "You know what happened. Nick told you, of that I am certain."

"He didn't tell me your version." Donovan waited.

Jeff crossed his legs and folded his arms before speaking. Donovan almost smiled at the efficiency with which the man closed himself off with his body language. Kate, too, became very focused on what was about to be revealed.

"It was very straightforward, really. Once upon a time, there was this small architectural firm, ninety per cent consulting and ten per cent construction. Almost everything was sub-contracted out. Jeb and I joined on, after Erin but before Nick, and between us, we grew the company from seven people to fifteen. It was nice. My father and uncle created a board of directors, created shares, and divvied them up among us. At one point, Nick finished school and joined the firm, and his hiring present was an equal number of shares as the rest of us. All this without lifting a finger." Jeff snapped his finger in emphasis as his tone rose.

"When he joined the company, he brought new ideas; some I liked, some I thought were stupid. My father and uncle thought they were all brilliant, and they mostly went with them. As far as Jeb and I were concerned, the ideas rolled in the door together with a bustling economy, so it would have been impossible for anyone, even a green architect like Nick to screw up. My ideas were just as good as his, but because he'd just finished school, and because his ideas sounded more cutting-edge, I suppose, they went with him.

"The payroll doubled, and doubled again. And again. The firm started trading on the stock exchange. Everything turned to gold and Jeb and I were pushed aside. But all that success would have happened whether Nick showed up or not. What's that football quote? 'Timing isn't everything; it's the only thing.'

"The next time the company grew, Jeb decided to lay his cards on the table. It was time to choose a new CEO, my father and uncle—Nick's father—were both stepping down, and Jeb pushed for the top job. I wanted the CFO position and Jeb issued an ultimatum. If we weren't appointed to the two top positions, you wouldn't see us for dust. Nick's father backed Nick, and, well, so did my dad. Erin got the CFO job, and Nick got the big prize. Erin stepped down six months later to take a manager's job, but I didn't know it at the time. Anyway, neither of us darkened the company door again." Jeff glared at Donovan, as if it were his fault.

"So, you took your shares and started over."

"That's right." Jeff's resentful glare turned to one of defiance. "I didn't become stupid all of a sudden just because I wasn't attached to the family business. I cashed in my shares and bought into an upcoming construction firm in Jersey. I transferred my skills over there. Three years later, we had some of the best bridges and road contracts in the area following the I-95 from Connecticut to Delaware. I retired—Freedom Fifty—a year ago."

"Sounds like you have a lot of residual anger built up."

Jeff's face softened. "Of course I was angry, mostly hurt. But every time I challenged my father, he said it was a business decision that was good for the whole family, including me. We were all raised to value the... advantages money could offer. As things worked out for me, my outlook kind of changed. For the better." He waved a hand to encompass his home. "It's not as if I starved or anything, after the fight.

"One day I came home from a long day, and there was a glass of wine poured, and two glasses of lemonade. They sat right there." Jeff pointed to a sideboard table. "I asked Katie if we had company, and Riley walked in. She came straight to me, gave me a big hug and told me she and Nick missed us. Things kind of melted away that day. Not so much for Jeb, but after that day I've been cool with how things went."

Donovan sat still, absorbing the layers of emotion he'd just witnessed from father and daughter. After a moment, he chose a different tack. "How did your brother get over the slight?"

Jeff shook his head. "He never did. Jeb cut off ties with our father as well as most of the relatives, really, and when he heard I was on speaking terms with most everyone—"

"With Nick," Kate piped up.

"Okay, with Nick, he soured on me as well. I haven't seen nor heard from him in a couple of years." Jeff's voice was dry. "You're getting a front row seat to all of our dirty laundry, aren't you?"

"I've seen worse. So, Jeb has a hate-on for everyone who walks and carries the Parker name. How strong is that hate? Strong enough to kill for?"

Jeff shook his head, his eyes locked on Donovan and unwavering. "No. I'd bet everything on that. Plus, he has an excellent alibi. He's been in Indonesia for the past six weeks. It can't have been him." He crossed over to the sideboard table, pouring two fingers of scotch with a hand that shook, just a bit.

Donovan scratched his chin, watching his list of Parker family suspects shrink. He saw his host glance at his watch and knew his time was running out. "I just have a few more questions." His eyes met those of the father and daughter. "Do either of you have any idea where Mr. Tannen, Erin's ex-husband, is?"

"Ike? I haven't a clue. He hasn't been around for years. Last I heard, he was in Mexico. Erin pressed charges against him and next thing you know he slipped across the border. Poof! He disappeared."

Kate found her voice. "Erin told me Ike tried to borrow big money off her, about seven years ago. She told him off and hung up on him before he could finish his sob story. She told me about it because she never wanted me to have any truck with him. 'Trash like that.' she said about him. I highly doubt he'd show his face around here. Aunt Erin was the only one who could stand him, and whatever the hell they had, well, it's not there now, for sure."

Donovan leaned forward. "Now, I'm puzzled. If she has such an antipathy for that man Ike, how could she stand Harry? Weren't they a lot alike?"

Kate grinned. "Ike was a bastard, but Harry was a suck-up and a charmer. He could play the loser card really well, and you'd have pity on him. The next thing you know, his hand is in your wallet and you're opening it farther, to make it easier for him." She laughed aloud, sharing this secret. "He's really good at it. Or, he was." Her smile faltered.

"So you think he was playing Erin?"

Kate paused, framing her response. "I'm not sure it was exactly like that. I had a feeling, once he ingratiated himself, they were both leaning on each other, all the while knowing each other's faults. I could be a hundred per cent wrong, but that's what I saw."

Jeff was less forthcoming. He sat beside his drink, rubbing the palms of his hands on his thighs, saying nothing.

"Anything you'd like to add?" Donovan waited.

Jeff shook his head. "My family has many flaws, but I just don't see murder among them. I believe you've wasted your time, sir."

"You've actually given me lots of information, shrinking my list of suspects a bit. If I don't have to spend three days getting this family information from others, then I haven't wasted my time."

"There's that, I suppose." He rose, effectively ending the visit. Donovan shook hands with his hosts and departed.

* * * *

Three blocks from the Jeff Parker estate, Donovan spied a green Chevy, two cars back. He remembered the same car pulling out behind him as he left the Parker place. There weren't numerous intersection options available, so Donovan didn't think much of it, other than to make a mental note of its presence. Three intersections later, however, the Chev was still there and his suspicions were fully engaged. He glanced around the tidy rental, and realized how vulnerable he was. *If it's the police, there's nothing I can do. If it's someone else, I need to pick up some toys. Let's head for the hotel*. He kept driving.

The second he put the signal light on to enter his hotel, the green car faded back, disappearing into traffic. Donovan parked close to his hotel unit and hurried up the outside stairs and along the balcony to his room. Sensing he didn't have a lot of time—and having no clue as to whether he was under surveillance or being stalked—he closed his hotel room door most of the way, leaving the security bar flipped out to prevent it from latching. He headed straight for his travel bag. Did he have something very tiny, something for infighting?

There was a challenge to be faced every time he flew. How to carry a gun in your luggage when you fly? You don't. Airport security sought out weapons on every flight, day and night. Whatever he brought had to look nothing like a weapon. Donovan reached into a corner of the bag and withdrew two unique items: the first appeared to be a small flashlight with a one-eighty degree head on it and a portable speaker with a tiny attachment affixed to the side. He unzipped the pocket at the end of the bag and withdrew earplugs and tinted swimming goggles with lenses that fit over each eye. Donning the ear-eye combo, he turned off the lights, looking foolish but safe. Sitting at the desk chair feeling somewhat senses-deprived, he waited.

The attackers weren't pros, and after a brief minute, he caught the shadow of one hovering just at the edge of his window. He picked the flashlight and speaker from the desk beside him, placed a thumb on each activation button and stared at the door.

It happened so quickly. Both men burst through the door, splitting up and preparing for an end run. They both carried pistols pointed across their chests, as if not expecting to have to deploy them. Donovan pressed both switches, pointing them at the men without necessarily having to, and crouched, partially obscured by the furniture.

The man closest to Donovan stopped in his tracks, bent at the waist, and began to projectile vomit across the floor. He dropped the gun and started scrubbing his entire body, like it was covered in fire ants. His partner followed suit, falling to his knees and rolling in the spew issuing from his stomach. Donovan collected up the guns and, taking care to minimize instances of puke on his shoes, headed for the door. He closed it and faced the suffering visitors.

Turning off both devices, he placed the guns within reach on the surface of the desk and raised the light and speaker combination in the air with a thumb above each switch. He shook the light, which he held in his left hand.

"This here is a visual cue to your brain that you are in the deepest throes of seasickness." He then shook the speaker in his left hand. "And this baby delivers an audio signal to your brain that every nerve in your body desperately needs to wake up and receive a good scratching. You can protect yourself from me by closing your eyes and placing your hands firmly over your ears. If you choose that option, I'll be forced to shoot you with your own gun. Or you can just sit there and clasp your hands on top of your head while we have a chat. What's it to be; this?" He turned on both devices long enough to return them to a heaving, writhing misery before shutting them off. "Or this? I thought so." He watched their hands creep up above their heads.

"Now, then. Since you were discreet enough to not shoot your guns, we may have a few minutes before the manager comes and kicks me out for all this puke. But be warned; if you hold back on me, on it comes." He rested his thumb just above the light switch, causing both men to close their eyes, wincing.

"The other thing I'd like to remind you of, I have your guns. As I said, if you don't cooperate, I can also shoot you. This is break and enter, right? Okay, you start. Who sent you?" Donovan pointed the light toward the heavier-set of the two, a man about thirty-five with a broken nose, unshaven, and wearing jeans that threatened to fall off his ass.

"Some guy. I dunno. It was all done with texts."

"How'd he get hold of you?"

"Friend of a friend."

"You're not being very helpful." To this, the man shrugged and Donovan turned on both the light and the speaker, sending the men into convulsions. When the man with the lighter frame recovered, he booted his companion in the side. Donovan waggled the light. "Let's start again. How can I get a hold of your boss?"

It was the second man; younger, blonder, and with better-fitting jeans. "His name is Ike. He's not in this part of the country. I got the impression he's in Canada."

Donovan leaned in and then withdrew as the stench of vomit assaulted him. "Where, in Canada, and how do you know that?"

"I was worried about getting paid, so I did a check on the cell number sending the text. The number went back to a guy named Rafuse."

"Ike Rafuse?"

"No, Harry. Then I found out this guy Harry is now living in Canada."

"Okay. So, how does Harry tie in to your boss, Ike?"

"Harry hooked me up with Ike. I just assumed they were both living in Canada."

Donovan tried to make a connection. "What's Ike's last name?"

"I haven't a clue. He'd just send a text and we'd do what the text told us to."

Donovan reviewed what he's been told. "First you said Ike was the guy giving you orders, but now you're saying it's Harry's cell phone sending the instructions. Which is it?"

The blond man shook his head. "I don't know, man. It's not like I ever heard them speak. Look, for all I know, Ike and Harry is the same guy. I'm just the peon here. Why don't you let us go? We'll give you all the money on us." His voice had descended to a whine and he reached for his wallet, stopping in mid-air as Donovan waved the light at him.

"We'll see. What were you supposed to get from me, and how were you supposed to tell your boss, Ike or Harry?"

Both men looked down at the same time, eyes refusing to meet those of Donovan. "Ah, we were supposed to send you a message—a physical message—to keep your nose outta people's business. When we were finished, we were supposed to send a text an' then we'd get paid."

"Would you get paid electronically? Maybe you should hand over the phone, and tell me how to phrase the message and then give me the bank information." Donovan's voice took on a lighter tone. "Just a little more cooperation and I'm actually seeing you two living through the evening. That would be a good thing, right? How much, by the way? How much does it cost to have me get beaten up?"

The heavier man mumbled something and then spat some remaining vomit onto the ugly hotel carpet. The blond fished a cell phone and his wallet from a back pocket. "Here's the phone. I'll tell you what I woulda said, honest to God." He dictated the message, which Donovan duly transcribed into text.

"That's done. How will you get paid?"

Again, the blond man pointed out the bank deposit process through the app that was installed on the phone. Donovan transferred the entire amount from the account into one of his accounts and accepted all of the cash from his captives. *No cash and no phone mean delays in communicating with their employer, even if they were lying about a second way to gain access to him. That buys me time.*

Donovan stood, pocketed the guns, the cell phone, their cash, and then gathered up a second cell phone from the sturdy thug. He then asked a final question. "Do you have any other contact information besides using this cell?" Both men shook their heads. Donovan gathered his things, popping them, together with his laptop, into the overnight bag, eyes never leaving the men on the floor. "Try to contact this Ike or Harry guy and I'll take a day or two to hunt you down. You don't want that."

Donovan stepped around the slimy mess and exited the hotel room. He stopped at the desk to report an intruder and then hopped in his car. Choosing his reliable mp3 player, he put The Mad Caddies on, smiling at the appropriateness of the song that popped up. *Lay Your Head Down* began with the words "There's a devil outside your window, and he's waiting for a piece of you." *I love a minor key*, he thought, as he pulled away.

* * * *

Once out of sight, Donovan parked in the closest beachside parking lot. He chose a busy street where a nondescript car could blend in with a host of other vehicles. A quick check of the attackers' cell phone revealed their employer duly posted their pay. This was transferred without delay to one of Donovan's offshore accounts. Taking out his laptop, he connected the cell phone to it and started tapping into internet service providers. This evolved into a focused search for the client sending the information.

Harry Rafuse. The late, I've-seen-the-evidence-and-he-is-dead Harry Rafuse.

Donovan raised his eyebrows. *So, dead men do tell tales. And, they are now actively hiring goons. Of course, this was appearance, not reality. What was another plausible reason?* Someone had Harry's phone. Stealing a phone for a day was one thing, but using it for a longer period required another: someone to pay the bill. He hacked into Harry's phone, relieved to see the username and password were auto-filled. Retrieving sufficient information to speak with the service provider, Donovan contacted them, and a moment later knew who was paying the phone bill.

Chapter 25

Niagara On The Lake

CLAIRE AWAKENED TO THE SOUND of. . .nothing. What she'd heard had been in her dreams. She had imagined footsteps echoing up emptied staircases, the drizzling gush of taps to the massive wine vats left opened to bleed unseen onto the floor of the darkened, uninhabited processing plant. The dream had conjured up black jeeps tearing through forty-year-old grapevines, engines roaring and faceless vandals careening sideways across fields and over freshly tangled, ruined vineyards.

She had pictured liters of salt held in black-gloved hands, the white grains of poison whispering out of sacks and into the wine barrels, and it was that which had begun to pull the young woman from a deep sleep. But then it was the imagined crash-smash of hammers against hundreds of four, six, and ten-year-old bottles of wine, all of them market-ready, that had ultimately awakened her. Now fully awake, however, Claire met silence, broken only by the catch in her breath, and the tick, tick of the clock.

And then, as was her habit, the second thought to enter Claire's mind was that of *maman et papa*, back in Arles, France. She felt their love, across the Atlantic and was reassured, but nevertheless fully awake.

Three o'clock.

The moon cast a benign pool across the floor beside her bed, and the pale cream light in the stillness provided the sole evidence of calm. This belied the turmoil running through Claire's head and pounding heart. Claire threw on a robe, dropping a security card into a capacious pocket, cinched the robe at the waist and, bare feet slipped into thin tennis shoes, set out to give the lab—her lab—a once-over before making a second attempt at sleep.

It is a remarkable thing, to witness a bustling winery at mid-day on a weekend. The restaurant is full, with chatty couples studying the accoutrements of the wine industry in the gift shop while they wait for a table. At the far end of the great room, customers are lined up for tastings of the pinot grigio and chardonnay, to be followed by the reds: pinot noir to start, then on to the blood-red baco, and to finish with the burgundy-hued cabernets. The hard-core clients want to try the high-end reserves, and these are the consumers who buy by the case. Gawkers stand in the middle, lost, awaiting a fresh-faced summer staff member half their age to tell them what they should try, what they will like.

But there was no hustle and bustle here now; it wasn't noon, it was the middle of the night with lights dimmed and doors secured. Claire could hear her sneakers scuff the slate floor as she transitioned from the public space toward the employees-only area.

She swiped the pass across the discreet panel beside the door and slid the handle down to gain entry to the production area. Swollen moonlight filtered through a bay of transom windows that ran the length of the east wall. It filled the room, save for the nooks and crannies and by squinting, Claire had no need to turn on the lights. Her feet knew the paths and, unthinking, she followed a route down the middle of the production site, slipping sideways down each tiny corridor to check between the lab tables.

Satisfied, she slid back the huge door that sat on rails between the lab and the vats and barrels. Opening the door just wide enough to pass easily through, she entered the next room, frowning in the dark. The moonlight didn't reach this area, so she turned to the door to slide it fully open and get additional light. She heard an audible knock even as she felt, or rather, saw a white light accompanying an equally intense pain at the side of her head and down she went. Just before slipping into unconsciousness, she heard a female voice muttering an apology. There was no opportunity to question this odd circumstance, as she was now out like a light.

* * * *

Jack Miller sat fully dressed atop the quilt of his made-up bed, reading glasses in his left hand, an unread novel in the other, and a mound of pillows at his back. He'd wanted to read it—the book had several five-star reviews—and sleep wouldn't come (it seldom did since the passing of his wife), but his thoughts kept getting interrupted. Why was he still getting paid by the RCMP—a paycheck to cover his leave until the fall—and soon a pension? On one level, this was an easy question to answer: he was officially old. On the other hand he'd always worked, most of it for the Mounties, so it felt unreal to receive money for not working. *That's how pensions work, fool.* Further, he had a new job, as Head of Security for this Canadian winery, Plenitude.

Which led him to his next question: Who was trying to destroy the winery? Was that too strong a term to describe the incidents that were beginning to add up? Perhaps. He put the book down, and chewed on a bow from his glasses. The list of suspects was regretfully short. He had none. This elicited a sigh. *What kind of detective can't detect? No wonder they put me out to pasture. Shit.*

Maybe I should take a little walk-about. It'll clear the head and I'll think up a plan. Might a mousetrap work? Generally, a mousetrap works when you know where to place it. And you know where to place it when there is an inkling of where the perp might strike next, and where in shit might that be? Jack shook his head. Anyway, a walk would do no harm, plan or no. A twinge in his back reminded him it hadn't quite healed from the Constanta job. Perhaps he'd take his walking stick. He fished it out from behind the door and headed out. Looking back into his room before closing the door, he noted the time.

Five after three.

Jack decided to check the perimeter first and exited the French doors of Dieter's office. He crossed the stone reception area overlooking the vines and skirted the building, choosing from instinct to walk in the shadow of the building. He passed the reception area, a couple of offices, the restaurant, the barbecue yard and stage, and headed back toward the production area. The morning birds hadn't begun to sing, and there was no breeze to cause the trees to sigh. He couldn't discern any traffic flow from the distant highway. The night was his alone.

Except.

Except, he heard a click, ten feet in front of him. It was followed by the faintest of taps, exactly like a door handle had reached the end of its tiny arc and the latch bolt was released. He took two quick steps toward the door and then waited.

The door opened away, and he took another step, which placed him beside the handle. He swung it wide, eliciting a gasp from the young woman coming out of the building.

Quick as can be, she was on the run, Jack in pursuit. *I'll never catch her!* He grasped his walking stick and threw it like a javelin at the middle of her back. The momentum carried her forward into a face plant and Jack reached down to grab an ankle. This action got him a kick from her free leg, catching him in the shoulder.

Grunting, she rolled to her knees and he spotted something shiny and metallic in her waistband. *She's not a girl; she's a weapon, pointing at me.* The assailant was about to spring off when he grasped the back of her hoodie. Not knowing what exactly he was dealing with, Jack showed respect for her possible fighting skills and didn't hold back. Jerking the cloth toward him with a powerful arm, he threw a powerhouse right to the jaw. The woman in the hoodie crumpled in a heap at his feet, leaving him standing over her, winded, rubbing his now-tender shoulder.

Out of the corner of his eye, he noticed a second figure approaching him. A partner-in-crime? *Shit*. But it was Claire, stumbling and then falling to one knee. Before he could catch her, she dropped face-first into the soft soil at the edge of the vineyard. In the moonlight, in her summery nightgown, she looked like an apparition. One, in this case, that didn't shimmer. The apparition didn't move at all, and he could see a smudge of blood at the back of her head, shiny and black in the night.

Chapter 26

Montauk, New York

DONOVAN WAITED IN HIS RENTAL car, a block away from the estate of Erin Parker, the former Mrs. Ike Tannen. The clock on the dash read two twenty, and the crescent slice of moon had long since slid behind a cloud bank, not to be seen again. *Would she be asleep now? Best to wait until three.*

That afternoon, he'd gone onto the City Planning website, and hacked into the Montauk Fire Department's restricted site. He pulled up the civic address of Erin Parker and downloaded the floor plans, including diagrams revealing fire escapes and alarm system wiring. Earlier, he'd visited the realty site that had sold her the property years ago. There was one discrepancy between the real estate listing of the floor plan and that of the Montauk Fire Department plans. On the latter, there was a tiny room that didn't appear on the city's official floor plans. A safe room? He didn't know.

The fire department had also noted something else. There was a notification that in January Erin had ceased paying for her security alarm system. The house wasn't armed. He'd seen the wiring going to the door and two of the windows, but wired up didn't always mean activated, apparently. There were no pets, and she'd advised him that her day staff didn't sleep over, if indeed any of them remained on the payroll. It was time for a visit.

Donovan loved the time between two and four in the morning. There wasn't a more private time in which to be alone with his thoughts (and his actions!). The bonus was that the inky nothingness between the moon and the stars augmented his sense of being in control. Similarly, it had been his experience that others did not share this opinion. Most night owls were in bed and fast asleep by two. They'd watched the late show and perhaps the late, late show, taking them to one thirty. They would have trundled up to bed and been out, minutes later. The early risers began to stir at four, some of them up and at 'em by four thirty. It had even been shown that B-&-E perpetrators were most active after four a.m. But Donovan liked the narrow window between two thirty and three. It was made for him.

He got out of the car, tossing on a body-fitting messenger bag. His shoes made no sound, and the distance to Erin's tattered estate was bridged in a few minutes. Seeking the corner of the property, he swung up the seven-foot wall and was over in a shadowy blink. Once within the perimeter he noted the time, studying the windows, each one dark and absent of movement. The verandah light was on—the sole evidence of light—and the rest of the lot was shrouded in darkness.

After three minutes of studying key windows, he dared to move toward the rear of the building. Donovan took another cautious minute to focus on the kitchen area, which contributed nothing of interest. He drew closer. The generic kitchen door lock took three seconds to solve. Once in, he headed straight to the hidden room. It was walled up, and the work hadn't been done recently. With a quick check on the pulse of the house, he moved to the library, noting the bare walls as he glided down the hallway. Once in the room, he pulled the door almost to and then stood a bit, waiting, listening.

Nothing.

The walls were naked; there were spaces where floor pieces had been removed, the desk had an untidy stack of bills on one corner, and all of the drawers were locked. Leaving it for the moment, he circled the room, hands sliding expertly along an area of the wall between four and six feet from the floor. There being no imperfections to the walls' finish, he returned to the desk and jimmied the drawers open. A pistol sat alongside a letter opener in the upper left-hand corner. There was no false bottom to the drawer, and he noted the gun was loaded. The drawer beneath the gun contained a thick sheaf of papers, and he flipped through them.

Donovan stopped riffling through the papers when a series of past-due payment notices appeared, most recent arrivals on top. The house was mortgaged to the hilt, and utilities were all accompanied by threats of cessation of service. He dug deeper, noting the absence of any storage bills. There were, however, months of horse race forms. He raised his eyebrows in the dark at that revelation. Toward the bottom he found a letter tucked into an envelope that had been slit open. The name on the upper corner stopped him in his tracks.

Tricia (Woods) Parker.

He tucked the letter into his messenger bag pocket, stopping for a second to listen. He heard…something. A glance around the room told him the alcove corner was his best bet. Using great care, Donovan pocketed the pistol and re-closed and locked the drawers, lifting each one to reduce any sliding noise. He glided over to the darkest spot of the room, in the alcove. A moment later, the door opened and a female form shuffled over to the desk. As the ambient light from the window touched her, Donovan saw her robe wasn't tied, and she reached into a large pocket, withdrawing a key.

With a great sigh, she unlocked and then reached into the top drawer and, without looking, fetched out a pack of cigarettes and a lighter. She headed to the window, slid the window open and then sat on a bare wooden chair. Lighting up, she exhaled with yet another sigh deep enough to cause a grief counselor to weep. Three drags later, she stubbed out the half-expended smoke and, leaving the pack and ashtray sitting on the chair seat, she locked the desk and shuffled back out of the room.

Donovan exhaled. He returned to the desk, jimmied the lock once again and replaced the gun. The exit was straightforward, and a minute later he sat in his car. Knowing his room wouldn't be ready and worried that his new hotel might be watched, he pulled away. A half hour later, he drove to an all-night diner to read the letter and formulate next steps.

A slice of apple pie and a cup of coffee before him, Donovan opened the letter. One sentence in, he pulled the page closer to his nose, glanced around the almost-vacant diner, and continued.

Hello, Erin,

Long time-no see! I'm sure you've been wondering what I've been up to, all these years. I won't lie to you, life's been hard, since I got the boot from Nick. I run a nail salon now, above the below and below the upper, as they say.

I'll cut to the chase. A couple of weeks ago, I was walking along Bleecker in Manhattan and spied a familiar painting in a gallery window. Familiar, because Nick had given it to me for our first anniversary. Owing to circumstances beyond my control (as you can well imagine), I had to leave it behind when your loving cousin tossed me out on my ass one night. But that's icy water under the bridge. I went into the gallery and lo! it was for sale by your dirtball cousin, Harry. Remember Harry? I believe he is what the world calls your gangster connection, able to do your dirty work while you keep your lily whites clean.

So I put two and two together and did my own little investigation. Jeb filled me in on the family's comings and goings over the years—yes, he's still sore at the way the family treated him—and I heard all about Nick lending you dozens of pieces of art, including the ones that should have been mine. 37 Pcs Art = $Much. I can do the math!

I think it's time I visited Canada, maybe let Nick know how much (little) you value his "loans". Of course, we can avoid all this unpleasantness, if someone was to, say, contribute to my retirement fund. Let's face it— running a salon doesn't get you rich at twenty bucks an hour per chair (on good days). I'll be leaving for the beautiful St. Andrews, Canada in three days. Or not. That's entirely up to you, my darling ex-in-law.

Donovan folded the letter and tucked it into his back pocket. Things were beginning to add up, and he could see some of the battle lines being drawn. Erin was being blackmailed...certainly by Tricia but possibly also by Harry. Nick was being bilked, so if he caught wind of it, might he also have had a hand in either of the St. Andrews murders? Were Jeff and his daughter Kate implicated and, if yes, on which side? His instincts told him they weren't. But no one liked to be attacked from behind, so he had to place them in the same column as Nick, Erin, and the ever-so-dead Harry.

Which reminded him of the pair of thugs sent over earlier. Who'd sent them? It appeared to have been Harry or Erin, and Harry was in no condition, being dead, to have ordered the hit. *So, Erin has claws. What else is she capable of?*

What was that saying? If you want answers, follow the money. He had to find the missing art. Clearly, at least one piece was sitting in the show window of an art gallery on Bleecker. He had to drive in to Manhattan tomorrow. Would he find the rest?

* * * *

This time, Donovan chose a generic hotel on Park Avenue, two doors up from the French cuisine restaurant *Fruits de Mers*. He booked a reservation there for that evening and grabbed a cab downtown, along Broadway. His thoughts grew wistful as the yellow cab crawled across Twenty-third St. and then inched its way through Chelsea and into the West Village. It would have been so pleasant to share New York City with Beth. But, business first. The cabbie passed Bleecker by one block, talking to the other cabbies with his horn, and turning right onto West Houston. As he rounded the corner, Donovan cast a longing glance farther down Broadway, toward Chinatown and Little Italy. Another day, perhaps. Two blocks in, as directed, the cabbie pulled over. He paid the cabbie and exited into brilliant, humid sunshine.

He walked north a block, spying young adults entering a film school, and thought of other lives he may have lived, other paths he could (should?) have taken. Why did this place, of all cities, induce such introspection? He'd been able, for years, to block out everything but that next gig, and he was so close to living the straight life, a life free of crime.

So maybe that was the crux of it.

If he was at the point where the door to clean living was within sight, wasn't he at his most vulnerable to screwing it up and losing everything, including Beth and the winery?

But he was fine, really. He wasn't here to steal something; he was here to save something. A life, perhaps, or a family. The art gallery sign came into view, and he decided upon a tack he'd use to garner some information. The plate glass doors parted to greet him with a puff of chill air-conditioned comfort as he entered, taking a first glance around.

The Martin Lawrence Gallery was a mere two blocks away, on Broadway, not far at all from the one he'd just entered. But this one was nothing like that…no limited edition Warhols, no open, modern spaces, all whites and chromes. Village Art was older in tone, homier, yet with an eye for mid-century modern pieces. No one rushed to greet him so he stepped over to the side, glancing from one painting to the next, ignoring the relatively few sculptures adorning the floor.

Donovan couldn't help himself. His eye went to the windows, the door, and the area traced by the crown molding. The alarm system. He noted the cameras—two—and the discreet inch or so of cable emanating from each glass pane. Based on his observations, there were also trip lasers available for the after-hours peace of mind. Homey the place may be, but based on what he saw it was impregnable and homey. And u*nlike Erin's, I'll bet a nickel this system is fully armed*. Luckily, he didn't have to steal anything. This time. He turned to face the door at the rear, hearing the soft pad of footsteps. An older woman passed through it and approached him.

Anne Coffey had been the owner and manager of Village Art, for thirty-five years, at first in partnership, then as sole proprietor. Donovan approached her, identifying himself as an acquaintance of her retired partner, Mavis Rockefeller. Coffey's face broke out into a smile that took years from her six decades of life.

"How is Mavis? I haven't seen her for almost a year! I miss her insights." She wagged a finger. "That one knew her art, don't you know."

Donovan allowed the small talk to continue for a minute and then steered the conversation around to the matter at hand. "I'd like to explain why I'm here. You have or had a piece for sale, perhaps it was consignment, I'm not sure. The individual who brought it to you was either Erin Parker or Harry Rafuse." Her reaction suggested it had been Rafuse, and her eyes led him to where the painting now rested. "You still have it."

She nodded. "Mr. Rafuse asked for a price near the top of its estimated value, so it's been sitting for just over a month. But it'll sell. It's very good."

"Did he indicate whether he was acting as an agent for someone, or were you to reimburse him directly?"

She picked an imaginary fleck of lint from her immaculate black dress. "It's not our policy to reveal too much information about our clients from either side of the sales equation, Mr. Donovan."

"Here's my problem. I'm trying to resolve some issues surrounding numerous paintings held by Ms. Erin Parker, but in fact owned by her cousin, Nick Parker. The one in the window is just one of several. It's my understanding you know the extended family, am I correct?" Without waiting for an answer, he pressed on. "I'm actually representing Nick and Riley Parker, but the extended family will wish to know what's going on here. You've spoken with Nick before, I believe?"

"Well, yes, but—"

He offered Anne his cell phone. "I have Nick's number here. You can speak with him directly if you wish. You should know as well, Mr. Rafuse has been murdered in Canada. It is believed the missing art factors into the overall mystery, and in fact, many if not all of the missing pieces are actually owned by Nick. Ms. Coffey, how many pieces did Harry Rafuse offer you?"

"Just the one." She hesitated. "He tried to offer several of them to my gallery, at one point. At first, he requested I buy them at half their value, but when I insisted on provenance and proof of ownership, he later phoned me and said he was going to offer them to another gallery out of state. I had the sense he wasn't being truthful, just a feeling, but of course, if he'd withdrawn his request, it was no longer my problem. At the end, he brought this one in with provenance, including a letter of permission from Nick." She took in a sharp breath. "You don't suppose the letter was forged?"

A worry line deepened on her forehead. "So, what do I do with it?" She pointed to the painting in the window. "Do I keep it for sale, or does Nick or one of the other Parkers own it? I want to do the right thing. But if there is a murder investigation, I not only want things to be perfectly legal insofar as this piece is concerned, but now I'm not even certain I want the damned thing in my gallery. Shit! This is getting complicated." She turned away from Donovan, thinking.

"Look. Have Mr. Parker—Nick send me a letter of direction regarding the artwork I have here, and I'll do whatever it says. I don't need this grief, you know."

"Imagine how Harry feels." Donovan thanked her and headed for the door. Once again, he sat in the car, thinking. Who ordered the hits, where is the art, and why was all this happening? He started with Jeff and his bubbly daughter, Kate. It just didn't feel right, ascribing all of the hurt on them. What about the sullen Jeb, who'd taken his fortune and started fresh? Were hurt feelings enough reason to murder relatives?

It all seemed to come down to Erin, and to Nick. Had it been Tricia alone who'd been whacked, he would have been tempted to include Riley into the family pot. But he just didn't see Riley caving in Harry's head with a shovel. Grimacing at the thought, it occurred to him if he was in Montauk with Erin, there was really no need to choose. He'd focus on the Montauk connection and pop the St. Andrews Parker under the microscope in a day or so, upon his return.

One other thing niggled at him. How big a coincidence was it that Palu showed up in Small Town Canada at the same time as a series of murders had fallen into Donovan's lap, in that same small community? Palu carried many flaws, but he had no evidence the Frenchman was a murderer. *What I caused the guy may have led him to becoming a murderer. I have to try to make a connection there, just in case.* It also bothered Donovan that he hadn't mentioned Palu to Beth. It was the quandary of keeping her safe by not having her worry about the man, versus endangering her by making her vulnerable to being blind-sided. *I'll have to think about which makes her safer. Man! It was so much easier when I only had to worry about me.* He started the car and headed out of the city.

* * * *

"What a lovely room, Ms. Parker. A little sparse in the décor, to my taste." Donovan had returned to visit Erin, and cast an idle glance around the room, noting the faint differences in shading where paintings had been hung, and the darker tone on the hardwood floor where statuary had stood.

Her anger at his comment boiled up, darkening her eyes and bringing color to the throat. She could barely contain the outrage—or was it rage?—from her response. "That was…insolent. I told you I have my artwork in storage. Must I repeat myself?"

He chose not to apologize, wishing, in fact, to goad her, to cause something to slip out. "In storage. I wonder where? There is no record of you having contracted with any storage service on the island. My associates in Manhattan also have no knowledge of having done business with you. Or Harry." It was a lie, one easy to refute, but Donovan was proficient at lying, and he could see whatever poise there was had fled.

Erin paused, practically willing all trace of red from the pallid folds of skin on neck and cheeks. "I...I placed it in private storage. Y-you don't know them. I don't have to tell you anything, anyway. Get out!" Her voice had risen steadily until these final words echoed through the now austere room.

Donovan sat, unperturbed, watching. "One of the paintings found a different home, Ms. Parker. A home on Bleecker, but you already know that." Again, he watched, as Erin's mouth opened and then closed. "Want to know what I think?"

"I don't give a damn what you think. Who are you, anyway? Nothing but a hired boy. I've bought and paid for a dozen just like you, in my time. And I may again, once I..." She stopped, stricken.

Her uninvited guest smiled. "Oh, don't stop there, Ms. Parker. You were going to say 'Once I sell Nick's paintings.' Say it. Confession's good for the soul, you know. I haven't tied up all the loose ends connecting the paintings to the murders, but I bet I'll soon find a ball of string and a pair of scissors with your name on them." He smiled, once again infuriating her. "I'm good like that."

Fear owned her eyes and she was drowning, rendered mute.

Donovan studied the face, body language, the paralysis within the voice, remembering every trick he'd learned years earlier as a security expert for the Canadian government. "I am a little curious, though. Who was the mastermind? I'm guessing it was Harry. Was he the organ-grinder and you the trained monkey?" He watched to see if her eyes dropped down and to the left, waited to see if, and how, the rate of breathing caught, changed tempo. He followed her pulse at the throat.

Something wasn't right. He hadn't drawn the absolutely correct inference, and his words didn't move her as they should have. Erin's reaction didn't follow that of a liar caught in their lie. He knew he was almost there, until he mentioned Harry. He knew it, yet…he'd got something that wasn't quite right, and she had a look of…triumph? Too strong. He thought for a second. She'd been caught on a hook and slid off, only to realize she was still swimming in a barrel. It may be only a matter of time until Erin knew she would once again feel the hook.So, why the almost triumph? Why did she still hold out hope of salvation? Where was the variable he was missing?

It was the art. Had to be. If he couldn't find the fortune in art, what did he have? It was back to the first rule of crime.

Follow the money; in this case, the art.

Chapter 27

Niagara-On-The-Lake

JACK MILLER FELT THE ONRUSH of fatigue, yet he had two women down and in distress in a field in the middle of the night. His hand automatically reached for the cell phone that never left his belt. He discovered to his chagrin it *almost* never left his belt, and he recalled placing it on his nightstand. There was no one within shouting distance, so he returned to the women lying on the ground. One was an unconscious criminal suspect and the other clearly hurt. A quick search of the suspect produced no weapon so he directed his attention to his friend and colleague.

He knelt beside Claire, checking first for a pulse and then to gauge the extent of the wound. There was a pulse, but the wound glistened fresh in the moonlight. Scalp cuts were notorious for bleeding, but there were no major veins or arteries above the ears and outside of the skull, so he knew she wouldn't bleed out. As to the extent of head trauma...

The first trace of lightening of the sky had begun. He patted Claire's hand, keeping an eye on the other woman, the one in the black hoodie. The black hoodie moved, and Jack heard a groan. Dropping Claire's hand for a moment, he sprinted to the side of the building, grabbing a loose length of the wires used to train the vines. He got back in time to grab a collar, shaking the wobbly girl like a terrier tackles a rat. Her feet flew out from beneath her and she landed unceremoniously on her ass. His growl was abrasive and carried in the empty yard. "Stay down, or I'll separate your head from your shoulders."

The retired RCMP detective wrapped the wire twice around her waist, bent the rigid metal at her ribcage and extended a length of wire to keep a reasonable distance from his captive. The captive moaned about the wires hurting. "Ah, girlie, you'll find that's the least of your worries." Warning her once more, he moved to pick Claire up, but she'd regained consciousness to an extent and waved him off. After a moment she stood up, weaving like a Saturday night drunk in a revolving door. With a jerk on the vine wire, Jack guided the tiny caravan of three. They turned away from the pinking sky and made their way, three stumbling mis-matches, back within the winery walls.

* * * *

Once inside, Jack studied Claire's scalp, pronouncing it not too serious. "Darling, you have to awaken Dieter to get you to the hospital and phone the police…but not in that order." He carried out a closer pat down for weapons on the intruder and then settled in across from the young woman and locked eyes on her. Claire went to the far end of the room to get to a phone, while Jack studied his captive. With the hood pulled back, Jack could see a woman, no older than the student-hosts offering the summer tastings. She had a black tee on under the hoodie and wore black tights and runners. Her glaring eyes and lips sported black makeup and the young woman's dark hair was short and spiky. Jack felt he'd met her before, somewhere…

He started in on the stranger, not holding back. Jack pointed down the room to Claire, who was holding a red-stained towel to the wound as she spoke on the phone. "D'you see that young lady? I'd go through a lot to keep her safe and, having failed that, I'm all about punishment. Applying truculence to the situation. Do you know what that word means? It means, I am so damned mad at you for what you did to her, if you say one wrong word to me, I'll end up in jail for the hammering I'll administer, got it?"

She said nothing. Instead, he could see her core begin to tremble.

"I think we understand one another. Now. The police will arrive, sooner or later, but I have at least fifteen minutes alone with you. I'm not police, so I have no compunction about stepping over the line, Missy. Let's begin with why you are visiting in the middle of the night." He leaned in, his nose almost touching hers.

"I-I don't have to tell you anything."

"No you don't. Especially not with a witness in the room, right?"

The trembling subsided, just a little, and Jack smiled. The smile, however, hardened, not having reached his eyes. He raised his voice. "Claire, why don't you step out, just for a minute. If you hear anything, I expect it's just this unwise young woman tripped on a hose, or something."

The woman's eyes widened. "No! Don't leave! I'll tell you why."

"Why?" Claire had just returned, a puzzled look on her face.

"Why she's here, in the night. Destroying something else. Go on, then. Speak up, before I lose patience."

"I've been doing things for a friend."

They studied the woman more closely. Claire gasped, pointing to her face. "*Je la connais. Elle travaille pour nous. Jack! Dieter l'a embauchée il y a un peu de temps.*" (I know her. She works for us. Dieter hired her a little while ago.")

Jack continued. "A friend, eh? Which friend might this be, then?"

"Kurt. Dieter's son." This revelation elicited another quick intake of breath from Claire. "I've been seeing him for some time, and he was telling me how that Donovan man stole the winery from his parents. Don't deny it! You're all in it against Kurt's family." Her voice was bitter. "Have been from the start. So I asked him how I could help."

Jack and Claire sat there, speechless. "What the hell!" "*C'est fou.*" (That's crazy.) They tripped over each other's words.

The woman twisted within her confines, raging. "Donovan waited until the Schmidt family was in financial trouble, and then he swooped in and stole the winery away from them. And this was after they took him in and trained him and everything. He's the bad guy, not me." She continued to speak, her tone not quite as manic. "You know, Dieter—Mr. Schmidt— won't arrest me. He'll understand I did all this for him, for his son."

Jack stared at her, trying to comprehend the reasoning, but then remembering what was important. "Perhaps you're right, Miss." Now it was Claire's turn to stare at Jack in disbelief, but he continued as if unaware of the incredulous looks sent to him from his young colleague.

"You began by pulling up the dozen grapevines by the road, correct? What did you do with them?" Jack sensed the young lady was impressionable and was parroting ideas hammered into her, probably by

Kurt, from his hospital bed. Could he acquire an exact tally of the trouble she'd caused? He was going to try.

"I threw them away. They were evidence, so I drove over to Line Three and tossed them into a ditch. Then I swept the truck so the dirt wouldn't incriminate me."

"I see. And the white crystals in the lab...?"

"Salt. Kurt said there was no need to ruin all the vats. All I had to do was toss a cup in one barrel and that would be enough. He said she—" the woman pointed at Claire, offering up a sneer, "...would probably over-react and throw out everything, and we had a laugh about how you would destroy your own winery."

"And of course the next thing was the—" Jack left the words go unexpressed, hoping she'd complete the sentence.

She did. "Yeah, the next thing was tonight. I was going to open the spigots and let the vats run out. It would have been funny, seeing fifteen, twenty-two thousand liter vats used as floor dye. I laughed when Kurt told me that one. But before I got started, I got interrupted." She glared at Claire, who moved her chair back, just a bit.

Jack feigned puzzlement. "I don't understand. Whose idea was this? You mention Kurt, but you seem to be the one doing all the work. Who's the boss, really? You see—" he grinned, a patient look on his face, "—I need to know who's going to jail for destroying a million dollars' worth of product and equipment. So...is it you running the show, or might you just be following instructions?" Before she had a chance to answer, a siren could be heard in the distance. Claire murmured Dieter told her he'd be at the door, waiting to let them in.

Jack patted the young felon on the shoulder. "Best get your thoughts in order, Missy. Who should go to jail, a young lady trying to help a friend, or a criminal with his mind set on destroying the livelihood of fifty people? Something to think about. Ah, here are our friends the police. Claire? Let's go get you cleaned up."

Chapter 28

St. Andrews By The Sea

RILEY PARKER STARED AT BETH McLean across an untouched plate of coquille St-Jacques. Beth returned the favor, looking without speaking. Riley picked up her fork, moving a fat scallop through the silky white sauce, but not lifting it. "I don't know why your nose is bent out of shape. You're not the one being hunted by a murderer." The women had ordered a late lunch on the patio of the Duchess Inn on Water Street in St. Andrews. Beth had spent the previous three hours tracking Riley down and neither was pleased with each other at the moment.

Noting the younger woman's peeved look, Beth tried very hard to avoid the sound of a teacher's voice. She swept a straight feather of auburn hair back behind one ear and leaned over the plate to keep her voice low. "I told you I can't watch your back if your back is running down every dark alley, shouting 'Hello, Mister Murderer, here I am, unprotected.'"

"Backs don't shout, and it's the middle of the day." The dark cloud above the young woman's forehead seemed to lighten, just a touch.

"Really? This is that wonderful opportunity to correct my metaphors? You're driving me to drink, girl." Beth sipped on a glass of water, wondering what else she could say. Her eyes drifted to a table of bottles sitting on ice. The label behind the bottles read: "St. George Water, the best-tasting in the world." *It's funny how the most inconsequential thoughts pop into your head when you least need them.*

"Look. You've clearly chosen to ignore the advice of the police, your dad, and me—" Riley rolled her eyes at that, "—which leads me to two contradictory next steps. You seem bound and determined to get to the murderer before they get to you, so I can either give up and let you go get yourself killed, or I can persuade you to let me come along. What's it gonna be, girl?"

Riley's face crumpled in defeat. "I just want to be doing something. I can't just sit and...wait. Ever hear the expression sitting target? Fish in a barrel? Target on your back? I've got a dozen of 'em, and they all refer to me. I know Dad and I are the prime suspects. I've watched enough detective shows to know where they look first. But I didn't kill anyone. Dad didn't. I'm...I'm sure of it. The police were by yesterday to see me, and it wasn't a social call. But if they're waiting for me to kill again—" she shuddered, "—then they're not focusing on taking care of me. So *I* have to take care of me, do you know what I'm saying?" She exhaled that same sigh every misunderstood young adult ever breathed.

"Look, I get it. But Jack had to deal with a crisis back in Niagara. And Donovan is working your case from the source of the trouble. And your dad, smart as he is, doesn't have the skill set in this case to do something about this. We're kind of a little under-staffed right now, with just you and me, and I'm not a fool. People get hurt every day, walking into the goo, thinking everyone is a nice guy and do-overs are available if you get in over your head. No. If you're going to risk my life, we have to have a plan, we have to take care of each other, and we have to come out of this alive. Mostly, I want you to pay attention to that last point; call me selfish."

Riley nodded, eyes pointing down to her plate.

Beth leaned in even closer, her food now stone cold. "Here's what we know. Both murders happened to Americans, on or near the water in St. Andrews. Tricia's body was probably dumped in as the tide was going out of Katy's Cove. Harry was brutally beaten to death, so someone either hated him, or they may have psycho tendencies. Both victims have ties to the Parker family, and both carried secrets to their graves. And here's what we can infer: trouble was swirling around and sticking to Harry like poop in a blocked toilet.

"Finally, every extended conversation around the case seems to touch on the world of art, somehow. And yes, we can also infer that you and/or your father are marked for...trouble." She got up and rounded the table to sit alongside Riley, leaning in so their temples touched. "If you have anything else to add—anything at all—Sweetie, you've got to tell me before we walk into Harry's toilet simile, except for real."

Riley sat still, her face a study in concentration. Finally, she glanced to her right and left, before speaking. "Let's pay the bill and go for a walk out on the wharf."

They passed the Scottish Woolens shop to their left and continued toward the pier, Beth keeping her eyes on the wide creosoted wharf planks just ahead. "Glad to see you're being discreet. This is good."

"I'm young and I don't know everything, but I do know a few things; for instance, that microphones can record a conversation from across the street. That's why pitchers talk into their gloves when they're working out a play with the catcher."

"You a ball fan? Yankees, I suppose."

"Yes, I'm a fan, but I like Detroit. I was a Red Sox fan, but that almost got me disowned. So…Go Tigers!" She offered an embarrassed smile, conceding that baseball small talk was inappropriate in a life-and-death scenario. Beth put an arm over her shoulder, and they continued walking.

A damp breeze had come up over the water, discouraging tourists from walking the wharf. It was high tide, and the occasional swat of wave on pilings sent little spits of salt spray up onto the wharf floor. They spied one boat with fishermen on it; the remaining few craft appeared to be unoccupied. The women sat on a bench, observing two men washing the deck of a forty-two foot lobster boat.

Riley nodded to it as the boat bobbed slightly, just fifteen yards away. "See that boat?"

"The *Mary-Ann*? Of course."

"See where it's registered?"

"It says it's registered out of here. St. Andrews." Beth turned sideways on the park bench to face her companion. "Where are you going with this?"

"I'll tell you in a minute. But first, I want to point out another boat. Farther out, by the turny-bend in the wharf? See the last boat, right at the corner?" Beth nodded.

"That's named the *Devil's Due*. It's registered out of the town of Machiasport, Maine. Everybody calls it Machias, though. It's a Canadian boat, with Canadian workers, but the owner has dual citizenship and works out of a Canadian dock. But. It's easier for that one—" she pointed at the *Devil's Due*, "—to skip across the channel than that one." She then pointed to the *Mary-Ann*. "Now, I have a story to tell, with these two boats being the punchline. I'm sorry I didn't trust you enough to share this earlier. But it's kind of breezy here. Let's go to the pub and talk there. At this time of day, we'll be able to find a quiet corner."

* * * *

They entered the Red Seal and ordered draft beer. It being late afternoon on a weekday, they had their choice of seating. The server brought their glasses over to a spot by the wall where they could chat in private, as well as see all of the comings and goings, of which there were none.

Riley took a sip, mostly foam, and sat back to begin. Beth thought the tangle of striking red curls surrounding the young woman's head was glorious and made Riley appear to be even younger than her twenty-plus years. Her youthfulness did, however, contrast with the solemn look on the young woman's countenance.

Riley started. "I've always hated Harry, ever since I was a kid. I didn't even have a reason, back then, other than that vibey-thing I felt. He just seemed one of those people who…who you just knew faced temptation on a regular basis and every single time gave in to it unless someone was watching. Father always said 'Give him a chance, he's family,' but I never trusted him. Erin was always giving him a break, too, and I never understood that, because she was always good to me. Well, if not good, she was at least fair. Ike, who was married to Erin, well, he was an out-and-out asshole. Just the scum of the earth. We were so happy when he left, even if it was with a pillowcase full of Parker money. Good riddance to bad rubbish, right? But the thing is, he left behind a souvenir, in my opinion. Harry. And I think they were…"

"Cut from the same cloth?"

Riley smiled. "Exactly. Harry might not have been as obvious in his awfulness, but it was there. I once heard a friend describe two boys I knew. She said one was a bad boy trying to be good, and the other was a good boy, trying to be bad. With Ike and Harry, I thought it was more like one was bad and couldn't hide it, and the other could sometimes hide it." She shuddered. "So, after the body was found—my...my mother—I looked around at all the possibilities, and around every corner, all I could see was Harry.

"He said he wasn't in town at the time of the murder. But just because he didn't show up until a few days later, didn't mean he wasn't around, or had someone who was around." Riley looked away, through the window to the bay, and the American shore off in the distance. Her green eyes moistened, and she blinked to hold back the tears. Beth patted her arm, and they paused for a moment.

"I decided that day to uncover him. That was my mission. I'd dog him until he coughed up...something, I didn't even know what I was looking for. A clue, I suppose." She smeared errant droplets across the back of her hand. "Every time he left the grounds, I'd scoot up to his apartment—he didn't have the nerve to install his own locks on Father's building—and I'd look around. I didn't get far at first, because I was too careful to leave everything in the same place I'd found it.

"In fact, I wasn't getting anywhere. In frustration, and anger, I suppose, I went up one evening as soon as his old rattletrap truck dragged itself out of the driveway, and I took the place apart. I started with the usual places: under and behind the furniture, under the cushions and even under the mattress. All I found was some porn, which was no surprise.

"I kept digging, and found it in the cookbook drawer. Funny thing, I find it, and the next day, when I go back, it's not there! I never found it again."

Beth's bottom had crept to the edge of the seat, her mouth poised to accept a sip of beer, but the glass had frozen in mid-air. "What was it? Where did it go? What did it say? What the hell?"

Riley's eyes sparkled, her mind clearly entranced by the allure of the chase. "It was a notebook. I had it in my hands, and next thing you know...

gone! But Nick didn't raise no fool. I photographed the pages I thought I needed and read them later, so I could digest them properly. The thing is, what I read wasn't clear. If it wasn't a confession, what did I have, really? So I had to, um, interpret what I had."

Beth quieted. In a lower tone, she locked eyes on Riley and asked a different set of questions. "What do you intend to do with these images? Why don't I have them already? The police…"

The young woman squirmed. "I know, right? If ever there was evidence to a crime, this is it. But I needed to know if—my dad…may have been implicated. I know! It's a terrible thing, to suspect your own father. But I couldn't be sure. Everyone so far who was involved, living and murdered, was in some way or other a Parker. And as I looked around me…"

Beth finished the thought. "You knew you didn't do it and when Harry got whacked, the list of suspects dwindled considerably. And if you're looking at Parkers, the list dwindles down to Nick, effectively."

Riley nodded, solemn, as Beth finally took a sip of her beer. Then they both spoke at once.

"When can I see them?" and "Would you like to see them?"

Beth put up both hands in surrender. "Yes, please. And is now a good time? Because now works for me. Send it to me so I can have it on my phone."

Riley retrieved her phone and, a couple of taps later, both were studying the images from the three pages on their respective phones. The first appeared to be an inventory list of books of poetry, or pieces of art. The second was a list of names, with addresses or phone numbers scrawled beside each. Beneath the list of names, Harry had indicated a number of dates, beginning a month earlier, the last inscription dated July twenty-seventh, two days from now. She noted a certain name, resting alongside a certain date and tried to hide her emotions from Riley.

She'd heard that name before, from Donovan's lips. Palu. Feelings of dread coursed up and down her spine.

"I'd love to print this off, as well as to send it to Donovan. He knows how to read the mysterious stuff. Can we do that?"

Riley nodded. "But, don't you want to hear the end of my story?"

Beth responded, stricken. "Oh, my God! Yes. Of course."

Riley pointed toward the end of the wharf. "Remember my pointing to the two boats out at the end of the dock? One of the names on the list you just saw is a guy by the name of Billy MacLeod. It turns out, he's the captain of the second boat we looked at. The one with the registration out of Machias. He's the man I've been following for the past three days."

Beth grabbed her arm. "What? You've been following a possible murder suspect? Alone?" She stared at the younger woman as if she she'd grown a second head. "Why didn't you call me to help?"

"I had to find out if he was somehow connected to my father. I had to!"

Beth locked onto her gaze. "And did you?"

Riley looked uncomfortable. "So far, I've found no connection to my father, but that's not the same as finding evidence that clears him, right? And this also compounds my crime of hiding evidence...the longer I hold these three pages, the more trouble I expect I'll be in.

"Anyway, back to the story. I'm beginning to get desperate. I'm worrying about that final date on the third page. It's a day and a half away and MacLeod doesn't seem to be doing anything but drink, when he's not on the boat.

"But there's one more thing. I got caught." Riley continued before Beth had a chance to do anything but gasp. "Last night, I was sitting as far away from MacLeod as I could, but still trying to overhear anything he might say, when I got a tap on the shoulder. It was a guy I'd seen before, from MacLeod's boat. It was one of his crew, a guy from Bocabec by the name of James Orr. He nodded for me to step outside, so after he left, I got up and followed him." She became defensive. "It's downtown St. Andrews, right? Nobody's gonna do anything to me on Water St., so I took a chance. Besides, I was busted. I had to do anything I could to avoid being noticed by MacLeod. The two thoughts running through my head were to hope this guy wasn't protecting his captain and to try to call you.

"But I just didn't have time. So out I went."

Beth sat waiting, fear for her new friend washing over her.

"I stepped out of the door and he'd sort of disappeared, so I looked up and down the street and couldn't spot him, and this was the scary part. When I finally spied him, he was across the open area, over by the cabins where they sell whale-watching tours. Which is fine during the day, but a bit lonely at night. Anyway, once you start something...

"Off I went. I stopped a safe distance from him and waited. He motioned for me to come closer and I shook my head. I can run really well, but if he got hold of me, I'd be in trouble. So I waited. Finally, he took a few steps out of the shadows.

"He asked me why I was following MacLeod, which I denied. He just looked at me, because he knew I was lying. Then, I told him I was attracted to MacLeod, and thought I might like to get to know him. Ironically, he bought that lie right away." She cast a knowing look toward Beth. "Men, right? Now, here's the funny part: all he wanted was to tell me MacLeod was a bad man. A very bad man that people shouldn't get to know. He said it wasn't safe at all, because he was capable of anything." Riley whispered the last word.

"He didn't say anything else?"

"He said 'It's your life, girl.' Just before I took off—because I was starting to become even more freaked, I asked him if he knew a fellow named Harry Rafuse. He said no, but there was this Frenchman hanging around MacLeod. The man had a cane."

Palu. Jesus, Jesus. I don't have a good feeling about this. At all.

Nodding, Beth patted Riley's hand. "So you got the hell out of there."

"Yes. That was last night. Now what? Do you think Mr. Orr told Mr. MacLeod about me? From what he said last night, and the way he said it, I think Mr. Orr's as afraid of him as I am."

Beth thought for a moment. "If we give the images to the RCMP, they'll take over following MacLeod. But if MacLeod is after something —" *and, based on our man Palu showing up unannounced, MacLeod is absolutely after something,* "—then, we have one day to figure all this out. I suggest we hand the images over, first thing tomorrow."

Riley's eyes narrowed. "You think MacLeod is after something. Is he the one who's trying to kill Dad and me?"

"Maybe. But I think it's more likely Tricia and Harry were killed because they somehow got in between MacLeod and whatever it is he's looking for. And he may not be working alone. In fact, I think he isn't."

Riley tried pressing Beth for details, but because everything was speculation at this point, she demurred. Riley had an appointment with the owner of the Rossmount Inn, so they agreed to meet at nine that evening, to recommence shadowing Captain Billy MacLeod.

Before returning to the Rossmount, Beth paid a visit to the new friend she'd met at the artists' reception the previous Friday. A few minutes later, she parked Donovan's sensible gray rental down the street by the liquor store, and walked back up the water side of the street in the late afternoon sunshine. She pushed open the door to the quiet gallery owned by Carlos Joba. He greeted Beth with a two-fisted shake that enveloped her small hand and drew her over to a pair of upholstered chairs that had been placed by the window. She noted he was wearing another Hawaiian shirt, and his sunglasses were again nestled in his jet-black, curly hair. It was clear he embraced island life, no matter where the location. "Coffee?" She shook her head, and he poured himself an espresso, smiled, and joined her.

"The lovely Beth, half of the charming team of Beth and Sean. What brings you here on this incredible summer day?"

Beth smiled an apology. "You know I have the best interests of the Parker family at heart, don't you? As I know you have, as well."

The broad smile on Carlos' face dimmed just a little. "This sounds a little more serious than I had hoped. Yes, I agree, you have their interests at heart, and Nick has said that to me since we first met. How can I help?"

Beth glanced around the room, including the spacious glass walls facing the bay, and began. "I believe Riley's life may be in danger." She raised a hand to forestall any questions. "She refuses to hide in her room, waiting for the case to be solved. Two of her relatives have been murdered in the past week. Because she has this—desire to help, I, of course, have begun following her, and in some instances, accompanying her. This is dangerous work, and I'm feeling particularly vulnerable without any, well, weapons on me.

"I don't want a gun, but something small and aggressive just might make a difference. I realize I don't know you well, and you're within your rights to shoo me out the door without saying another word. But in my recent past, I've come to realize that my life might be saved if I had the smallest element of surprise in my back pocket, something I could defend myself with. Can you think of anything—anything at all—that I could carry to reduce our chances of getting killed if we're caught or ambushed?"

Carlos sat for a long minute, all traces of his smile vanished. Finally, he stood up. "Wait here." And he was gone.

The gallery owner was away for almost five minutes before she heard the private door to his residence open. He carried a canvas bag in one hand, his face filled with purpose. He returned to his seat, and leaned forward, opening the bag to reveal a compact wooden box. To begin, he placed it on the coffee table between them. The cover back, Beth peered in to reveal…a toy!

"Um, I'm not sure…this is—"

He grinned. "It is not exactly what you had in mind? What are you going to do with a four-inch toy, right? But, what if I told you it is a scale model crossbow, and it actually works? It has two bolts, each one holding a serious irritant on the tip. If you had a moment to set it up and fire it, you would have a very distracted person on your hands. And here's the second weapon. It doesn't look like much, does it?"

Beth held out her hand and Carlos handed her a small screwdriver. *A screwdriver?*

Reading her thoughts, he said it aloud. "Yes, a screwdriver. Note the small handle, the drilled hole in the end, and the relatively short length." He paused, pulling a silver chain from his pocket. "If one were to drop this nineteen-inch chain through the end of the screwdriver, and place the chain on your neck, the screwdriver would sit discretely, um…" His grin broadened.

She tried it on, and the tool rested, unobtrusive, between her breasts.

"Note the chain—"

"Yes. I can snap it off my throat in one second. Perfect."

Carlos looked uncomfortable. "I have one more trick. Before I offer it, can you once again assure me you have Nick's best interests at heart?"

In response, she handed him her cell phone. "Absolutely. Please give Nick a call, and ask him about me, without revealing I am now 'armed,' so to speak. You will surely receive an endorsement from him." Beth looked at the canvas bag, eagerness on her face.

The gallery owner peered into the bottom of the bag and pulled out a stubby marker, half the length of a typical pen. "Be careful of this one. It contains pepper spray; the technical name isoleoresin capsicum. It's not very accurate, but up close, I wouldn't want to be on the receiving end of this spray. Just make sure it's pointed at him and not at you."

Beth turned it end-for-end. "I'm not trying to stereotype this part of the country, but wouldn't something like this normally have bear spray in it?"

Carlos nodded. "Yes, but if it was to be actually used as a bear spray, it would be stored in a snub-nosed pistol with a fat barrel, not this tiny thing. And pepper spray is actually more concentrated than bear spray. No, this is the one for you, my darling." He demonstrated how to hold it, how to activate it and, with a shrug, told her these were his best ideas, for better or for worse. "And now it's time for cheesecake, no? I make mine with ricotta and blackberry compote."

Beth thought about refusing, but the memory of the cold, abandoned lunch that had been filled with creamy scallops and white wine sauce weakened her will, and she surrendered to "a thin slice, please."

* * * *

Back at the Rossmount, Beth carried a tall glass of milk and a toasted Portobello-and-sundried tomato sandwich up to the second floor, pulling up a fat, comfy chair to the window overlooking Passamaquoddy Bay. As she ate, she noted the deer wandering through the mid-July raspberry bushes at the residence between the inn and the bay, and waited.

Her sandwich finished, Beth sipped on the milk until it, too, had disappeared. Still no call. A dozen glances at her cell phone and at last she willed it to ring, opening the line before it had completed its first ring. "Are you safe? Why haven't you phoned? Did you get the three pages I sent you?"

Donovan's voice carried over the line; patient, calm, music to Beth's ears. "Wait, wait, please. I couldn't call until now, but just know I'm finished up here for now. I'm on my way home. Tomorrow we can start fresh, okay?"

"No. Not okay, Sean. Tomorrow we have to give everything over to the police or risk getting arrested. I'm not sure you'll like being married to a jailbird, Sweetie."

Beth could hear the laughter in his voice. "What's the alternative? I can be there in a few hours, which means the middle of the night. What's happening that can't wait?"

"I sent you three images from Harry Rafuse's notebook. They have not been shared with the RCMP and when they are, I'm vulnerable to a charge of withholding evidence. Worse, if that's possible, I'm pretty sure Riley and I will be cast aside and they'll take over."

After a pause, Donovan began again. "Would that be so bad, to ride the bench on this round? It sounds like the safer route. MacLeod appears to be a tough cookie, and I should have mentioned this as soon as I spotted Palu in St. Stephen, but—"

"You saw him and didn't tell me? I'm aware of how much he hates you, so which of us were you trying to get killed; you or me?"

She noted a greater length to the pause that followed her words. "I thought I'd be home in time to sort this out without you or anyone from the Parker family getting drawn in. Look; give me just a few more hours and I'll be there. If you want to be involved, we can tackle this together. But for God's sake, keep Riley from doing anything foolish."

Beth sighed. "Wish me good luck with that. She's convinced the police are sure it's Nick, and she won't be placated. I'm afraid I'm going to have to start without you. I'll ping my location every step. What have you learned that could help me?"

"I'll be quick. Harry was a piece of shit who deserved what he got. He might have been in cahoots with Erin's ex, Ike, who may or may not be in the picture. Palu is cruising around St. Stephen-St. Andrews, and there is a large shipment of art, much of it owned by Nick, that has conveniently disappeared from New York. I won't be surprised if it's in a Maine coastal town, probably Eastport, waiting to find its way into Palu's clutches. In fact, we have to be on the lookout for your sailor MacLeod and for Palu, and they might just be together with or without Ike when you find them. So just watch your step."

"Why do you think the art is in Maine?"

"A conversation with Erin, together with the images from Harry's notebook."

"Ah. So you studied them."

"Yes, I did. Here's what I got from them. Harry knew Palu, and Harry knew MacLeod. Obviously, he's known Ike for some time, them being relatives of sorts. It appears there's a connection between Harry and Eastport, Maine. And he named some dates. Unfortunately, too many for me to narrow down to the exact one. Pull up the images on your phone. See the dates in the second picture? Harry scribbled down a half dozen days, all right around today. However, he also wrote some words alongside of them, such as fog, moonlight, tide times, rain, something about B's Mood, and lobster season. It looks to me as if there's a specific date they need, in order to accomplish something, but there are factors—variables—that will come into play to decide that date.

"Now that I know there's a shipment of artwork involved, and Palu is in town, I'm guessing the artwork is trying to make its way from New York State to Charlotte County, and then on to Montreal. The problem is, Eastport doesn't just have a single warehouse, so the boxes could be in any one of a hundred storage buildings and fishing sheds anywhere along the coastline between Calais and Machias. Campobello Island would seem to be perfect for smuggling, given that it's jointly owned by Canada and the US, but that's also the reason it's patrolled so heavily.

"But since we don't have an address…"

Donovan finished the thought. "…We need MacLeod to take us there, or we need to greet him upon his return."

"Which is the safer of the two options. Yes, let's have him lead us to the artwork, but let's stay in Canada if we can. It sounds like we have a plan. Sean? Please get here as fast as you can. Oh! Riley's messaging me. She says MacLeod is on the move. I gotta go now." She ended the call, wishing he'd already returned to New Brunswick.

Chapter 29

Niagara On The Lake

JACK MILLER SANK BACK INTO a leather club chair in the George Bernard Shaw Room, one of the multi-purpose rooms below ground at the Plenitude Wine Estate. He sat across from Dieter Schmidt, wondering if there could possibly be a more somber and worried look on a man's face. Dieter's wife, Anna, was absent, having accompanied Claire to the hospital. The EMT had told Claire it was a probable concussion and that the doctor would possibly close the gash with eight to ten stitches. Satisfied he could do no more for Claire at that moment, he sat down with Donovan's partner in Plenitude, and together, they focused their attention on the youthful break-and-enter assailant and the upheaval she'd caused the Schmidts and everyone around them.

Jack sat, his eyes narrowed to slits, waiting for Dieter to gather his thoughts before opening the conversation. At one point, Dieter raised his eyes and Jack knew he was as ready to hear this as a father could be.

"Jack, what happened?"

He didn't try to soften the information. "The young lady confessed. In her statement, which the police are taking down as we speak, she says Kurt put her up to it. Essentially, she says he convinced her that Sean had stolen the winery from you. That Sean had to pay for this, and the best way would be to ruin the winery."

At this, Dieter lowered his face into his hands. "But that would also ruin us! All of us! That's crazy." He paused for a moment. "I can't believe Kurt was involved in this. He never left his bed for months. What did she say she'd done? Did she tell you what the extent of the...damage was?"

"There were three discrete events. The first, as you know, was the destruction of a dozen vines over by the road. She dug them up and threw them away, with no chance of recovering them alive. The second time, she dropped some salt into a barrel, ruining the contents, which was just under two hundred liters. The good news here is the damage was limited to that one cask. Tonight, she was going to open the spigots on the vats and cover the floor with the wine waiting to be bottled. This would have been the major act of destruction. Claire caught her red-handed this time, though, and she paid a price."

"I'm so sorry. I'm just…I can't even absorb all this."

"Clearly it's not your fault, Dieter. Your son must have been traumatized by his year-long illness and the impact it's had on himself and on your family. He really doesn't even know Donovan all that well, so it wasn't hate or resentment. It must have been built up from all those months, lying in a bed. At the moment, it's the word of a very immature young lady, but she seemed sincere. She may have believed she was helping her friend without actually telling him what she was up to. I don't know. A pair of RCMP officers are over at the hospital, interviewing Kurt, and others have the young lady at the detachment headquarters, taking her statement. They'll get to the bottom of this, and then we'll know which way the wind is actually blowing."

At the mention of his son being questioned, Dieter jumped up and paced back and forth. "I've got to go…be with my son. But before I leave, let me take a moment to thank you for helping me get through this. May I ask one more question?"

Jack nodded.

"What is Donovan going to say? He'll hate me for this. How will I ever be able to meet his eyes?"

Jack frowned. "To begin with, he knows you are not your son. Secondly, he knows your son has had the worst year of his young life. On the one hand, nothing got ruined; on the other hand, poor Claire has received physical trauma, together with a considerable shock. And they came within a hair's breadth of ruining an entire winery. So, I don't know. But you should go be with your son. Call me if you want to ask me any questions you may have, after you've spoken to your son.

"In the meantime, I'll fire off a brief note to Sean, without details, telling him the case seems to be resolved here." He twisted in his chair. "I saw the sun peeking up just before we came downstairs, and I haven't been to sleep yet, so I'm going upstairs to have a nap. Wake me if you need anything, otherwise, we'll chat over dinner. I'm going to bed."

Chapter 30

St. Andrews

"GET IN." RILEY'S CONVERTIBLE HAD decelerated so abruptly, Beth was surprised the tires didn't screech. She sat, impatience written all over her as Beth climbed in. They started down the long, sloping driveway of the Rossmount Inn. Instead of turning right to head into town, Riley careened left, and the rear end of the car dipped, tires chirping as she punched the accelerator.

"What's going on? Isn't this the way to Saint John, and when did you get your car back?"

"Thalie finally picked up her new car, and we're not going that far. My new snitch friend James sidled up to me at the Red Seal and told me his worker Devin just took the *Devil's Due* out. MacLeod never loans his boat, according to James, but supposedly he's delivering it to a place in Bocabec. He didn't know why MacLeod isn't taking it there himself, but James says MacLeod will be picking it up from there. Doesn't it sound to you like MacLeod is getting ready to take a boat trip?"

"It's possible. What are you thinking of doing, once we get there? This car doesn't drive on water, so it's going to be dicey, tailing them."

Riley gave her a look and then focused back on the highway, which was being eaten up in great leaps by the small, powerful convertible. "I'm not crazy. Imagine being on a boat with a murderer. What do you suppose would happen to us? My thinking is, we go to where he's picking up his boat, watch him leave as he heads out of the bay and we figure out as best we can what course MacLeod has set. Then we do one of two things. If we're optimistic, we sit and wait back at the wharf until he returns, which should be in the middle of the night. Or, we wait until he's out of sight and we call the Coast Guard."

"And what would we tell the Coast Guard?"

"We'd tell them the *Devil's Due* is on its way over to Maine to pick up contraband, and it'll be crossing back into Canadian waters before dawn. It's the truth."

"What if we're wrong?"

"In a worst case scenario, they'll get him for leaving the country without checking in with Customs. But I know he's off to get the art. The thing is, we have to get there in time to see him leave. This'll be all about timing. And look how it's beginning to cloud over. So, he'll be scooting along the border between Grand Manan and Machias in the dark of night, plus clouds and maybe fog and rain." She stared up at the black-bottomed clouds, scudding in from the east. "No wonder he picked this evening."

Beth sat back as Riley picked up the pace. She noted the car was ascending hills more than easing down the inclines. The tires began to protest with each corner, but Beth's mind was elsewhere. Where was Donovan now? Did he catch his flight? When would he show up? Perhaps in time to receive the boat upon its return? *This business of analyzing everything is a waste of time. How can I be useful, right this minute?* She took out her phone and pinged her location, noting the time, and then sent him a message to advise him of their intention. And she checked her weapons: the crossbow, the pepper spray, and the tiny screwdriver. All of a sudden, they seemed so…paltry. She moved the spray to her shoe, tucking it on the inside between her anklebone and her heel. Finally, she placed a gentle hand on Riley, encouraging her to drop the speed a notch.

"I'm cool with you being a speed demon, Sweetie, but we actually do need to get there in one piece. Besides, the last thing we need is to get pulled over. How much farther will it be to get us to the shore?"

In reply, Riley leaned on the brake and jerked right, into a fresh new subdivision that had been cut right out of the forest. As they eased along the road, Beth noted driveways slipping discreetly into wooded lots that revealed very little of the estates within. She also noted there were very few driveways, indicating large and very private lots. The car swooped down curves that cut through rock face, and arced back upward, only to angle around a steep corner. A quarter of a mile in, they executed one last curve and found themselves in a tiny, pebbled parking lot sporting a sign advising that the beach was private.

"I don't see a beach. We're in the middle of the woods. But I know this place. We know this place. It's the main path to the place where the police found Harry."

"That's right. Let's go. It's quite a ways to the shore." They'd just exited the car when they were startled by the headlights of a vehicle pulling in behind them. The truck ignition shut off and the wooded parking lot returned to quiet. Beth could hear the still-ticking engines cooling down. The doors to the truck opened, and she heard the unmistakable sound of a pistol cocked. Riley looked at her, unable to move.

"What have we here?"

Riley mouthed the name "MacLeod" to Beth, her eyes round. Beth was about to respond when she heard the passenger side door to the truck close. First one foot, then another hit the crushed rock of the lot. A second later, she heard a third sound. A cane.

Palu.

Beth knew from the presence of the gun that one of them—MacLeod, probably—had made Riley. She found her voice. "What we have is two women whose friends know where we are, meeting two strangers who haven't broken any laws. Yet." She stared through the arc of the headlights, trying to determine if the men were buying what she was selling. Her answer came in the form of a low chuckle, making the hackles rise on the back of her neck.

"I think you should come with us for a ride. It's a lovely boat, is it not, Mr. MacLeod?" The captain grunted and came around the car to gather up Riley.

Beth's heart sank. They were abandoning a deserted stretch of beach that could lead to a hundred American and Canadian places. Much worse, the man with the French accent wasn't being cautious about identifying his partner. *There's one reason why kidnappers don't care if they've been identified by their captives. They don't expect us to blab. This is bad.*

Palu's voice dropped a tone. "Quickly now. We have a tide to catch and we're losing light. Leave your purses in the car. You never know what mischief they might contain." MacLeod shut off the lights and left the truck parked right behind the car's bumper.

MacLeod pushed Riley ahead of him, driving the young woman hands and knees onto the crushed rock surface. He grabbed her by the hair but she rose without any assistance. Beth moved to walk alongside her, but got a gun barrel in the ribs for her trouble. Palu whispered: "I like single file. Let's do that." They headed toward an opening in the woods, leading to a set of weather-resistant stairs built in the style of park platforms. They took the first set of stairs, and by the time they were ten feet into the woods, they had dropped eight feet and the daylight from the open area of the parking lot diminished to the point where they had to watch where they stepped.

The pattern was similar the whole way down. For every ten feet forward, they dropped eight steps. By the time they could hear the first waves hitting the beach, Beth estimated they had descended a hundred feet. The tide was coming in, and the sand inhabiting the tiny cove had begun to be eaten up by the inexorable waves that rolled one after the other, closer with each uniform splash.

Beth couldn't see much in the waning light, but she did notice a single line of footsteps coming from a gray tender that was anchored at the water's edge. *Devin must have left them the boat. And he's gone.* A sense of isolation increased as she was nudged toward the boat. Feet in the frigid bay water and with one hand on the gunwale of the craft, she tried one more time. "If you force us into this boat, the whole thing goes from a misunderstanding to kidnapping. Is that what you want?" For her troubles, she felt the barrel of Palu's pistol crash against the side of her head. With a moan, she half-climbed, half-fell into the little craft, with Riley slipping over the side to sit alongside her.

Palu got in next, taking his time as MacLeod held the boat steady. Then he used a single oar to pole out to a buoy that rested halfway between the little tender and the fishing boat that sat in the now black water. He told Palu to grab the buoy and pull until a line appeared and then to grab the line. "No need to start the outboard if we don't have to. Gimme the line and I'll pull us out." Once they reached the *Devil's Due*, they took turns, Palu first, climbing an aluminum gunwale boarding ladder until all were aboard.

"Sit there and don't move." MacLeod stepped down below the forecastle and started the diesel, leaving all the running lights off. He set the engine to idle at seven hundred rpms and burbled in the general direction of the anchor. Once he got almost on top of it, he activated the winch and weighed anchor. Turning the boat around to face the open water, he eased his craft directly away from shore. Night had now dropped like a pebble into a well and it was not possible to see the older couple scramble down the last stairs to the tiny cove, staring as the *Devil's Due* pulled away from shore.

* * * *

"Hurry! Do you know how to use that thing?" John and Peggy Whiteway had just passed the Tim Horton's coffee shop at the outskirts of St. Andrew's, with Peggy driving and John navigating. Donovan had sent them Beth's GPS coordinates, based on her cell phone ping, and they were now chasing darkening highway past Chamcook Mountain, toward Bocabec. Peggy took a bump a bit faster than the car was designed for, earning a reproving look from her husband.

"The satellite is slow giving us a signal. Just keep driving until it catches up to us. It would be nice to arrive in one piece, Pegs."

"That's all good and fine, but if those girls have done something silly, every minute will count, you betcha."

"You do understand I have no gun, right? If we walk straight into something, all we'll be doing is crowding the whole kidnapping market. Have you ever tried hiding in the bushes, when there are no bushes to be had? You can't invent perfect hiding spots." John continued to grumble as they sped along. The GPS kicked in at some point, and they found themselves a mile from their end point.

John pointed to the entrance to a new subdivision as Peggy exclaimed: "It's a gated village! This is the sort of place I'd like to spend my summers, since we can't live Nick's lifestyle. I wonder how far we are from here to the beach."

"Not far, if we're looking for a lobster boat." John's voice was grim. "Now, slow down. We don't want to drive right up their behinds. Our job is to find them, figure out the situation, and get back to Donovan. If he can't get here fast enough, we're to call the authorities. But most important, we can't get caught. We're no good to anyone if we're caught."

"Or killed." Peggy's voice was small. She topped a crest and glided down the ensuing hill. Rounding a bend, they spied the parking lot with the two vehicles. She stopped their car in the middle of the road. "What do I do?" It came out as a whisper, still loud in the idling car.

"Pull a U-ey and park over there. If they're in that truck, they've already spied us. I'll go take a look, and if they grab me, you go get help. If the vehicles are abandoned, come quickly. This is the parking lot that takes folks to the beach, and if both vehicles are abandoned, we've got to see if they have the girls, or if the girls need backup. Watch for my signal."

"Look at you! All brave and in command." She gave him a somewhat forced smile of encouragement as he exited the car. In a second, he waved her over.

"Their purses are in the car. That suggests they left in a hurry. But the truck appears to have arrived after them. That's not good. Let's go!" John headed for the stairs, with Peggy right behind him.

They arrived at the bottom, out of breath and in near-darkness, to see the outline of a fishing boat on the horizon, barely a dot at this point, chugging northeast toward the lower end of Grand Manan Island. In front of them, the tide was no more than ten feet from the foot of the stairs, rising fast.

Peggy took a deep breath, letting it back out in pants. "What direction would you say they were headed?"

"I'd say they were headed south, toward Deer Island, maybe Grand Manan. Hard to say, since they could pull off at any point, maybe strike shore at Minister's Island. I'd be curious to know if they were going to circle Grand Manan, or if—"

"So…somewhere south, then. Let's get on the phone and have a chat with Sean. He'll know what to do."

"I agree. Then we have to call Nick."

"We can't call Nick."

John turned to face his wife. "And why not? She's his daughter. He'd never forgive us if anything happened to her and he wasn't even told she was gone."

They started back up the stairs, still huffing. "I understand, darling, but if you had two kidnap victims on board a lobster boat and a coast guard cutter was bearing down on you in the night, what would be the first thing you'd do?"

John stopped and turned again, his face stricken. "I'd weigh them down and toss them over the opposite side of the boat from the coast guard."

"That's right. Look. Let's talk with Sean, and see what he has in mind. But first, we'll get up these stairs and see what the girls left in the car."

At the top of the stairs, they noticed again how the truck must have arrived last, to have blocked the convertible so effectively. Peggy peered over the side of the car. "It's too dark. Can you fetch a flashlight?"

John returned in a moment, shining the light across the empty back seat and then sweeping the front from left to right, pausing at all the crannies. "Two purses. That's it." Peggy opened the glove box, noting nothing out of the ordinary.

Peggy opened the purses and found the tiny crossbow. "That's odd. Why would Beth carry a toy in her purse?"

John spoke up, his voice seeming loud in the still of the evening. "It's not a toy, it's a replica. I've seen images of these on-line. That actually works. I'm afraid it's here because Beth hoped she'd have it on her, if she was…"

"Taken."

John nodded. "Let's message Sean to call us. You can give him some of the information in the message, but nothing incriminating, in case he has to—"

She finished his thought. "In case he has to commit a crime to save her. He is capable of that. But he also seems to get the job done. Anyway, I catch your drift." Peggy had her phone out and was already texting, thumbs flying. In a moment, she looked up from the phone, crestfallen. "He's in mid-flight from Montreal. He won't arrive in Saint John for half an hour. Which leaves him more than an hour away."

"What does he say we should do?"

"He told us to sit still and to not tell anyone. He said telling Nick or the police now will get the girls back, but the men will get away with the murders. He needs to catch them with the art on the boat. Does that make any sense to you?"

He shook his head.

"Sean also said he told Beth what to say, to keep them safe. He says they have an ace in the hole. Now, whatever does that mean?"

"It means I'm going to age ten years in the next two hours. That's what it means. Come on, dear. Let's go wait near the wharf until we receive further instructions."

Chapter 31

BETH HUNKERED DOWN WITH RILEY on the deck beneath the portside gunwale of the *Devil's Due* and braced as she felt the throbbing of the Cummins diesel come to life. The throbbing matched the ache in her head from the assault by the gun barrel. MacLeod had jacked the engine up to cruise speed, and the craft cut the water like scissors through wrapping paper. A full, dark-sky mass of clouds had descended until they threatened to become a fog bank, but the lower barometric pressure kept the waters calm, and swells were non-existent.

Riley grasped Beth's arm at the bicep, refusing to let go. Palu stood by the captain, murmuring something, and Beth took the opportunity to tell the young woman what she needed to know. After confirming Riley knew exactly what to say and how to say it, Beth sat back, trying to establish where they were, where they were going, and what advantages she could conjure up.

Without being obvious, she touched her wrist to the hidden screwdriver, taking comfort she wasn't completely unarmed. At the same time, she felt the uncomfortable sensation of the tiny canister lying just behind the malleolus bone of her ankle. *Not much to scare someone with a gun, but they are something*. Beth decided to distract Riley, who had fallen silent.

"Sweetie, let's say we're travelling between Grand Manan and Maine. What would we see if it was a sunny day?"

Riley smiled at her, grateful for the distraction. "Well, we've just left Bocabec, and we're headed in that general direction, but we probably won't be going to Grand Manan, unless that is actually the destination. First off, we leave Big Bay, heading into the Passamaquoddy, which is a First

Nations word. Soon, on the port side—" she touched Beth's left arm "—you'll see Deer Island. But before that, we'd either bear left and scoot between the two big islands, or go hard right and travel along the international line between New Brunswick and Maine." Her brow furrowed. "I hope we don't go that way, especially on a cloudy night."

"Why not?"

"There are lots of rocks and shoals. And then there's the Old Sow."

"Old…?"

"Yeah." Riley's voice was dry. "Picture this: you've got a gigantic bay with miles and miles of water. It fills and empties twice a day with the tides. Now, make the entrance to that bay, The Bay of Fundy, quite narrow, so that countless millions of gallons of seawater rush through each time. Passage through that narrow opening has the water coming in so fast, it makes the highest tides in the world. Can you picture that?"

Beth nodded.

Riley continued, her voice low. "Okay, now, at the end of that insanely large bay is our smaller one, the Passamaquoddy, which is where the highest of the high tides are. In between Deer Island and Eastport, Maine is a spot, underwater, where these crazy tides hit a small mountain, at full speed. Twice a day. Underwater. So, just before high tide, which, remember, we are almost at now, all that water hits the mountain and causes a permanent whirlpool. The Old Sow is that whirlpool, about forty feet by a hundred and twenty feet, at its smallest."

Riley looked at Beth, her eyes straining in the darkness. "If that bastard scoots this boat between Deer Island and Eastport, and knowing we have to bypass all the shoals through that passage, we've basically got to shoot the whirlpool. I did it a few times, at low tide and in a slightly bigger boat, and it's just like being hit by a massive hammer—first one side, and then the other. MacLeod's an experienced pilot and since he has dual citizenship, he's plied the waters on both sides of the line. So he knows it as well as anyone." Her hand tightened on Beth's bicep. "But I've never shot the Old Sow in a boat this size."

Beth had to ask. "What if the boat doesn't make it all the way through?"

"Boats have been lost. Passengers have been thrown out."

Distracted by all this, Beth stared straight ahead, past the pair of curled ropes, to the other side of the boat. *How can I use this Old Sow as a weapon?* Over the side, she could just make out a ghostly shadow, the outline of slate rocky crag and then it was gone. *Where are we? And more important, where is Donovan?*

* * * *

Donovan grabbed his carry-on bag and hurried from the small commuter plane. A simple question ran through his mind as he headed from the tarmac to the lobby: Can I get *a chopper?* He'd made the request during the flight and would know the minute he landed. His last message from Beth contained her GPS coordinates. His last message from Peggy was to ask for additional instructions. Should they wait at the wharf? Call the Coast Guard? Tell Nick? He'd messaged her to wait at the wharf and to give him a couple of hours before notifying anyone. He had an idea...

Checking his watch, and noting the time the boat had left Big Bay, Donovan was satisfied with his decision that travelling by car just wouldn't get him there in time. The helicopter pulled away from Saint John airport at ten and headed west to St. Andrews, nose down and accelerating. He had twenty minutes to think. By the time he and the pilot rolled over Blacks Harbour, he'd decided what to do. A comment Jack had inserted into his report convinced Donovan what MacLeod's plans would be. He chose not to share them with John and Peggy, for fear they might walk into the middle of it all. If only he could chat with Beth, to reassure her he'd been thinking of her! In the meantime, he'd given them what he'd hoped was that critical, life-saving piece of information, but would the kidnappers believe it? Even as the chopper sped along, they began to cut through low-flying clouds. Would his pilot be obliged to abort the flight if the clouds thickened? Would he have to return to Saint John?

Donovan called the US State Troopers, introducing himself and explaining as much of the situation unfolding on Passamaquoddy Bay as he felt they needed. Then, he directed his pilot to pass over St. Andrews and head straight to Eastport, reassuring him the state troopers were waiting to welcome them. The pilot reached for his radio, but Donovan put his hand over the transmitter and cautioned him the boat with two kidnap victims had access to radio frequencies as well and the lives of two women would be snuffed out at the hint of trouble. The pilot nodded, a grim smile on his mouth, and the nose dipped once again, as he picked up additional speed.

Chapter 32

Between Deer Island and Eastport

"WHAT ABOUT THE ROCKS OFF Deer Island? The fog's like pea soup out here." Beth's back rested against the port side of the boat, Riley sitting on the same side, but closer to the bulkhead. Both men were under the standing shelter, MacLeod at the wheel and Palu talking without pause. Despite the need for privacy, the men dared to operate a single running light. A second weak beam illuminated the dash in front of the wheel, beside the navigational equipment: sonar, compass, and GPS.

Riley squirmed. "We're all but past Deer Island, except for the Point. Did you notice the engine sounding a bit differently, a ways back? The sound bouncing back off the island changes the tone a bit, lowering it, somehow. We're almost to Eastport, and we're about to pass The Old Sow, so hang on tight."

But there was no interaction with the mid-water whirlpool yet. Instead, the boat cut to half-speed, heading to starboard. Palu stopped nattering and shuffled back to the women, relying on his cane and the gunwale to keep from upsetting. Despite the relatively calm seas, it took almost a minute for him to traverse the six steps from the standing shelter to the aft area where Beth and Riley crouched.

He half-sat, half-leaned on a wooden crate used to house ropes and faced his captives, a shadowy smile on his face reflected in the light of the electronic equipment. "I'd like to begin by telling you how incredibly inconvenient it is to have you here. Of course, we're going to kill you soon, but it's only your good behaviour keeping you from going for a swim right this minute. Now, be good girls and hand over your credit and debit cards."

Beth's gaze never left his face. "Do you recall pushing us away from the car, back in Bocabec? The purses are still in the car. Sorry." She didn't muster an ounce of apology in her voice.

Palu's look darkened, if that was possible. "I should kill you right this second, but we're picking up some…Christmas presents. You are going to load the boat with them." His cane slashed down, taking a vicious swipe near Beth's foot, missing it by an inch.

"You don't want to kill us. We're too valuable to you." Riley had begun to parrot the lines Beth had rehearsed with her a half hour ago.

Palu placed the cane between his legs, leaning down a bit to rest his chin on his hands, which covered the top of the handle. He rubbed the thigh of his game leg, instrumentation light playing off the right side of his face. "I'll bite. Amuse me. What can you possibly say to convince me to let you live another hour?"

"You're about to stop near Route 190, on the highway to Eastport, right? You'll pull in and someone will be waiting for you with a truckload of wooden crates, filled with art. That art belongs to my aunt Erin, it's from her house in Montauk. Here's the thing—most of that art was purchased by my father, Nick, and given to Aunt Erin. Once she had all her money stolen, she sold a few of the originals and then bought some replica paintings. What some might call knock-offs, but you and I know them as forgeries."

"I know a forgery from the real thing." He spat the words out, and his thick French accent returned as a snarl. Beth watched the interplay, noting how tightly his hands were curled around his cane.

Beth waited, praying Riley would remember how to respond to this challenge. If they could prove their value to the men, they stood the slightest chance of getting off the boat alive. And if they could get to shore, Donovan would be there.

Hopefully, he would be there…

Riley then recited the next line she'd been fed by Beth. "I'm sure you know a lot. But how much is your reputation worth? One scam to the wrong buyer and your reputation would be in tatters. Word is, you've already suffered a setback to your…career." Her voice had softened, and carried with it just the smallest trace of mocking rebuke.

Outraged, Palu rose, his cane over his head. It dropped with a vicious whistle, catching Riley on the shoulder and forearm. At that moment, the *Devil's Due* was hit full bore by the force of the Old Sow, alternately freezing and lifting the craft. The assault brought home Riley's words: "the highest tides in the world running smack into the side of a mountain." Beth had pulled out the bear spray and as Palu lurched toward them, she caught him in the eyes. As if in slow motion, Palu half-stumbled, half flew over their heads. MacLeod, in full concentration to keep the boat going straight through the whirlpool, stole just a second to witness the women cowering down on the deck, as Palu appeared to launch himself, cane and all, over the side.

With the fog offering visibility of no more than twenty-five feet, they were able to watch Palu flail about, without being able to do a thing. Beth got up to toss a rope to the man who was already circling the drain. With a curse, MacLeod half-turned, a cocked pistol in one hand.

"Don't fucking move."

Beth sat beside Riley, staring as Palu surfaced once, twice and then left them, his eyes locked on Beth and his air bubbles mixing with sea foam. Turning, Beth checked to see the extent of Riley's injury inflicted by the cane.

With the right shoulder dropped, it was clear her collarbone had been shattered. Beth took off her hoodie, tied it above the opposite shoulder and fashioned a sling of sorts. She showed Riley how to cradle the vulnerable arm to minimize the pain, and they sat still as the craft powered out of the pull of the Old Sow and straight to the Maine shore. Minutes later, MacLeod cut the engine and dropped the anchor.

He pointed the gun at Beth. "Pull up the tender and get in. Wait for me, and don't start the outboard. I not only have a hostage, but you'd be full of holes before you could gun the throttle." He then hauled Riley to her feet and shoved the young woman into the trunk cabin below deck. He turned to face Beth. "Let's get going. We have more than a dozen crates to load, and I want it done in seven minutes."

MacLeod ignored the outboard and inserted small oars into the oarlocks. Beth hadn't rowed more than fifteen feet before the shore assumed shape through the fog. He made her course-correct to port and the tender made a whisper soft landing twenty feet from a laden pickup truck, its tailgate down. MacLeod waved the gun. Beth jumped out and headed up the beach sand to the truck.

A man, face partially obscured by a hoodie, stepped out from behind the truck, stubbed out a cigarette and grabbed the closest wooden crate from the back. He refused to make eye contact with Beth, so she continued up the bank and took another crate. On the second trip, she whispered, desperation in her words, MacLeod was going to kill her and her friend. Again, no eye contact. The zodiac managed to fit every crate on the second trip to the beach, and after doing a re-count, MacLeod passed a fistful of bills over to the man who disappeared into the truck and rode away, never having spoken a word.

Subdued waves splashed every three seconds, making little noise, and Beth wondered, if she shouted, would anyone be close enough at that time of night to come and save them? Aware of how empty that stretch of highway would be at this time of night and concluding there was no one out there, she moved to get back into the zodiac, but was greeted by a pistol.

"End of the line, darlin'. There's no more use for you, so there's no return ticket."

Beth stared, hands on her hips. "You may want to re-think this, jerk. For starters, Riley will not cooperate with identifying the forgeries if I don't come along. Secondly, killing me on American soil will only multiply by ten the number of law enforcement officials on your ass. Finally, our DNA is all over the back of your boat. They'll get you."

"That's all well and good, but once Palu took a header into the Sow, everything changed. I'll find a new buyer, tell them some of the shit is reproductions, eat a fifty grand loss and walk away with millions. Even with the Parker woman's share, I'm out of the fishing business. I sell the *Devil's Due* there's my fifty grand back. Enough chit-chat. Take a step back, I don't want any blood on the boat."

As dark as it was, she could still see a smirk beginning to form on his face. And she could also see his trigger finger tighten as he ceased weighing his options. And, even as she knew—just knew—she was bearing witness to her last moments on earth, a ridiculous thought entered her head.

Why, if it had been pitch black all night, was she able to discern his facial features? And then it registered.

She was able to see his outline by the tiny, perfect red glow of a laser, illuminating the pocket of his plaid shirt. Over his heart. A moment later, a hole the size of a dime shredded through the pocket and forced a mess the size of a baseball to explode out of his back. In what seemed like an instant of directional craziness, a second shot hit him from behind. With a single convulsion, MacLeod pulled the trigger of his pistol as he recoiled from the impact. The slug carried off into the night, and MacLeod tipped over the side of the zodiac and into a foot of salt water. Beth, knees rubbery, heard several sets of feet rushing past her to the shoreline.

A familiar pair of hands, strong and sure, sat her down on the beach, as state troopers rushed past her. "Why must I always find you in these dramatic situations, Sweetie?" With a shudder, she clasped Donovan's shoulder.

Chapter 33

Katy's Cove

DONOVAN PROMISED TO VISIT THE Eastport State Police offices the next morning and then helped his additional two passengers into the helicopter, following them in. A few minutes later, the helicopter landed on the wharf in St. Andrews, dropping off its passengers. John, Peggy, and Nick were there to greet them and to take Riley to the hospital. Donovan asked Beth to stay with Riley, whispering she should request a guard to stay with the Parkers for the remainder of the night.

Beth arched an eyebrow. "It's not over yet, is it." It was a statement.

He shook his head. "Loose ends. Give me an hour. I may need to call you, but I'll have to see what's unfolding when I get there."

"Get where?" Beth's voice sounded calm, but he could tell she was anxious.

"I'm going fishing. Katy's Cove."

He drove behind the Algonquin Hotel and headed down and then up a low hill to the cemetery, parking his car on Cemetery Rd. After a quick search of the trunk of his car for supplies, he began to trudge the remaining distance to the shore, crossing the graveyard until he came to Quoddy Shores Drive. He turned left, following the road.

The heat that had been trapped in the asphalt through the day escaped upward, and he reached down for a second to feel the warmth. Clouds had dropped and socked everything in. The fog obscured the moon and stars and, at times, it was necessary in the absence of a flashlight to use his feet to feel the shoulder of the road. He heard a snuffle fifteen feet away, in the brush. A deer. Ahead, he caught the gentle lapping of waves on the pebbly beach. *Getting close. I'll be able to put on a light soon.*

Before reaching the end of the lane, the clouds parted, just for a moment. Hazy moonlight revealed a pickup pulled over to the side, two wheels off the road and resting in the shallow ditch. Donovan stood and watched for almost a minute. The air was cool, humid, and carried the smell of smoke. American cigarettes. By peering intently into the dark toward the driver's window, he was able to pick up the appearance of a glow from the end of a cigarette every fifteen seconds. He knelt down, opened the green canvas backpack that seldom left his side, and withdrew a tiny vial.

Holding his thumb over the tip, Donovan crept up to the truck and, when he was close enough to hear the man cough, he dropped his crawl by half. It took minutes to inch the final ten feet, until he found himself on the ground beside the rear quarter panel, listening to the nasal wheeze of the man's breathing. Scootching inches closer, Donovan reached up and, without brushing against anything, dripped a colourless, odorless fluid onto the shirtsleeve of the smoking man.

A long four seconds later, the man started, as if he'd sat on a thorn. With a curse, he fumbled with the door handle, but Donovan's back was pressed hard against the outside. The thrashing weakened with each push the man attempted, until the night was once again motionless. Donovan opened the door and the man poured out and onto the ground. By the light from his phone, he spotted a pistol with a silencer that had fallen to rest alongside the unconscious man. No cab light had come on when the door was opened. *This man did not want to be noticed.*

Guys with guns in the night are always up to no good. He reached into the man's back jeans pocket and retrieved a wallet and a passport. The identification produced a name Donovan didn't recognize and an unfamiliar New York state address. The money compartment held twenty-one hundred dollar bills. He checked the time on his phone. Eleven. There was only one building on this part of the lane. It was under construction, and sleepy St. Andrews lived up to its name.

Donovan sat on the ground beside the drugged man, his back against the quarter panel of the pickup. What did the man's presence mean? There was nothing in the cab of the truck, and he hadn't seen anything in the bed behind the rear window. So, the stranger was waiting for someone or something. *Both, I think.* Who would he find on the shore, waiting for the fishing boat: the elusive Ike Tannen?

He heard footsteps coming up the rough path that led from the shore to the lane. After a moment, the crunch of gravel quieted to light steps on asphalt. The person approached with confidence, and Donovan noticed a faint light preceding the footsteps. *The man knows where he's going. This is the boss.*

Lifting himself up to a crouch, he padded backward to the rear of the truck and waited, one hand fumbling in his bag for a focused-beam flashlight, the other hand holding the borrowed pistol. Thinking things through, Donovan eased around to the passenger side and lay down in the ditch, peering across the undercarriage of the truck as footsteps drew closer.

Based on the weight on gravel and his gait, he determined it to be a small man, his pace deliberate. Was he one of the players? He had to be. *I don't know much about Ike, but this doesn't sound like a very big man.* He caught himself holding his breath, thinking of the Olympic shooters who timed their shots, not only to coincide with breathing, but heartbeat. And he waited.

The man's steps slowed, and he paused to shine a tiny light on the bundle crumpled beside the truck. "Shit!"

What? A woman! She took a step closer; close enough for Donovan to see her boots and aim at the lower part of her leg. He squeezed off two rounds, each one catching an ankle before the stranger fell, cursing. He noted the shot through the silencer sounded more like a clink than a gunshot, not a lot louder than the spent shell hitting the asphalt.

As she hit the ground, though, the woman fired a couple of rounds back under the truck toward Donovan. The first hit the unconscious man but the second bit into Donovan's side, catching mostly clothing and a bit of muscle.

Shining the light on his attacker's arm, Donovan fired a third round, destroying her gun and piercing her palm. In a quiet, intimidating voice, Donovan called out. "I'm coming around, watching you as I go. I don't need you alive, but if you have a preference, just stay as you are." A second later, he had his knee on the woman's kidney, fishing out a wallet.

"Son of a bitch! It's my new friend Erin. How did you race me here? I have to tell you, ma'am, the pieces of this puzzle are falling into place with remarkable speed and clarity." He fished a short rope from his canvas bag and, after repositioning her belt with the buckle at the back, tied Erin Parker's hands to the leather belt. Then, he took a moment to tie her to the unconscious man.

"So, how crippled are you? Not too bad, I hope. I hate carrying people, so if we have to go anywhere, it's into the truck bed with you, darlin'." He received a curse for his troubles. Katy's Cove was isolated, an excellent place to chat. The tiny park on the water just down the hill was all locked up for the night, and except for the one under construction, there were no houses for a quarter of a mile.

He swung her legs around so she could face him, which elicited another round of moans. Donovan began again, his voice conversational. "What makes this particular part of town so popular at this time of night? Are we waiting for someone?" The narrow beam of light from Donovan's flash revealed Erin's eyes and forehead. The woman shook her head.

"I have to warn you, the last time I had a conversation with a thief and a murderer, it took three or four strategically placed slugs before he sang. But, I had a hate on for him and it was a pleasure separating him from his thumb. You? You're merely a woman trying to kill off all of your relatives. One was a distant cousin, I suppose, but still."

"I didn't kill anyone, nor did I steal anything. Do you see me holding a bag of loot?" It came out as a snarl.

"Ah, but the night is still young. I don't have all the details, but here's what I do know. You used to be married to Ike Tannen and after he cleaned you out, he vanished with a load of cash. Later, he returned for some artwork, and his willing helper was the ne'er-do-well, Harry. Next thing we know, the hapless Tricia goes for the long swim. And now, here you are, literally waiting for your ship to come in. When is it due to hit shore, by the way? You see, my wife was a passenger, and the voyage didn't go well for everyone, so now I'm in a bad mood. Isn't it funny, Erin, how you began the evening wishing for millions of Nick's artwork to sail right back into your mitts and now, you'll be wishing for the arthritis to not settle into those ankles of yours.

"While we're waiting, let's get back to Tricia. What's the story with the strawberry blonde?"

"I don't remember Tricia. It's been years."

A narrow beam of light hit the ground at Erin's feet, creeping up the body until it rested on the hip. "Some shooters swear by the kneecap as the way to deliver the most pain from a bullet, but you'd be surprised how much it hurts to take a slug in the bursa of the hip, or in the bony part of the shoulder. Shall we explore this? You could decide after we acquire a clear understanding from each shot. Maybe on a scale of one to oh-my-god-that-hurts."

"All right, All right. I'd see Tricia now and then, in the years after Nick kicked her out. She was always broke, always looking for something to get her out of the messes she was always getting herself into. She fell in with Harry, at some point, which provides a great example of her good judgement and the messes she loved to embrace. That was around the time…"

Donovan spoke up. "Now isn't the time to be shy. You're already in it up to your rapidly aging neck. May as well spill it all." He waited.

"Ike left me, but he didn't go away. He never knew when enough was enough. After he took all my money, I thought that would be that. But no. He came back trying to take my art, and he hit me. He hurt me to the point where I needed a couple of bones set. I knew the police couldn't catch him before he killed me, so I told my family I fell off a ladder, and they seemed to believe it. A visit to the hospital, coupled with his threats made me understand that one of us was going to end up dead." She stared into the flashlight beam. "Why should it have to be me? I mean, really, why?"

Donovan chose that moment to ask about her gambling. "Was he the reason you were broke? Or was it the horseracing?"

She responded with a grim smile. "I was actually quite good at picking the ponies. But all it did was serve to slow down the bleeding. It was almost as if Ike knew when I had a few dollars ahead. He could smell money, that one." The rage in her voice carried across the inky darkness.

"So I killed the bastard. Well, I had him killed. He was quite inexpensive, in fact." She paused, collecting her thoughts. "But. And there always seems to be a 'but' in stories involving bastards and murder. Did you ever notice that?"

It seemed to be a rhetorical question, so he waited for her to continue.

"In my case, Harry knocked on my door one day. He'd run into a mutual acquaintance of mine, a yappy one, who mentioned me having got Ike whacked. From then on, I basically had one blackmailer replaced by another. Harry seemed to be a bit more reasonable, at first. He said that, rather than bleed me dry, he'd split the profits on the sale of all my artwork. Later, though, like all greedy individuals, he changed our agreement. Instead, he said he was taking all the profit from the sale, and I could keep the insurance money. At least, that's what he said; what I heard from his words was I'd end up in jail, penniless and charged with insurance fraud."

"So, that's how Harry wound up arguing with the mouth of a shovel?"

Donovan raised the light to shine on Erin's face. She wore a grin entirely devoid of humor. "At that point, Harry was no longer useful. The sale was brokered, but if Harry's mouth could be permanently shut and if he could be identified as the fall guy, I could actually get most of the money from the sale of the artwork. But the best part—I'd be finally shed of bloodsucking blackmailers and people would assume Harry had stolen the art. I'd be rid of the pair of them at last.

"And for the record, it wasn't me who killed Harry, either. Harry had found the art broker in Montreal. The guy came here and I saw his name in Harry's notebook. I had a guy steal it from Harry's kitchen, just before he died. Well, I contacted the man and he was the one who killed Harry. They must have had a falling out. A Quebecer, I don't remember his name.

"But up 'til then, all Harry had to do was open his trap and everything would turn to shit. What stupid bastard keeps notes in a scribbler?" Erin's tone was incredulous. "Can you believe how sloppy that was? Anyone could have found it, but they didn't. I did."

Donovan recalled Riley having taken photos from it, but didn't correct this error. "And Tricia?"

"Ah, Tricia. Sweet, stupid Tricia. As I said, she was in on things from the beginning. She needed a nest egg to start a new business, and she didn't want much, so I was cool with her taking a slice and disappearing. Unfortunately, she bumped into her daughter, somehow and changed her mind, right there on the spot, about everything. From that moment, she wouldn't have anything to do with the plan and therefore couldn't be trusted. So I got Harry to kill her. He dropped her into the water just over there—" She pointed to the shore on the right, "—and let the falling tide carry her away."

"Just like that?"

"Just like that. Friends are friends and business is business."

"This guy sitting beside you. Muscle?"

"Yeah. I brought him up to Canada to help shift the artwork to Montreal. A lot of good he did me."

"And who else is involved?" Donovan had turned off the light. He was confident he had all the information he could glean from her, but thought he'd press, anyway. The night was quiet except for the crickets, but offshore, he thought he detected a low throbbing sound.

Parker sat tight. "That's it."

"You do remember I have a gun. And you do know I'm aware a fishing boat is supposed to land here at some point before dawn. You want me to assume it's navigating itself? Sounds like we're going to test my bursa theory."

She raised a hand in supplication. "No! I'll tell you. There's just one guy. It's a local fisherman, name of MacLeod. That's it, I swear."

Knowing he'd got as much from her as he could, and conscious of the passage of time, an awful thought entered his head. What chance would the women have had, if Palu and MacLeod changed their plan? But the thought came and went, as everyone who could do Beth harm has been taken into custody, or killed. He no longer had to think of that possibility.

Making sure he'd severed no arteries in the lower parts of her legs, Donovan then checked the ropes and pulled out his phone. "Hello, Beth, can you ask the RCMP to follow an ambulance up the hill overlooking Katy's

Cove? Near the cemetery. Two criminals, one sleepy, one with holes in her ankles. Yes, I'll be back at the inn as soon as I give a statement."

Chapter 34

Epilogue: One Week Later, In Niagara

THE TASTING ROOM AND RESTAURANT at Plenitude buzzed with the sound of visitors and one floor below, Donovan and his friends entertained each other in the private dining room. The room was decorated in "wine cellar chic," with ample red-brick arches and Edison light pendants lining the ceiling along one long wall. He'd chosen a mix of East coast Canadian musicians: Emily Curran, Kill Chicago, Hey Rosetta, and Garrett Mason, but the music was background to the animated conversations taking place around the table.

Trays of food had been brought in, admired and attacked, together with bottles of viognier and pinot noir. Donovan and Beth sat surveying their friends. They'd partaken of king crab legs, cracked lobster, and flash-seared scallops, accompanied by flight trays of seven sauces. Jack had chosen a butter-and-blue cheese-drizzled porterhouse that had won the fight for space over a twice-baked potato and seasonal yellow beans. Somehow he'd made it all disappear.

Jack sat to Beth's right, across from Claire and her mother—all the way from the south of France—and beside them, Beth's mother. To the left of Donovan, Nick and his daughter, Riley, her arm in a sling, struggled with the pleasant problem of how to finish a sampling of wings in a fiery buttered Stevie sauce, Tennessee-style ribs, red beans and rice, and pineapple corn salsa. Riley was the last one to finish, owing in part to the sling, as well as to her interest in everyone else's conversations.

At the end of the table, John and Peggy Whiteway sat holding hands and beaming. They finished their food as well, although John kept a firm grip on an oversized bottle of Picaroons Blonde, a craft beer he'd fallen in love with in New Brunswick. Conspicuous by their absence were Dieter and Anna Schmidt.

Jack caught Donovan's eye and nodded toward the door. Excusing himself, Donovan left the room, with Jack in tow.

Donovan, who'd brought a wineglass of red with him, tipped it in Jack's direction as soon as they found a couple of club chairs in a discreet nook near the bar. "We haven't had a chance to chat since Beth and I flew in yesterday."

"Exactly. I just thought it would be nice to get caught up alone, rather than asking questions in front of Riley. I know what MacLeod was up to and how he died, but what's the chance of getting a few more details? The detective in me needs to know what happened." He'd brought his glass of Guinness with him and unconsciously rotated it in his hands as he spoke.

Donovan thought for a moment. "Let me take you to New York, first. This is what I learned there. You know by now Erin was being blackmailed by her ex, Ike, and she put out a contract on him, in true New York fashion. It turns out Harry caught wind of it and picked up where Ike left off. Erin got in bed with Harry, at least in terms of insurance fraud and off he went with all of her art and a bunch of stuff he'd nicked, and shipped the stuff as far as Eastport, Maine. In the meantime, though, Nick's ex, Tricia was also supposed to be in on the heist, but she had a change of heart, brought on by bumping into her grown-up daughter. So she had to go, and Harry took care of her. He slipped into the country, did the drowning, and left the country. Then he returned a day or so later.

"In the meantime, the artwork landed in Eastport and was held by a lowlife Harry knew. It sat there until Harry could line up a smuggler and an art broker, which he did. First chance she could, though, Erin hired the art broker to murder Harry, which he did in a pretty definitive way. It was brutal."

Jack stared down at his beer. "Seannie, this is my first drink in a year and a half. Cheers." He took a long quaff, wiping a bit of foam from his mouth with the back of his hand. "Continue." He put the glass down on a nearby table.

"From then on, Palu, a thief from my past, actually, and MacLeod, the boat captain, bided their time until the weather and tides were right. By that point, Beth and Riley were shadowing them, and I wasn't confident I could get back to Canada in time to keep them safe. So—and you already know this part—I got hold of you and you convinced the local RCMP to place a man in the cabin on the boat between the time Devin left it in Bocabec and the time that MacLeod, Palu, and the women set out for Eastport. I arrived with the Maine state troopers in time to pick up the Eastport guy with the pickup truck and, not coincidentally, to save Beth. MacLeod was shot at the same time by the RCMP officer from the boat, as well as the lead officer on the shore." He noticed Jack's glare. "Yes, I did cut it close."

Donovan continued. "Riley did her part perfectly, getting Palu upset enough that Beth could overpower him. He landed in the drink, and MacLeod wouldn't let them pull him out. He was a very bad person, but so were Harry, Palu, and Erin, not to mention Ike."

"And the artwork?"

Half of it was Nick's, with the rest being works stolen over the past seven years. The haul was worth millions." Donovan paused for a second, looking pensive. "It would have been nice for a fella to get his hands on it all…"

Jack grinned. "If a fella was a thief, which you aren't." He didn't phrase it like a question, and Donovan didn't elaborate. "So, what now?"

"You go back to work tomorrow morning, keeping Plenitude safe. Beth takes her mother touring around the Niagara Peninsula. Beth's retiring, by the way. It seems she wants to take up winery management.

"And as for me? I have to hire a winemaker for a bit, until Claire gets her skills up. We're sending her back to France, to school. Dieter is done. He says they want to retire. As well, I think I need to know more about wines. Mornings in the lab, afternoons in the field, and evenings with the books. There may be a glass of wine in there, somewhere."

Donovan stood up. "I didn't have a great upbringing and as a result, my family was fractured, in some ways the same as the Parker clan and their secrets. But here, it feels as if I may well be with family. In my home. I never thought I'd utter those words. That seems to have been someone else's dream. But here I am, with the right girl, in the right house, and now, with the right family. Cheers, Jack."

DONOVAN: THIEF FOR HIRE

Make sure to catch Chuck Bowie's other novels:

Three Wrongs

Sean Donovan will steal anything for a price. The combination of thrill plus profit will take him—and you—on a journey of travel, food and wicked crimes.

AMACAT

It's trouble in triplicate for this thief for hire, as he rescues, returns and steals his way through four countries.

Steal it All

Donovan has seen hauls worth stealing, but he's never had the chance to steal it all.

ABOUT THE AUTHOR

CHUCK BOWIE is a genre writer whose strengths lie in writing smart fiction, warm passages and crisp, clever dialogue.

Chuck began writing short stories, essays and magazine articles. He currently sits on council as the Atlantic Canadian Representative for The Writers' Union of Canada.

He's just finishing the manuscript for the first in a Cozy Mystery series, and will begin writing Book 5 in the Thief4Hire series later in 2018.

Underwater Road is the fourth in his **Donovan: Thief For Hire** suspense-thriller series, and the first with scenes set in his home province of New Brunswick.

He's married to Lois Williams, and has two grown sons: Jonathan and Matthew.

Did you enjoy The Body on the Underwater Road
If so, please help us spread the word about
Chuck Bowie and MuseItUp Publishing.

It's as easy as:

•Recommend the book to your family and friends
•Post a review
•Tweet and Facebook about it

Thank you
MuseItUp Publishing

Made in the USA
San Bernardino, CA
02 June 2019